SERPENTS IN PARADISE

Also by Nancy Phelan

THE RIVER AND THE BROOK
WELCOME THE WAYFARER: A TRAVELLER
IN MODERN TURKEY

Serpents in Paradise

Nancy Phelan

MACMILLAN . London . Melbourne . Toronto
ST MARTIN'S PRESS . New York
1967

MACMILLAN AND COMPANY LIMITED
Little Essex Street London WC 2
also Bombay Calcutta Madras Melbourne

THE MACMILLAN COMPANY OF CANADA LIMITED
70 Bond Street Toronto 2

ST MARTIN'S PRESS INC
175 Fifth Avenue New York NY 10010

PRINTED IN GREAT BRITAIN BY
NORTHUMBERLAND PRESS LIMITED
GATESHEAD

FOR
KYLIE TENNANT AND RODDY

One

AN Egyptian sunset was going on in the east. Crimson-flooded sky, black silhouette palms, vast flat foreground were all in order, but the scene lacked brooding Arabs slumped on camels, the desert moved and glimmered strangely.

The illusion held; then the sun slid up, revealing Aratoa, administrative centre, port of entry for the Peaceful Islands Colony. The lagoon flared, coastlines turned green, mountains developed blue shadows. Fowls, pigs, children gave tongue. Scented smoke of coconut husks drifted from cookhouse fires. Men set off from villages to fish, to work in garden or forest, on nets or canoes. No Europeans were abroad. For the moment the island belonged to the islanders.

But not for long. As the sun rose the ship lying off-shore moved in through the reef-passage. In mud-coloured houses by the port bare feet brushed pandanus mats as morning tea came round. Brown supple hands set down cups by beds—at the Residency on the hill where His Honour lay thinking about retirement; at the meteorological station where the Cornicks and Jacksons still slept; at the white coral house by the church where the missionary's snoring chorale defied mosquitoes wailing outside his net and his wife's diminished face reproached the smile in the bedside glass. In the houses of Medical Officer, Customs Officer, Native Development Officer showers ran, shirts were groped into, tea drunk on the move. Soon men in white shorts were driving towards the boat harbour while dressing-gowned wives thankfully returned to peaceful second cups.

No human activity disturbed the small wooden house

1

outside the town but in its *flamboyant* trees the day's brawls were well advanced for the mynah birds. Fluttering, screeching, they rattled the scarlet flowers, snatched at food, pushed each other off branches, bounded aggressively across lawns. The angry voices penetrated the hot little bedroom where Leicester Whiteway struggled to detain receding sleep.

'I can't!' he protested. He sat up suddenly, hot, confused.

'Toa! Where's my tea?'

The mynah birds clattered and shrieked.

Leicester dragged his *pareu* from the sheets, groped out of bed.

'Toa!'

The housegirl was not in the kitchen but life seethed round the refrigerator. A procession of dedicated ants moved up and down the legs, a sooty question-mark hovered above the back vent.

'Toa!'

The fuel stove exposed ash-smeared teeth, the refrigerator shelves their acrid smell, the ice-tray its warm cubes of water.

Helpless, frustrated, Leicester retreated.

In the bath-house cockroaches drew back respectfully. When the movement of black forms subsided he stepped fearfully under the shower, skin roughened in anticipation.

Cockroaches did not attack but from above fell dried mud, insect corpses, a spider curled in a protective ball. With face defensively lowered beneath the lukewarm trickle Leicester reached for the soap, snatched back his hand. No soap, but a soft furry body in the soap dish.

Disturbed by the incoming stream, the smell in the drain uncoiled and rose. Leicester held his breath.

How could you expect natives to learn decent habits when white men set such an example? The cottage belonged to Government, had housed only Europeans. THE BATH-HOUSE IS NOT A LATRINE! With his posters in each village school and dispensary, must he be victimized in his own shower?

2

Familiar half-hearted bangs, rattling stove-lids announced Toa's arrival. As the shuffling steps reached his door he put down his comb.

'You're late!'

Toa shrugged. She offered a cup of cool grey tea.

'Stove no good. Don't burn.'

'Why don't you use the primus for tea, like I told you?'

'Frightened of primus. I told you.'

'I said to come early this morning. I must go to work early.'

'My baby sick. My old father not good.'

'You know today is important.'

She shrugged. First things came very much first with Toa.

'Today is just as important to you as to me ... to you and your baby and your old father. Specially your baby. The people coming today are going to work for them. Make them better; teach you how to look after them so they don't get sick. Help your baby grow big and strong. Teach the Peaceful Islanders to grow more food, catch more fish ...'

'You have your breakfast now?' said Toa.

He glared, exasperated. She gazed guilelessly back. Dark tragic eyes; pretty, fragile, pathetic with drooping hem, hopeful frangipani behind her ear. He flushed. How nervy he was, how irritable. It wasn't her fault, after all; she was a child. They were all children. He must be more patient.

'My car's at the garage. I have to walk over the mountain. Mr Holmes will not like it if I'm late.'

If his tone was now too servile, Toa did not notice.

'Why don't Mr Holmes come and get you in his car?'

'Mr Holmes has gone down to meet *Marinda*, to meet the Experts from Ha'i Koma ... from the Pacific Islands Development League.'

'Why he don't take you? Mr Holmes very mean.'

'You mustn't say that! He's my Chief. He's a good man. He works hard for you all. Why should I go? It's not a party. It's business.'

A*

Her shrug weighed up and dismissed the Native Development Officer and his hard work.

'Okay, I get breakfast now. I cook you eggs.'

Trudging over the mountain, shirt glued to back, Leicester's harassed expression returned. Toa's comment about the Chief was ungrateful, unfair, uncalled for, but disturbing. Of course it was right that Holmes should meet the Experts but Leicester was, after all, his assistant. If Toa thought it strange, what must the Europeans think, since normally it was he who must rise at dawn to meet *Marinda*. Were they all talking about it ... wondering what it meant? Had he done something wrong? Or was it because ...

He flushed miserably, jabbed by an overheard comment: *'Whiteway's an excellent N.C.O. but not officer class.'*

On the plateau at the top of the slope he rested. Too hot for walking, too breathless and sticky; and there was the forest. You walked into it and a curtain dropped behind. Vaguely disturbing. Never quite coming to terms with you, for all your efforts to understand. Not hostile, like jungles; just aloof, indifferent, uncaring. Like the islanders.

Shocked, he sat rigid. That was the sort of remark made by Old Island Hands; the very attitude he had come here to fight. Cynicism, negative thinking; and untrue. The islanders were sleeping beauties, unawakened, unaware, awaiting the kiss of enlightenment.

His heart bumped in his chest in a doomed way. The warm air penetrated painfully into his lungs. No good. He must do some deep breathing to quieten his nerves.

Below was the island. In the vitreous lagoon, enclosed by the line of the reef, lay *Marinda*. Aratoa's two whaleboats waited to unload cargo; a few canoes hovered idly ... no oriental swarming and staring, fleets of sightseers, Tahitian welcomes. The Aratoans took the ship calmly. She was part of their lives. Once a month she brought passengers, mail and supplies and carried away copra, tomatoes, *kumaras*,

4

whatever the islanders had produced. Voices rose up, the rattle of Aratoa's truck blundering to the port with its cargo for loading. On this still humid morning the reef was silent, the cries of terns sounded close and clear.

Beyond the anchorage, across the now glittering sea, were the rest of the Group ... Manu, Pinoi, Hinoa ... far out of sight; beyond again to the east, French Oceania; to the west, the Southern Cooks. Here and there in between, volcanic islands rose and sank. In the nineteenth century the Admiralty caught and charted one in passing. It had vanished by the time the Handbook came out.

It was beautiful; beautiful. It was the Garden of Eden; and it was full of serpents. Sickness, ignorance, apathy....

'Look closely!' He heard the Chief's voice. 'Look at the landscape, so admired by the tourist! Does he know the significance of those wedges cut in the coconut leaves? Does he recognize them as the mark of disaster, the rhinoceros beetle that eats out the heart of our trees? Does the tourist connect his carelessly jettisonned tin and the swollen filarial legs of the villagers? Does he realize he is helping to breed the *anopheles* which is destroying the race? If the European with all his advantages is unaware of these facts, how is the islander, in his ignorance, to understand? We must educate ... educate ... *educate*, first and foremost, by every means in our power, using every form of instructional media at every level ... in school and village ... film, filmstrip, poster, flannelgraph. All the resources of Fundamental Education must be mobilized. Community Development teams must be formed. We must seek the guidance of Experts....'

That had been twelve months ago at the P.I.D.L. Session, at Ha'i Koma. Now the Experts were here to join battle with ignorance, sickness and apathy. It was immensely exciting, a privilege to be in it; and yet...

And yet, what?

No doubt about it, the Chief was keen, frightfully keen. No one could be more keen. It wasn't that; it was just that sometimes ... sometimes one couldn't help wondering ... Of course one paid no attention to the cynical talk of traders and sea captains. It was not in their interest for the natives to progress. They claimed one could never know the true attitude of the islanders, who said only what they thought Europeans wanted to hear; but these days, with so many techniques for assessing reactions, measuring emotional climates ... so many objective criteria to work from ... so much Expert information.... Still ... how much *did* the islanders take in? Sometimes there was the sense of a charming, courteous wall. Would one ever penetrate ... learn the mystery of the Polynesian soul?

A pair of angelic terns circled overhead. Unafraid, they swooped low, peering with shining black eyes. The warm air carried sweet scents. Among feathery kapok trees, pink hibiscus, scarlet *flamboyants* shone out. Leicester thought of life in Wellington, his years in the Education Office of Island Territories. Had he ever imagined then he would work for an International Organization in a paradise like Aratoa? He had not. It had all been miraculous. Rung in as last-minute substitute for a sick offsider, he had accompanied the New Zealand P.I.D.L. representative to Ha'i Koma. It was a new world ... a new life! The island delegates! The gaiety! The romance! The worthwhile cause!

'Try for it!' Mother had commanded when in due course the Peaceful Islands Colony advertised for assistant to Holmes. 'Nothing venture. And with your background. Those little Readers you do for the schools. They'd be lucky to get you.'

'I haven't a chance. It's a British Colony, not a New Zealand territory.'

She could not see what difference that made, nor could his friends in the office.

'The Colonial Service is frightfully hard up for staff. They can't get people.' 'Who wants to go to the end of the earth for that sort of pay? And what sort of future ... with all this self-government?' 'Since the war the British Colonial Service will take what they can get. Anyone. Even Australians.'; and

6

Mother: 'An International Organization! It might Lead to Something!'

He had tried for it; they had taken him, and here he was, Colonial Service, seconded to P.I.D.L. ... working for the islanders he had admired, and apparently, after only four months, expecting to find them changed. Was he already so used to their charming ways that, like other white residents, he saw only their faults ... the faults of careless, improvident children? It was natural, inevitable that one's first reverent awe for Old Island Hands should progress through reasonable acceptance to disillusionment. The Europeans, pleasant enough in their way, had done nothing to foster, even preserve a newcomer's respect. Oblivious to its existance, they blighted by scepticism, cynical apathy, would-be-humorous resignation to the bloodiness of island life; but the islanders ... that was different. They did not deserve to be so dismissed. They were like birds ... sweet island birds, singing, loving, living for the moment, without thought for the morrow. Their youth was brief; their beauty faded like flowers; but gay, generous, vulnerable, they sang on to the end.

Despite humidity, Leicester's sweat was emotional rather than thermal. Shame, self-disgust prodded. He jumped to his feet. How dared he waste time questioning when there was so much to be done.

Eager to start afresh he began the descent to the town.

At the boat-harbour, cars were moving off from the copra-stacked wharf.

'Au revoir then. I'll see you at the hotel!' The Native Development Officer slammed the door and stood back. Gears jarred; the Land Rover kangarooed forward. Holmes's smile, etched in acid, seemed uncertain how to behave. More feral than human ... red face, hair, moustache—even eyes had a red foxy gleam ... his natural humour was choler. When—as now—occasion demanded he would throw back his pointed snout and emit short barks and snorts; but this ferocious joviality, more frightening than bad-temper, convinced no one.

'Anything wrong, Holmes? Got your Experts ashore?'

At the voice of the Medical Officer, Holmes's smile knew what to do. It took itself off.

'If you'd just move your car.... I'm late as it is. Whiteway's waiting for me at the office.'

'Watch your blood-pressure now. Don't want a stroke just as they arrive.'

Damn Vincent! Damn his impertinence! Jeering; always jeering. And furious now, of course, about the new Infant Welfare Expert. What sort of Infant Welfare had he provided? What sort of Health Department did he run? Drunken, second-rate G.P., hiding his failure in the islands.

'Territory must be getting pretty scarce for Experts these days, Holmes. Competition's keen, I hear....'

'If you'd just move your car.... *Thank you.*'

'...Have to look out, you know. You'll have the French crashing in here if you're not careful. Well, I'm going home for breakfast.'

Breakfast! At this hour! No wonder the Colony was in such a deplorable state. The French! *Conseil de Recherche pour l'Avancement du Pacifique*. The French indeed! And what had they done, in actual fact, for their Pacifique *sujets* and *citoyens*? A few metal bands round the trees in Tahiti....

'Can't say I care for these dawn risings. Well, you've got your PIDLing Experts at last. Ha-ha! Cosmopolitan bunch, I must say. Well, ta-ta.'

Resentment, of course, and sheer envy. Cheap jokes. Nevertheless the Pacific was getting too crowded. Apart from P.I.D.L. and C.R.A.P.—and of course the South Pacific Commission, brooding passively over the whole area—there was that gang at the South Pacific Health Service in Suva, those chronic itinerants from the Australian National University in Canberra. Not to mention United Nations,

8

F.A.O., W.H.O., I.L.O., UNESCO observers; and all the eager Fulbright, Ford Foundation, Rockefeller scholars who filled in the gaps. All poaching. So far, thank God, not in this Colony. P.I.D.L. had won the race for the Peaceful Islands fair and square; but one never knew. Specially with U.N. and A.N.U. fieldworkers, forever measuring heads, inspecting coconuts, sending out questionnaires in other peoples' territory.

The sun was already warming up Native Development's pale iron roof. Within, where yesterday's heat had matured to a rich soporific miasma, ammunition for the assault on ignorance awaited mobilization ... battery wirelesses, kerosene projectors, tape recorders, silk screens, crates of powdered milk; books and posters at village level on flies, hookworm, pit latrines, mosquitoes, scabies; mats, bedspreads, carved *tikis*, wooden bowls. The film cans contained footage on hygiene, breastfeeding, Co-operatives in Africa, Safety Measures in Factories (sent by mistake), Fruit-farming in the British West Indies, Better Boneless Cod for Canada and Bench Terracing in Cyprus.

'Good morning, Mr Holmes.'

Aporo, trainee assistant; the New Peaceful Islander. Eager to learn, to lead his people; eventually, to Take Over.

'Good morning, Aporo. Mr Whiteway is late.'

'Today, Mr Holmes, I am very early. I am very anxious always to come to work, to learn all I can, you see, Mr Holmes.'

'Yes, I see. Tell Mr Whiteway I wish to see him when he comes in.'

'Yes, Mr Holmes.' Aporo made his daily request. 'Mr Holmes, when I am good at these lino-cuts posters and these flannelgraphs you will send me to Art School in New Zealand? Then I could come back to teach My People ...'

'We'll see. You get to work, Aporo, and rewind those films.'

New Zealand indeed! That was all the Peaceful Islanders thought of ... joyrides to Auckland to see their relations. As

9

for Whiteway ... Still, he might have been an Australian. No doubt one was lucky to have him—the only applicant offering...

For oneself ... Barely started on retirement after service in Africa, overnight one had found oneself translated to the Pacific, implementing this great P.I.D.L. project. Janet's cousin in Whitehall behind it, of course; still, none the less gratifying. And a challenge. The islanders—members of the great Maori family—were not Africans; work for an international organization less restful than Colonial Service in these days of chronic concern for tax-payers' money; nor had the Peaceful Islands government shown eagerness. Only fear, one felt, had obliged the Resident Commissioner to accept the project.

'Davidson hates me,' Holmes told Janet. 'But he's in a cleft stick. He's afraid of exposure; of losing his job.'

'What exposure?'

'For God's sake, the state of the place; the state of the people. They're a Dying Race.'

Janet said, 'They say the natives like him.' (This was early days.) 'But he must be due for retirement.'

'Long overdue. He keeps getting extensions. Doesn't want to retire. Wants to hang on to his salary as long as possible.'

'Really, I can't think why. A widower. No children to educate. And that sister who acts as hostess for him, she has private means, I believe.'

'Salting it away. He'll do anything to hang on. Can't afford to draw attention to the place; not since those Articles.'

'Ah yes. Those Articles.'

An American bastard had wormed himself into the Colony and produced a pictorial essay—(*Serpents in Paradise*)—for *Life* Magazine. It showed up everything, even what was not there. Vincent, of course, made a joke of it ... '*Yaws, Sores and Whores to the Fore*'. No one else saw the joke. It said the Peaceful Islanders were a Dying Race, that the Resident Commissioner was strangling the Tourist

Potential, trying to turn the Group into a museum. There had been a fuss. A Question had been asked in the House. United Nations Experts had come and reported, scandalized, that the Peaceful Islanders had no shoes. Anthropologists, social scientists, do-gooders had turned up in shoals. There had never been so many parties, so much gossip, so many rows. When the P.I.D.L. finally secured exclusive rights to the Colony and set up a Native Development Section the Europeans had felt as much relief as resentment.

'Let them resent!' Holmes bit his pipe with small butterscotch teeth. 'They can't ignore the fact that progress has been made. Restoration of Native Culture; Women's Interests; Handicrafts; Housing; Rhinoceros Beetle; now the three new projects—Infant Welfare, Fisheries, Co-ops; and the linguistic survey to come....' If only one had a decent Resident to work with. If only Davidson would retire!

Two 🦢 🦢

AT the Residency, His Honour looked up from a poached egg and said to his sister, 'How much do wireless licences cost at Home?'

Miss Davidson stopped pouring tea.

'I was thinking this morning in bed,' said her brother. 'If I cut out the daily paper, that should save 3/6 a week. 3/6 a week is 156 shillings, plus 26 shillings, that's 182 shillings ... let's see, that makes £9. 2. 0. a year. I could do without papers; I could go to the library each day.'

'They all have TV now at Home.'

'Television! I can't think about television. Do you realize, Imogen, just how much of a struggle it's going to be on my pension? It's all right for you. But you seem unaware ...'

'I'm not unaware. You tell me so often. But *you* seem

unaware that you should be early today at the office. It's
boat day. And those Experts are here.'

'Experts! Holmes and his gang.'

'And we have to have them for dinner tomorrow.'

'There you go. You see? One expense after another. Well,
I'm not going to have them, that's all.'

'Yes, you are. I'm official hostess here. I say you are!'

'The newcomers ... all right. But those others ... that
Holmes and his wife. And Vincent, guzzling the whiskey.
Why do we have to have Vincent? And his sister? What's
she here for anyway? Place is becoming tourist-ridden.'

'His wife's cousin. Miss Pollock; from Sydney. She's come
for a holiday. You have to have her because she's a visitor,
also because she's a journalist. Cheer up. Whiteway and the
Hitchcocks don't drink much.'

'But it all adds up. And Hitchcock's appetite is enormous.'

'Well, you've got to have Hitchcock. He's hostile enough
as it is without alienating him further.'

'When the Church starts playing politics,' said H.H., 'it's
time to watch out. Hitchcock will overreach himself before
long. Interfering; laying down the law.'

'He has a good deal of influence with the natives.'

'I know how Henry II felt about Becket.'

'Well, you can't have Hitchcock murdered and you have
to include him tomorrow night.'

'Broken-down barnstormer.'

Before getting the call, the missionary had done time in
provincial Shakespeare, in the Sheffield district.

'You can't afford to have open war with the L.M.S.,' said
Miss Davidson. 'And he's never forgiven you for letting the
Baha'is into the Group.'

'Rubbish. I had no choice. One in, all in. You can't let in
Mormons, Seventh Day Adventists and keep out the
Baha'is.'

'You should never have let in the Mormons and the
S.D.A.s in the first place. That's what he says. He's saying it

will be Jehovah's Witnesses next. You made your first mistake when you let the Catholics in.'

'Let them in! You make it sound like a zoo. What about freedom of worship? Hey? The London Missionary Society doesn't own the Peaceful Islands.'

'No, but they got here first.'

'Peaceful Islands! Every European at somebody's throat. And one has to entertain them, provide them with food and drink. Night after night!'

'Where shall I put them at table! That's the thing.'

'Don't put Holmes or Vincent anywhere near me. Or Holmes's wife. Can't stand Janet Holmes's great teeth. And that cousin's a journalist! I don't trust 'em. If I'd known she was on a paper I'd never have let her in. And journalists drink whiskey like water.'

'It would be easier if you could eat alone.'

'Suit me. Suit me admirably.'

'Such a mixture. The Fisheries Officer's German ... *Offenbach* ... can you believe it! And that mothercraft woman from the New Hebrides....'

'She's not black, is she? They speak English.'

'And a Turk!'

'An Egyptian Greek. Constantopoulos. Don't ask me why we have to have an Egyptian Greek Co-operatives officer. Stumbled into the Service through some training scheme, I suppose. Whole show will be run by blacks before we've finished. Look at Africa.'

'God knows what one talks to them about.'

'You got your degree. You're supposed to be educated. Talk about current affairs.'

'Too risky. How do we know this Greek isn't a Communist?'

'Mrs Hitchcock will be pleased if he is. Don't put that madwoman near me at table. Her husband either. Talk of local affairs.'

'It's her time of life. Local affairs, are you mad? Sunday sport? Girl Guides fornicating in uniform after meetings?'

13

'Anyway, one thing about not having a knighthood ...
the tradesmen. They put the prices up, you know, for poor
Featherstonehaugh. Hadn't a penny piece beyond his pension; but the shops charged him almost double for everything because of the title.'

Judy Pollock said to her cousin, 'You're busy. I'll drop in
to see Ken Forbes. He came to the ship but I didn't have
time to talk to him.'

Dolly Vincent said, 'Mind you, I know it's not for me to
say but it seems such a waste, a clever fellow like that, living
like *that*!'

'Like that,' meant giving up newspaper photography in
Sydney to settle in Aratoa; 'Like *that*!' referred to the
native mistress and children.

Judy rolled her eyes up.

'He-likes-it-it-suits-him-he-hated-the-city-he's-happy.'

In the workroom behind *Ken's Kurio Shoppe* ... (Island
Souvenirs, Ansco Films, Orders Taken) ... Forbes was
breakfasting. Among pearlshell cut into brooches and earrings, conch shells fitted with forty-watt lamps, coconuts
carved into ashtrays and cups stood a bottle of whiskey, a
plate of corned beef, cold cooked taro and kumaras in a
pie-dish, a loaf of bread, a jug of fresh lime juice.

'Leicester Whiteway,' Judy said presently. 'I remember
him, when I covered the Grand Session. Those rimless
octagonals.'

'Of course, he's a New Zealander; but he means well.'
Forbes waved the bottle. 'Another drink?'

'There's a slight taste of hypo. Could it be the water? He
means terribly well. And so eager; so earnest. He told me he
was A Citizen of the World.'

'Wellington. But he's not bad. It's not his fault, all this
Native Development jazz. I sometimes wonder if he swal-
lows it all.'

'He struck me as pretty docile.'

'Docile enough, and keen, as you say. Idealistic. Burning to serve the islanders, if they'd let him. Impressed by Holmes. But I don't know how long it will last. Holmes is a self-seeking little bastard. I don't fancy Leicester looks as happy as he did.'

'What does this Native Development *mean?*'

'Oh . . . all sorts of projects. . . . Fundamental Education . . . health and agriculture at Village Level . . . you know the drill. Then there's Revival of Maori Culture. They're going to put back all the missionaries wiped out when they came . . .'

'Everything? Heathen gods? *Maraes?* Bare breasts? Public defloration?'

'. . . Starting with the old Peaceful Islands Maori, which no one can speak or understand. It's like reviving Cornish. Then there's ancient handcrafts; archaic dances and songs. The Experts don't like the natives doing the Twist and singing Beatle songs in Maori.'

'Where will they get these songs and dances? Who's going to teach ancient Peaceful Islands Maori if it's extinct?'

'Museums. Anthropologists. A linguist is coming. And poor Leicester goes up into the mountain and tries to dig out old people who might remember.'

'What do the Maoris think?'

'They just smile and make speeches. They can't see any point in making *tapa* when they can buy *pareu* material at the store; why they should sit on the floor when they can have a wooden chair; why life has to be made difficult again just when it's getting nice and easy. They don't want handcrafts. They like bicycles, sewing machines, movies. They're bored stiff with all this ancient history. But they're too polite to say so. And they don't really care very much.'

'History's discouraging. All those missionaries . . . building, preaching, converting. Then, just as they get the islanders all cleaned up in hats and dresses, sitting on chairs, eating corned beef, going to church, along comes Social Development and wrecks it.'

'The missions are blamed for everything now ... putting the natives into clothes and coral houses (it gives them T.B.); spoiling their teeth with wrong diet....'

'Killing their spirit. They're a Dying Race, don't forget.' Forbes thumped the table.

'They were happy enough before the missionaries came ... singing, dancing, working as little as possible. Trusting and credulous. Living by love. If they weren't making love to each other they were sharing their property and possessions, bringing each others' children up, looking after decaying elders. Of course, they didn't love God. But that was soon fixed. In no time they were weeping, confessing their sins, wearing mother-hubbards instead of grass skirts, embroidering texts instead of carving idols....'

'And now it's all to be put back by Mr Holmes. Because of that African.'

'What African?'

'A U.N. observer, at a P.I.D.L. Session. He said the Peaceful Islanders were a Dying Race because they had lost their Indigenous Culture. It was the same with his people. They had sewing machines and cinemas but nothing Deep Down. Life blood drained out. He was a sensation ... of course, he was black. But that's how it started. I heard it from journalists who were there.'

'But why Holmes? Why a Public Works man from Africa to restore Maori Culture?'

'Don't be naïve, Ken. It was probably Britain's turn. You know how it is in International Organizations. No matter how much you know, how good you are, if it's Nicaragua's turn for an appointment, Nicaragua gets it. I suppose he was cheap. And you can get a lot out of books these days.'

'A native team's being trained—no one knows who by— to Community Develop Manu! There's a frightfully bad-tempered old Dutch priest on Manu been doing community development for thirty years without knowing it. He's hostile enough to Government as it is. The leader's to be a

16

fellow called Aporo, in Holmes's office. Like a bull-calf. Fat, conceited, stupid, sexy, lazy. Bulging bovine eyes.'

'I suppose Holmes is greatly loved by the European community.'

'He's so bloody bumptious! Treads on everyone's corns, inferring nothing was done till he came. Vincent loathes him. He tells Vincent how to run the Health Department. Wilson—he's Agriculture Director—has never got over Holmes saying he could clear up rhinoceros beetle with Visual Aids.'

'It's progress. It's the Age of the International Organization. They're all cutting each other's throats to develop the islands. I doubt if there's a Group left in the whole Pacific that isn't swamped with good works. Except perhaps a few remote French islands where they still go to hell the gay way.'

'Don't mention the French to Holmes when you meet. It might bring on a cerebral haemorrhage. And don't mention Holmes to Vincent, Wilson, Hitchcock or His Honour.'

'There's something about this place! The peace and beauty; the harmonious spirit of brotherhood ...' Judy began composing sentences: '... Traders and sea-captains abuse and ridicule Government! European wives dislike each other, distrust native girls! Protestants against Catholics, Catholics against Seventh Day Adventists, S.D.A.s against Mormons. All resent the Baha'is, who, being last in, are considered interlopers....'

'If you start writing articles about us you'll be thrown out of the Colony.'

'Is there friction between the British and the bloody colonials?'

'Of course. The British patronize the New Zealanders. The New Zealanders patronize the Australians. The Aussies have no one to patronize—apart from the natives, which they wouldn't dare do—so they're bloody-minded to everyone. We all drink too much, don't take enough exercise. Most of us have bad livers. It all increases general irritability ... rubs up prejudices, brings out your worst qualities. Are you here to do articles?'

'I'm here to enjoy myself; but I may write something. I may write a book.'

'Be careful, that's all. Don't publish till you're sure you never want to come here again.'

'Don't you tell anyone. But you can give me information.'

'The hell I can! I have to live here. This is my home. It's all very well for spectators. But you be careful. They're terribly touchy since those Articles.'

'I won't betray you. I think I'll go round the Group and see the Outer Islands ... Manu ... Pinoi ... Hinoa.... Lovely names.'

'That you won't It's forbidden. Since the American. They're in a terrible mess. No one on Aratoa cares what goes on there.'

'What about the District Officer?'

'He spends all his time on Pinoi ... he's an anthropologist. Writing his Ph.D. thesis on Pinoi pre-puberty sex-games. He can't spare much time for the rest of the Group. They struggle along under Native Magistrates. The American articles wanted to know why. It's a sore subject.'

'Still, I feel I must see them.'

'You can't go without H.H.'s permission. And he won't give it.'

'You think so?' Judy said absently.

Three 🌊 🌊

IN Aratoa, the government freezer took the place of the parish pump.

Phyllis Cornick, wife of the Radio Officer, had just collected her meat when Thelma Jackson, the Meteorological Officer's wife came in.

18

'Ah! What did you get?'

'Topside. There isn't much else.'

'I had topside yesterday,' Thelma gladly informed. 'It was tough as a boot.'

'Was it?'

They really had nothing to say to each other. Their's was an on-again, off-again friendship, born of propinquity and husbands not being Colonial Service. They huddled together, drawn by, hating each other because of their common social inferiority. The fact that both were New Zealanders did not console.

Their husbands, George Cornick, Kev Jackson got on well enough. And why not? as Dr Vincent said; their dreary mediocrity was so similiar they were interchangeable. Shut your eyes and you couldn't tell which one was speaking. This was not quite accurate. George and Phyllis had once lived for a year in Western Samoa, where George worked at Apia airport; whereas the Jacksons had never been anywhere, apart from the Peaceful Islands. You could tell from the way Phyllis said *Sa*-maw that she had been there. She also used words like '*musu*', '*talofa*', '*aiga*' and so on. She and George often spoke of their life in *Sa*-maw. In Wellington Phyllis had done Adult Education courses; lectures on geology and the regional novel and Which Way Thailand? She had belonged to a playreading circle and once spoke in a discussion on The Art of Patrick White; so altogether she was fairly advanced and very broadminded about Colour whereas Thelma, from Auckland, was utter suburbia ... cakeforks, indoor plants, lace tablecloths, anti-Maori prejudices. Her husband, Kev, sent up balloons in a valley behind Aratoa. People made jokes about Kev's balloons and Thelma had to work hard on the social side because of this, as well as not being Colonial Service.

'The ship's in.'

'Yes.'

'Are you having a party for them?'

'Oh, I don't *know*.' Thelma's over-taxed-hostess voice. 'I

19

suppose I'll have to do *some*thing. Kev thinks we should have something for Dolly Vincent's cousin.'

'She'll be here for a while. There's no hurry.' Phyllis did not care for Thelma's possessive note. She became lavishly off-hand. 'I suppose we'll have to have them all in for drinks.'

'The Vincents and the Wilsons and the Holmeses will grab them first,' Thelma said lugubriously. 'There's a dinner tomorrow night at the Residency.'

Phyllis did not need to be told of Residency dinners to which she was not invited. She said, 'H.H. won't kill them with hospitality. When we were in *Sa*-maw ... the dinners at Vailima ... Very different!'

'Well, I'll jack up something for Judy Pollock,' said Thelma. She was sick and tired of Phyllis's affected talk of *Sa*-maw nor did she believe the Cornick's ever dined there at Government House. She said, 'There's you and George; and Leicester; and I'll get the Crumps.'

Ern Crump worked at the Public Works garage. He came from Brisbane. His voice was atrocious, his wife Marje was Common. Phyllis knew Thelma knew how she hated Marje Crump. She knew it was just spite. She thought bitterly of the British dining tomorrow night at the Residency in long skirts and cummerbunds. She only got asked to more democratic functions when everyone was included.

'It's nearly half-past. Are you coming to the hotel?' said Thelma.

Ten-thirty at the hotel was a highlight, when government personnel collected for tea. Today, the newcomers added excitement.

'I might as well, I suppose,' Phyllis's reluctance did not deceive. 'I need a cup. This frighful weather.'

'I'll just get my veggies,' Thelma offered generously. 'Then I'll come with you if you like.'

No matter how carefully dressed, something was always

missing from Mrs Hitchcock's appearance: the nut or piece of cheese dangling from pink tassellated claws, to be carried off to nest or lair. Marsupial eyes, circular nostrils, downy quivering whiskers, scuttling movements perfected the impression; but in fact she had never carried off anything, not even Mr Hitchcock. He had selected her for qualities needed in the Mission Field. No baby marsupials had consoled her, no penitents, aged parents, ailing friends. Other white women kept their safe civil distance; the island women showed little gratitude for her ministrations.

Life, however, was not empty. Besides her husband, her work in the Field, there was need for endless vigilance. She had always believed that the Communists meant to take over the world, that Rome would prevent them; that these two black forces would fight themselves to exhaustion, leaving the world fit for clean-living Protestants; but lately she had learnt that Catholic and Communist were in league, that their antagonism was a clever blind.

And now, an Egyptian-Greek Co-operatives Officer in Aratoa! Greece was full of communists; and Egypt ... there were pictures of Nasser, smiling at Khrushchev....

'Or he might be a Catholic,' she said, deeply troubled.

'More likely Greek Orthodox; perhaps Moslem,' boomed her husband.

'I don't know. There are lots of Catholics in Cairo.... All those Austrians.'

'Who said?'

'I read it somewhere. Or someone told me.'

'Pop-pea-cock!' He declaimed it in the Shakespearean manner. Mrs Hitchcock sighed. That beautiful voice, wasted on ignorant natives, uncaring white residents, deserved at least a cathedral and lawn sleeves.

'I shall make it my business to find out,' she said.

'Well, be careful. You know how they gossip.'

'I'll be discreet.'

She looked discreet enough. Four foot eleven, mouse-coloured, tear-shaped, pointed head, sloping shoulders,

21

spread hips, short heavy legs ending in platform feet. Mr Hitchcock, tall, enormous in girth, with imperial features, called her Nutkin.

He frowned. 'There's the Residency dinner tomorrow.'

'Oh!' Nutkin's paws flapped. 'Oh Theodore, if only one needn't go!'

'One must!'

'Oh, I know. But I do so dislike accepting hospitality, the way things are. All that unpleasantness over the Baha'is; then the question of Sunday sport. And that disgraceful business of the Girl Guides. I feel the first mouthful will choke me. I shan't enjoy it.'

'One doesn't go for enjoyment. One goes to remind others that one is here. There is too much laxity in high places in this Colony. Someone must uphold the standards of decency, morality, clean living.'

No one had ever analysed the morning-tea mystery; why those who sat all day in the same office, in mutual dislike and boredom, rose up so eagerly and flocked across the road to drink weak tea and eat limp arrowroot biscuits together. At first sight they appeared to be off to a party, and from afar, voices, rattling crockery did suggest a wild, illusory gaiety.

On the hotel verandah tea was drunk in traditional groups. In a corner, the Resident Commissioner held uneasy court with selected Heads of Departments: Secretary to Government—at present away on leave; Humphries, Director of Education; Wilson, Director of Agriculture. There was no conversation. When not silent, H.H. talked jerkily of early days in the Colony. On the outer edge, junior officials, eager to show their worth, laughed distractedly: (*'Oh, that's good, sir! Damned good!'*) or displayed respectful astonishment: (*'Really sir! How absolutely extraordinary!'*)

In the renegade Dr Vincent's circle the Assistant Medical Officer, Dental Officer, Director of Public Works laughed ferociously at coarse jokes. At a refined distance, senior clerks, typists, school mistresses chatted about womanly topics; lesser females bunched together in defensive hostility, watching like cats. Now and then, dislike and distrust gleamed out like the colour in shot silk. Only the fact that all could be overheard prevented everyone openly discussing everyone else.

Tea had already started when the Radio and Met. men's wives wormed their way into the basilisk group. Beside them sat Mr Hitchcock's cross, two elderly American Baha'is, munching, smiling, pregnant with universality.

It was the custom to pour one's own tea and help oneself to biscuits but today a strange woman stood at the trolley handling the mountainous pot. Sandy-haired and moustached, she had bright blue eyes, an air of command. A plump dark figure moved with a soup plate of arrowroots among the women.

'That's Miss Arbuthnott; Infant Welfare,' whispered an elderly typist. Her voice revealed indecision: should the newcomer be condemned for assuming authority, or cherished for her uncompetitive plainness?

'And that?'

'That's Co-ops. *Armenian!*' Tightened lips showed she for one would not be got round by slimy dago tricks.

The younger women seemed to favour being got round. Undone by compliments, flashing eyes, already they planned privately gifts to be showered, sweaters, socks to be knitted.

'I suppose it's his way,' Leicester answered Holmes's sarcasm. Introduced, Constantopoulos had shaken hands with eager protestations of pleasure, fervent hopes of friendship. Fingers sank into his soft plump palms as into dough, his eyes were black olives, his feet sleeping doves. Smooth, rounded, tapering form, dark shining hair further evoked feathered images. In brown striped suit, with two gold teeth, he emanated all the warmth of heart so often accompanying fulsome manners, a flair for back-stabbing.

23

'Where's Offenbach?'

Informed that the Fisheries Officer was already at the bottom of the lagoon, Holmes was stunned.

'As soon as he landed,' said Miss Arbuthnott. 'He looked round and started giving instructions. Then he unpacked his gear and began to dive.'

'Poor Heinrich,' said Constantopoulos. 'He works far too hard. I hope he comes up again in time for the party tomorrow.'

Miss Arbuthnott found little wrong with working hard. She showed no fear that Constantopoulos would overwork.

'It is pleasant,' she informed Leicester. 'To hear English spoken again after months of French. Apart, of course, for the vernacular.'

'You and I must have some *tête-à-têtes* in French,' Constantopoulos offered. 'At home, in Egypt, French was our second language. I went to the Brothers' school.'

'I don't speak French,' Miss Arbuthnott said. 'Apart from what I require for my work;' but the snub was lost. The typists had risen like starlings and Constantopoulos was swept into a flurry of hands to kiss.

'I shall take off the rest of the day to unpack,' Miss Arbuthnott announced. 'I shall report for duty tomorrow.'

Leicester's antennae, conditioned to apprehension, picked up his Chief's displeasure; but Holmes, smiling stiffly, claimed to have been forestalled.

'I shall expect you at nine, in my office. To discuss your terms of reference.'

'I shall be ready long before nine,' Miss Arbuthnott stated. 'I'm an early bird. And I am quite *au fait* with my terms of reference. I have my work all mapped out.'

Holmes blinked but did not argue. As Miss Arbuthnott blandly departed Leicester perceived there would never be argument where she was concerned.

Four ❧ ❧

MOST people went home to lunch at midday but Leicester ate at the hotel. The food there was bad but Toa's was worse. Boat day, being mail day, was always rushed. Interrupted, delayed by the Experts' arrival, it was after five when he picked up his car from the Public Works garage where Ern Crump had been checking a whine in the diff.

'She'll be right, Less. How's she going, boy? You got your Experts okay?'

'Thanks, Ern. Yes, they're here.'

'Dolly Vincent's cousin from Sydney's here. Writes for the paper. She must be a smart girl. Marje and I were thinking of having a bit of a rort for her. How about it?' He narrowed his eyes, waiting.

An ambush in the perennial war. Leicester, incapable of convincing excuses at short notice said cravenly, 'Thank you. I'd like to.'

Ern unnarrowed his eyes. New bloody Zealanders. But old Less was okay.

'Seeya then. She's right.' The flat of his hand descended on the boot of the car as on an equine rump. 'Takeraway.'

Leicester obeyed, wondering why Australians were so touchy, so determined to find themselves patronized. A night at the Crumps was a high price to pay for their reassurance. It was no good saying Never Again. There would always be an again and he knew it. He spent most of his time appeasing those he liked, even, such was his lack of spirit, those he cared nothing for.

'Old Less looked pretty gloomy today,' Ern told his wife Marje, a Brisbane girl with bad teeth.

'Ah,' said Marge. 'He's got his troubles, I guess, I wouldn't like to work for Holmes. And his housegirl's no good. He ought to get someone else.'

'If you ask me,' said Ern. 'He's got his eye on Temata, Ben's daughter.'

'No kidding,' said Marje. 'Temata, in the post office? She wouldn't go out as housegirl. She's too grand. She calls herself a princess.'

Ern had not meant as a housegirl.

'Go *won*! You don't say!' said Marge. At once Ern regretted his indiscretion. Feeling men should stick together he said, 'Don't spread it round.'

'Oh no,' Marje said fervently. 'I won't breathe a *word*.'

At the Session held on Ha'i Koma, Leicester had been fascinated to find all the Peaceful Islands delegates were Chiefs and Princesses.

The princesses, in white with gardenias behind their ears, were exotic, romantic, graciously democratic. They had been photographed, interviewed, recorded on tape. They made speeches about their People, their Way of Life. Words like breeding, race, ancient tradition had peppered the reports of susceptible journalists.

It had been rather a shock to see these patricians in their native setting. The most beauteous and aristocratic had lost several front teeth. Sallow, very pregnant, she wore an old maroon cardigan over a tight cotton dress. She worked in one of the trade stores; had forgotten Leicester's existence. Temata, the younger and gayer princess, who registered parcels at the post office, was offhand. She did not remember his name.

There had been other shocks. The Chieftains who at Ha'i Koma had called him their brother, wept at parting, offered hearts and homes, had not bothered to show up when he reached Aratoa, though aware of his coming. Discovered at menial occupations unworthy of their princely status, they had displayed little interest in whether he came or went.

Temata, at least, had been polite, prepared to chatter about herself, her aspirations: 'I went to school in New Zealand. I had a scholarship. I should like to return there and go to University. Then I could come back and help to lead My People.'

Leicester found it touching, admirable, in view of her background. She was so fresh, so well-groomed in her white shift, hair massively coiled, with frangipani or hibiscus over the ear, or, at home, in *pareu* and long shining plaits. Her family were less particular. The mother, the endless vague female relations out in the cookhouse were toothless, obese, with swollen filarial legs, dressed in shapeless garments with gaping plackets, sagging hemlines. Ben, the princess's father, wrapped a *pareu* round beneath gross pendant bosoms and for formal occasions chose a tattered athletic vest with ragged shorts and sweaty felt hat. The swarming good-looking children—(*My little brothers and sisters*) were dirty and often had sores. They wore torn washed-out hand-me-downs or nothing at all.

There had been instinctive shock at the royal domestic setting. Garbage lay outside the cookhouse, flies were thick. Though at meals Ben and Leicester were served by the women with the best food, the best china, mission-embroidered linen, he was always uncomfortably conscious of the family, squatting out at the back, gnawing cold taro and tinned corned beef. But with familiarity came acceptance, even changed vision. Relaxing climate, South Seas indolence dimmed critical faculties; flowers, songs, soft hands, murmuring voices obscured flies and sores; Polynesian generosity, easy-going good humour became the ideal; even squalor seemed picturesque.

Through it all Temata moved gracefully, Ha'i Koma first impressions magically transcending bare feet, garbage, pigs. It had not taken Leicester long to fall in love. She was so pretty, so charming, so respectfully attentive; smiling, playing her coconut ukelele, singing sad gentle songs.

He was overwhelmed at love's generosity in visiting him for the first time in so idyllic a setting. Not one traditional prop was withheld ... moonlit nights, sighing reef, waving palms, scented air ... unbelievably, he was living a South Seas romance; but early training made him ungracious to Venus. It did not occur to him to take advantage of Temata's compliant sweetness. One simply could not regard her as one of the natives; she bore no relation at all to the freely accessible village girls. Like a loved and respected European, she must be offered no less than marriage.

It had all seemed so simple at first; but now the thought of marriage brought embarrassment. It was not so simple, after all. Complications must be considered. He had been considering them for some weeks without result, beyond increasing uneasiness with Temata.

As though reading his mind she had lately shown signs of withdrawing, was less inclined to listen to talk of development projects, benefits in store for her People. At times she seemed restless, almost bored. She had begun to look at him in a way he did not understand, did not like. Was she disappointed? Waiting for something? Summing him up? Presents, inspired by guilt and remorse, solved nothing. Temata accepted blandly, retaining inscrutability.

'Hi, Leicester!'

The verandah roof sagged like a hat pulled over eyes. Its wooden posts suggested loose teeth. Coral walls sprouted damp-loving plants, coral floors crumbled to rubble. Leicester slowed down.

'Hullo, Ben.'

'Coming in?'

Fowls, piglets scuttled away as he parked by a breadfruit tree. Tins, coconut shells crunched under his wheels.

'Temata?'

'Not home. She gone out. She gone up in the mountains to her sister's.'

'Oh ... will she be long?'

The man in the blue-and-white *pareu* smiled.

'Back tomorrow. You have *kai* with us maybe?'

Leicester shook his head, not in the mood for those long aimless evenings on Ben's verandah. Without Temata it all seemed suddenly so untidy, almost squalid.

'Well . . . I think if you don't mind, Ben, I won't. It's been busy today and I'm tired. Toa has *kai* ready for me at home.'

'Okay then. Okay.'

'Will you tell Temata I came?'

'Okay. I tell her.'

Disappointed but strangely relieved, Leicester started his car.

'Ben,' he said automatically. 'Can't you stop them throwing tins and coconut shells about?'

'Okay, okay.'

'They fill with water when it rains; mosquitoes breed in them. They shouldn't be here.'

'Okay Leicester. Okay.' Ben looked surprised at the almost querulous tone. 'Goodbye Leicester.' He waved without malice or interest.

Refusal of Ben's hospitality was pure perversity. Nothing could be more depressing, less enticing than dinner prepared by Toa. Boiled taro and cold corned beef last night; fried chop, breadfruit chips tonight. If only he could have chicken or fish. Other people had chicken, they had eggs and pork, but these were hard to find in the hurricane season and Toa was too stupid, he was too busy to search. Meat from the freezer was well enough until she cooked it. Sometimes Leicester was so hungry he drank too much whiskey and woke with a headache. He feared he might become alcoholic; suspected an ulcer; and why did the hotel always serve Irish stew in the heat, and that lukewarm tinned grapefruit? He needed a wife.

Dinner was ready, too early. Leicester gulped resignedly at his drink and went to the table. He was still contemplating the warm greasy chop when he realized Toa was hovering.

'Pictures tonight?' he obediently called.

From the dark verandah a bashful giggle. She came to the door.

'And you want to go?'

'Yes please, Leicester.'

'And you want me to hurry up?'

Chin, eyebrows were silently raised.

'All right. But don't go till you've washed up, will you?'

'Yes.' (Yes, I won't go.)

They'd been playing this game for months. Gentle hints, discreet hoverings, hopeful eyes were as close as she got to requests. He would bolt down his meal and hand over his plate; but tonight, out of boredom, he said, 'Are you going with friends?'

'No. All alone. By myself. I have no one to go with. Unless you come with me?'

Slut as she was, her Polynesian good manners still charmed.

'Thank you, Toa. Not tonight. Some other time.'

'Tomorrow night you will come?'

'Tomorrow I'm going to dinner at the Residency.'

'After tomorrow? After tomorrow is one picture called *Black Arrow*. You will like it.'

'You have seen it?'

'Oh yes. But I see it again. I take you.'

'Thank you. Some other time.'

Now he could never sack her—as though that were likely! Dark tragic eyes ensured continued employment, not to mention illegitimate baby, useless old father, dependent young brothers and sisters, the derelict ruin she lived in, her own malnutrition.... She would go on exploiting his weakness, refusing an orthodox broom, straggling through the house with her bundle of twigs, offering him grey boiled taro, picking flowers for her hair, playing her ukelele, helping herself to his stores.

She was at the door again.

'I go now, Leicester.'

'You washed the plates?'

'I washed. I go now. Good night.'

'Good night, Toa.'

The pale dress flitted away down the path. Leicester moved to the verandah with his whiskey. For the moment, greasy meal, impending indigestion were forgotten. Sweet-scented flowers breathed out their hearts by the steps; among the *flamboyants*, sleeping mynah birds muttered. In the villages yellow lamps would be swinging, candles shining in jars. From far away came sad Maori singing, in the background the sigh of the reef.

Released by whiskey, stirred by nocturnal beauty, Leicester permitted self-pity. Lonely; alone in this paradise. Must he always be alone? Was he losing Temata? Suppose she married a Maori? That would be just punishment for procrastination. His heart told him he was a fool not to snatch her; his cautious nature reminded that it was not so simple, so simple as that.

The truth was, no doubt, somewhat ignoble. When you had been a nonentity all your life it was hard to throw away popularity. At home, shyness, passing exams, helping Mother had cramped your style. There had been no time for learning to dance, no money for clothes. A harassed night student, you crept through the university, unsought, unnoticed.

Later, there had been wholesome bushwalkers, almoners, workers in worth-while causes, some ready for maladroit kissing—oh, the dodging and clashing of lenses—others even prepared to go further, entangled in sleeping-bags; but one could not pretend to have been a success.

But on Aratoa you found yourself pursued by women. At the hotel, housegirls padded into your room after dark, climbed into your bed; white spinsters showered tributes ... Tahitian shirts, handknitted socks, sacrificial offerings of liquor rations. How could you fail to enjoy it? How could you bear to lose it?

But lose it he must if he married Temata. In his first months of island life he had learnt this hard truth. No mat-

31

ter how godlike the status of eligible bachelors, how deep the warm bath of competing approval, there was a price to be paid. To survive, they must love all; prefer none; not marry natives.

For all its dazzling seas, waving palms, sleepy lagoons, trade winds and flowers, Aratoa life was not like Somerset Maugham. Passion, intrigue among Europeans was directed into administrative channels, affairs of social precedence rather than of the heart. Respectable, settled, unadventurous, the matrons played tennis, competed with coffee and tea parties, made cakes, gossiped, complained of island life and kept within their own compounds. (Husbands who strayed did so discreetly with Maori girls, which though deplorable didn't count). The spinsters kept themselves to themselves. They had come seeking marriage and though island life turned out to be mainly spent between the walls of government offices, hotel bedrooms, though perfumed nights and twanging guitars were rather pointless without male company, they clung to their pride, did not contemplate married men or native boys, and bided their time.

Into this arena of crouching lions Leicester had stumbled, to witness a frightening observance. The last dental officer, eager newcomer, fêted and petted, indulged in his wild oats, had just married his native mistress. Overnight, the eyes of Aratoa's white women, married and single, had glazed in his presence, voices grown cold, metaphorical skirts drawn aside. It was no moral judgment. To marry a native was the unforgivable act of rejection, affronting all European womanhood. The men, though less censorious, showed contempt and, fearing their wives, became cool. The wretched Carruthers was now back in Auckland alone, they said, since his wife had returned to the islands, drinking, his whole career shattered.

Shocked by the speed of the tragedy, the implacable law that had broken Carruthers, Leicester had tried to rationalize. If the dentist had shown defiance, stayed on, stuck it out, would not hostility have eventually died—a diminished status been granted, such as accorded sea-captains and traders with native wives? Perhaps; but sea-captains who married island girls did not thereby slight white woman-hood. Their very ineligibility protected them. It was different for government personnel, especially junior newcomers. For all his modesty Leicester knew his value, his danger. Could he stand up to disapproval, ostracism, gossip, ridicule? Had he the guts?

Each day, shaving, he studied himself in the glass. He knew it all by heart. Without glasses his eyes were not bad, though myopic. Fainted-mouse hair, face longish and thinnish; nothing too bad or too good. Mediocre, ordinary, uninteresting. A worried expression. Not grubby but not fresh-from-the-tub. A meaningless face; a face to forget. Worse, a face not to see.

Once or twice he had groped into self-analysis but always retreated, appalled at what he uncovered. A mother who blamed him for existing had bred a chronic desire to appease, doomed him to a lifetime of eagerness not to offend. He saw himself as a cripple, a formless nonentity, an apology too abject to be contemplated. Only by resolutely ignoring self could he gain balance, and that precarious. Any stronger, uncaring will could demolish it at a glance.

What chance would he stand in a normal society where single men were not regarded as trophies? Who would want him? Had he the strength to abdicate? Above all, had he the courage to stand martyrdom for Temata? These were questions he had not yet been able to answer.

At the hotel, Offenbach, redfaced from his exertions on the sea-bed, had silently eaten dinner and vanished.

'An early night for us all,' Miss Arbuthnott said, sweeping out of the dining-room.

'Oh ... but *coffee* ... on the *verandah* ...' the Baha'i missionaries seemed to swoon at the thought of missing this treat. 'That's if it won't keep you awake. It's Instant.'

33

'Nothing would keep me awake. When I'm ready I sleep like a child, no matter where.'

'How wonderful. Well then ... coffee.... And *you* ... Mr ... er ... You'll take coffee? On the verandah?'

'I am a *Greek*, my dear lady, and you ask me if I'll take coffee!'

Oh, how gay it was getting at the hotel. The typists had put on their prettiest dresses and sprayed their hair; the housegirls were all smiles. And what was this charming gentleman handing round now? Turkish Delight! Egyptian cigarettes! Sugar almonds!

'A little sweet, Miss Arbuthnott, to go with your coffee?'

'Thank you, no. I do not eat sweets.'

'But you will, Miss ... ?'

'Miss Manders. And this is my colleague, Miss Jones. Why, thank you.'

'Would you care to wipe your dainty fingers? Your beautiful knitting ...'

'Oh, how thoughtful! Your own handkerchief! What a bewdiful perfume!'

Miss Arbuthnott wrinkled her nose. Oriental bazaar!

'And you live here, madame, you and your friend? You are working perhaps in the government? Or you are *touriste*?'

'Why no, Mr—'

'My friends call me Costa.'

'Oh. Why no, Mr Costa.... We are pioneers for the Baha'i faith.'

'Indeed. How interesting that must be. Excuse me, dear lady. I must hand round the cups.'

'Why, Mr Costa, the girls will do that!'

But he had gone with his Turkish Delight to the typists.

He was gone but his ear was still tuned to them. Everyone, everyone liked him but that Miss Arbuthnott. On the ship he had, when not seasick, been enormously popular. Only she, with her moustache, her bottle-shaped calves had resisted. Taking a blow round the deck, feet well apart,

34

hands dug into pockets, she had despised him, limp in his long chair. She did not find him charming, this big ugly Englishwoman. That was the arrogance of the British. Everyone else, man, woman and child; but not she.

He wished to dismiss her but she was a thorn, a jabbing splinter. Through the prattle of enslaved typists her loud English voice boomed across. What in God's name was she talking of?

'Sometimes they go on breastfeeding until the child is six! It's appalling. By that time the milk is no good and the mother is quite exhausted. Of course usually there are several more children by then, but I have found in some districts...'

The Baha'is sucked their sugar almonds and clicked their knitting needles.

'...Still, better wean too late than *not breastfeed at all*!'

At the thought of those fecund black bosoms, shining and sweating and bulging with life-giving milk Miss Jones and Miss Manders slightly shrank. Unlikely, alas, to feed anything now but mosquitoes, they reminded themselves that they had come voluntarily, at their own expense, to serve for a year in the islands and this was the sort of thing they must get used to.

And here was that sweet Mr Costa again, *kissing hands*!

'If you beautiful ladies will excuse me, I shall retire. Good night, dear Miss Manders, Miss Jones. Miss Arbuthnott: good night.'

Not a hint of his petulance, dissatisfaction. A courteous bow when Miss Arbuthnott replied, schoolmistressy, 'That's right, Constantopoulos. Off to bed, for an early start in the morning.'

In his striped underpants Costa stood, idly stroking the wombat bristles erupting through his aertex vest. No woman had ever resisted before. Could it mean he was slipping, losing his charm? Must he be penned on an island

B*

with a constant reminder of failure? No, no, it was she, un-
natural creature; there was nothing the matter with him.
But it was not agreeable to be so rudely rejected in public.

Encased in the rocketting birds of his favourite pyjamas
he dabbed cologne on his hands, smoothed his sleek hair
and got into bed. In the dark he lay smoking, staring out at
majestic peaks, black against white immense stars. Strange
that all the raptures of typists, Baha'is, housegirls could not
relieve the smart of this hideous masculine Englishwoman.

He put out his cigarette and lay down. Briefly, he slept, to
wake with a start. Stiff with fear, he heard a faint brushing
on the mats. Burglars? Wild animals? Terrorists? He
opened a terrified eye. A human form showed against the
window. Should he pretend sleep or sit up and tell where
his wallet was hidden? Heart arrested, eyes closed, he
awaited attack.

A gentle hand fell on his face, moved blindly to rest on
his hair. A whisper: 'You awake? You awake, Costa?' A
scent of frangipani and coconut oil as a figure bent over
him, long dark hair swept his skin.

He sat up suddenly, put out his hand for the light.

'What is it? What is wrong?'

'No no, don't put light on,' the gentle voice said. 'Only
me. Nothing wrong.'

The girl who waited on his table!

'What is it?'

She sat on the edge of the bed and looked down at him
through the darkness.

'You like me come in with you maybe?'

'In here?'

'Yes. I come in if you like.' Already she had begun to
undress. A frangipani crown plopped on the floor; little
warm hands paddled over him, soft giggles sounded. Costa,
recovered, moved over enthusiastically.

Five 🌊 🌊

WHEN Leicester reached the office next morning Miss Arbuthnott was already with Holmes. Neither Costa nor Offenbach were visible. The latter was down on the sea-bed, the former still in his hotel bed.

Leicester's day had not begun well. Slightly hung-over from his evening of drink and self-searching he had met Judy Pollock, in a shift screen-printed with gas-lamps. Fair stringy hair, clever boot-button eyes were as he reluctantly remembered from their meeting at Ha'i Koma. She had asked for a lift and at once begun making impertinent remarks.

'How's the Morris Dancing? How's Maori Culture? How's Mr Holmes? Oh dear me, how the sun does glare on those government roofs! Tell me, Leicester, why, with his dedication to native handcrafts, is Holmes so wedded to corrugated iron? So dear, so hot, so ugly....'

'Those roofs were there before he came.'

'But the others ... all the others. It's his ambition, he told me at the Session, to have every Aratoan in a wooden, iron-roofed house before he retires. I suppose it's his Public Works background.'

'Leaf houses get shabby. They fall down. Pandanus thatch harbours rats. It doesn't last....'

'There's lots of materials, free for the gathering. Everyone helps with the thatching. Apart from the look of it, and the coolness and suitability....' She had been unspeakably tiresome.

Aporo was waiting.

'Good morning, Leicester.'

'Good morning, Aporo.'

'See Leicester, how well I have done this screen printing.'

He held up a poster. 'The *anopheles* mosquito. It brings filariasis,' he explained.

Leicester contemplated the horse-like image.

'Very good.'

'See how I cut the legs! That was difficult. I am getting on, you think Leicester?'

'Oh yes, you're getting on well.'

'Soon Mr Holmes will send me to New Zealand. You will ask him ...'

'Whiteway!' Holmes opened his door. 'I'd like a word with you. Aporo, fix up Miss Arbuthnott with whatever she wants for her work.'

'I shall work in my hotel room for a start.' Miss Arbuthnott rolled up behind him. 'At this stage, mine is mainly a scissors-and-paste job. Adapting my filmstrips ... posters ... flannelgraphs,' she nodded at Leicester. 'Local idiom and vernacular. May call on you for advice.'

'Miss Arbuthnott will be in your charge,' Holmes said when she had bounced away with her scissors and paste. 'She wants to get the feel of the place. When she's ready you'll take her out with you on location.'

Leicester sensed Holmes was, for once, a mouthpiece.

'I'll look after Constantopoulos ... show him round ... introduce him to the villagers. Offenbach seems to be settling all right. Meanwhile ...' he opened a file with the air of a cat scenting fish. 'There is plenty of work in other directions. Sit down.'

Leicester sat.

'You remember I wrote to Joseph, schoolmaster on Manu, asking for a report on the situation there? I have his reply. He, of course, wants all sorts of impossible things for himself but out of it all I find quite a number of subjects that do come into our province.' He ticked off items as he read. 'People won't use latrines. The school children stay up too late and go to sleep in class—all good for posters— There's no arts or crafts; no one making mats or *tivaivais*. No traditional dances, no women's interests—all that will be excellent for our Community Development Team—and as for health ... Infant mortality; filariasis; yaws; TB ... even leprosy!'

Leicester shifted uneasily at the note of triumph.

'Excellent opening for health education materials ... a combined-media job, I should say ... posters, films, film-strips, flannelgraphs.'

'We did send some TB posters several months ago. I never heard if...'

'Someone must go to Manu,' said Holmes. 'I'm sending you.'

The big chance! The longed-for opportunity! An honour, a mark of the Chief's confidence; and he could only think of excuses. Impossible to leave Temata, the way things were. He said feebly, 'But what about Miss Arbuthnott and Constantopoulos? They'll be on Manu.'

These two were to act as the spearhead for the Community Development project, to soften-up Manu for the native nurse, schoolmaster, Women's Interest Leader, Hand-crafts Instructor, Filariasis and Agricultural Officers who would come later, when their training had fully equipped them; but Holmes said impatiently, 'Manu's a big atoll. Joseph's on the main island. The Experts are going to Arumai, miles away, a separate islet. The people don't mix much. Manu village is a very bad area. The natives spend the money they make from pearlshell diving on drink, buying useless luxuries. They're not easy to handle, I understand. It will be your first big challenge. You must rise to it.'

Leicester wondered how he might best do so.

'Your first job, of course, will be to establish felt needs, make the people articulate. But we'll go into that later, when the time comes. There's no question of action till after the hurricane season, when shipping resumes. You will probably go with the others.'

Leicester relaxed, but Holmes, dismissing Manu, said, 'Look here, Whiteway, those posters for the rhinoceros beetle. Call Aporo in. He'd better hear this.'

39

Aporo stood, awaiting compliments, as Holmes unrolled a poster bearing a great glowering beetle.

'These are useless,' said the Chief. 'Completely useless.'

'Useless?' Leicester was startled. 'But why, sir? What is wrong? The beetle was drawn from life.'

'I can't imagine what you were thinking, to let Aporo draw this absurdity.'

'But what is wrong with it, sir? What is wrong?'

Holmes flung aside the screen-printed insect.

'The villagers say they have never seen animals like this in their lives.'

Leicester said indignantly, 'Then they're not telling the truth. The beetle is correct in every detail. Aporo went to no end of trouble and Mr Wilson said it was perfect. . . .'

'Yes, Mr Holmes. The Director of Agriculture congratulate me on my work. . . .'

'Entomologically it may be perfect, but you have overlooked the literal mind of the native. *Scale*, Whiteway! What about scale? The villagers are looking for creatures this size. Big as cats. They say they have nothing like this in their coconuts, only little black beetles which they don't bother to catch or bring in. People are laughing at you, Whiteway. If *I* had been designing the poster I should, for instance, have shown the beetle in the palm of a hand, to give the idea of scale. . . .'

Leicester, protest deflated, went scarlet. His hand moved nervously to his mouth. Idiot, unspeakable idiot! How could he make such a stupid mistake!

'I'm sorry sir. I didn't think of scale.'

'You did not think! It's your job to think! Well, fix it up. Redraw the whole thing; but better let me see it before it goes out this time.'

'Yes sir.' Leicester manoeuvred the stupefied Aporo out of the room.

At his desk he found all the clever replies he never could think of in time. He groped for consolations. Everyone made mistakes. That was how you learned. He was lucky to be able to profit from his superior's knowledge and experience; but philosophy shrivelled under Aporo's insistent gaze. Constipated with fury, the New Peaceful Islander awaited vengeance, all thoughts of Art School swamped by brutal loss of face. Leicester feared he might burst.

'Get on with your work Aporo,' he said impatiently. After all, his loss of face had been greater. But of course he was spineless.

So clearly did Aporo reflect this thought, Leicester had to avert his eyes.

Leaving the freezer Phyllis Cornick ran into Marje Crump. Of all the luck!

'Did you get onions?'

'Of course not!' said Phyllis. 'They're out of them.'

'Go won!' Marje said. 'Every year it's the same.'

'They never order enough,' Phyllis said peevishly. 'You'd think they'd never heard of hurricane seasons or shipping shortages.'

'I'll say!' But Marje wasn't really concerned. She came to the freezer mainly for its social life. Plump, with amalgum corners on her front teeth, she was not much sought after by Aratoa hostesses. Phyllis, despising her, found her Brisbane accent appalling. She said now, 'I'm really so tired of this place. When we were in *Sa*-maw we didn't have to put up with this sort of thing.'

'Ah well, now you're talking. S'moa's a big place ... Apia's a city. My brother, has a store in Raro—in the Cooks— goes there for his buying sometimes instead of New Zealand.'

Phyllis did not need Marje Crump to tell her Rarotonga was in the Cook Islands. She said coldly, 'Well, I'm going. Goodbye.'

'Bye-bye. Hey, Phyl, could you give me a lift?'

'I'm not going your way.'

'Oh, I'm not going home. I'm going to the hotel for tea. Come on with me. It'll do you good. Take you out of yourself.'

'I don't need taking out of myself, thank you. I'll drop you off.'

Marje was impervious.

'Have you heard,' she said, climbing into the car. 'About Leicester?'

'Leicester Whiteway? What about him?'

'Don't tell anyone, but I'm that worried. Ern says...'

Seeing Temata leave the Post Office Leicester flushed, then paled as adrenalin cascaded into his blood.

'Temata!'

She gave him her beautiful blank Maori stare. Would he ever know what was behind it?

'If you've finished work I'll drive you home.'

'All right. If you like.' You could not say she was over-joyed.

'Did you go to your sister's?'

She jerked up chin and eyebrows.

'You look tired. You were late last night?'

'I don't come if you lecture me, Leicester.'

'I'm sorry. I'm sorry. I won't lecture you.'

So pretty, despite the dark circles under the eyes. So pretty and so unfathomable.

'Would you like to come for a drive?'

'No. I go home, thank you Leicester.'

'Do come.'

'I go home. My mother is waiting.'

There was nothing you could put your finger on, yet uneasiness remained. Was she annoyed? Was it just Polynesian moodiness? She was so withdrawn....

'Temata,' he said humbly. 'Have I done something to upset you?'

Perceiving sincerity, her incredulity became scorn.

'I like a new dress for Mrs Hitchcock's concert,' she said experimentally.

'Oh! Oh, of course you must have a new dress! You go and get what you want. I'll give you the money. You tell me how much...'

Calm acceptance cut off eager apeasement.

'Okay. I tell you how much. Tomorrow. I get off now.'

The slight smile granted was gratefully aceepted but as he drove on his uncertainty returned. Was it really as simple as that ... just a matter of a new dress? How could he ever find out what went on in her mind? Ever know what she thought?

A dim monotone competed unequally with the scarlet trees' clamour: Toa, on the verandah step, with her coconut ukelele. A large stolid baby, propped against the wall, breathed adenoidally.

'This is Daniel. My son.'

'Ah.' His mind on Temata, Leicester stepped over Daniel. 'Did you iron my shirt, Toa?'

'Oh yes.'

'Where is it?'

'In there.' She jerked her head at the bedroom. 'I go now?'

'Yes. No. Get me some ice for a drink.'

'No ice. Fridge gone out.'

'Gone out! You let it go out!'

'Oh no. It go out by itself.'

'Well then, make me some tea.'

'Stove gone out.'

'What the hell have you been doing all day?'

Daniel drew in his breath, shut his eyes tight and went black in the face. A piece of grey taro fell from his open mouth.

Toa snatched at him protectively, defensively.

'What's the matter with him? What's he crying for?'

'Frightened. You frightened him. Shouting.'

He controlled his exasperation. 'I'm sorry. I'm sorry.'

She crouched, reproachful eyes staring over Daniel's head. Brute; bully; tyrant! Leicester sighed.

'All right. Take him home, Toa.'

'I make you some tea?'

'No, don't bother. Get me a whiskey. Then, take that baby home.'

She stood up gingerly. Daniel hiccupped, drew his breath in and roared.

Leicester said suddenly, 'Why is Daniel here? Why did you bring him?'

'My father gone fishing. Daniel all alone. I bring him.'

'Well, don't do it again. Understand? Just this time. Not every day.'

Agreement cost nothing. She raised eyebrows and chin.

He went gloomily to the bath-house, ashamed of his anger. Dreadful to frighten a native; a child! It had been a bad day but it wasn't her fault. Too nervy; too touchy. All on edge. The posters! The weather! Temata!

Must be gentler with Toa: have more patience. He groped from the shower, pressing his face into the towel. At once he pulled back. Slimy and damp! Had she used it for washing the floor?

'Toa! What have you done with my towel?' he yelled. 'Toa! What the hell?—*Toa!* Bring me a clean one.'

The shrieks of the mynah birds were the only reply.

Six ❧ ❧

MEETING Judy in the square on his way from the lagoon bed to the hotel, Offenbach fixed her with his bloodshot blue eyes and said, 'Tonight I drink viskey mit you at the hotel.'

'Oh?'

'*Ja.* You vil to hotel kom in mine room and ve drink viskey. *Nein?*'

'*Nein*. Not tonight. Tonight is the Resident's party.'

'I vould rather drink viskey mit you tonight than eat dinner mit governor.'

'Yes, but you can't, Heinrich. You're a guest of honour.'

'So. You like viskey?'

'Oh yes, I like it. But not tonight. Some other night.'

'I do not see you since the ship. Vot you doing? To-morrow at 7.30 kom. Ve drink.'

'We'll see.'

'You can't say Offenbach beats round the bush,' Judy said to Dr Vincent as she drove with him and his string-coloured wife to the Residency.

'Whereas Constantopoulos invents bushes to go round; and behind,' Dr Vincent suggested.

'Oh,' Dolly Vincent said affectedly. 'I'd be *petrified* with Constantopoulos. He's a wolf.'

'Mediterranean men have to make conquests. I bet you'll end up eating out of his hand.'

'I shan't. I hope I shan't have to sit next to him tonight. To be honest I really don't think I'm going to enjoy myself. The Holmeses—the Hitchcocks—it's such a shame. I so longed for these new people to come and now they turn out to be wolves.'

'Well, Judy will enjoy herself, if no one else. She'll enjoy H.H.'

'I'll enjoy myself. But will His Honour enjoy me?'

'His Honour never enjoys anything when it involves giving hospitality. He suffers every time I look at the whiskey.'

Dolly said indulgently, 'Oh Bill, you're awful. He's not all that bad.'

'Yes he is. He's bloody mean.'

'He worries about his retirement,' said Dolly kindly. 'How he'll manage.'

'I met him,' said Judy. 'He was at the P.I.D.L. Session. I thought him a pleasant old chap, but peculiar. The boys

45

said he used to pinch all their pencils. Perhaps he has some kind of complex?'

'Oh no. That's for his memoirs. He's going to write his memoirs when he retires.'

'With our pencils?'

'Yes. He believes there will be a depression or the cost of living will go up and his pension won't be enough,' Dolly said. 'He expects to live in penury when he retires. That's why he's so careful with money.'

'But the *pencils*?'

'Well, he won't be able to afford them, you see. So he's collecting. He does the same with paper.'

'Are you making this up?'

'No, it's true. Perfectly true. He collects paper. They say at headquarters he keeps all his old drafts, to use the backs, and that he's always requisitioning for more paper than he can use. They say he stores it away. Some people say he pinches the telegram forms from the post office . . .'

'Oh Bill!'

'. . . but I don't believe that myself . . . there's printing on the back of telegrams.'

'Perhaps I could give him some pencils and paper,' said Judy. 'I have plenty with me.'

'If you did he'd eat out of your hand. I wouldn't go so far as to say he takes *bribes* . . .'

'Bill!'

'. . . but he does accept presents. He's not expensive, they tell me. A few stamps for his collection or shells from the reef and he'll do anything you want.'

'There's the Residency car at the door,' Dolly said. 'It must have gone down to the hotel for the Experts.'

'Experts!' said Dr Vincent. 'Experts!'

His wife looked apprehensive.

'Promise you won't drink too much tonight, Bill. It makes you so tactless.'

46

Christmas had come, in the Residency hall: cellophane, coloured paper, plastic ribbons crackled and shone.

'Good evening, dear lady.' Miss Davidson snatched her Vice-regal hand back from Costa's lips. 'So delightful. Such a pleasure. For you ... and for his Excellency.'

The Queen's representatives helplessly stared at the sweets, cigars, handkerchiefs, scent piling up on the hibiscus-wood table.

'Ah, Miss Judy ... Doctor ... Madame ...'

'Is it somebody's birthday? We didn't know....' Dolly stood thunderstruck in the doorway.

'Greeks,' said Miss Arbuthnott, in beaded blue chiffon, 'bearing gifts.'

Amorous black olives, seeking sympathy, swept towards Nutkin, on guard by her husband. A flicker, and she ceased straining to see if the chain round Miss Arbuthnott's neck ended in pendant or crucifix. Poor fellow, he looked so crushed. That woman need not have been so sweeping; nor did he look like a communist in his white mess jacket.

Miss Davidson took Miss Arbuthnott's arm. It was Stanley and Livingstone.

'Come,' she said. 'Come to the verandah. Let us all have a drink.'

Drink had not circulated enough to smooth out rough edges when Leicester arrived in his ill-ironed shirt. Almost at once the company moved to the table, thankfully, since it was easier there for enemies and those not speaking to keep apart. Miss Davidson's seating arrangements—an afternoon's work—had been thought out with care. Holmes occupied neutral territory between his hostess and Dolly Vincent, opposite Leicester. Judy Pollock was next Dr Vincent; then came Mrs Hitchcock, Costa, Janet Holmes, Offenbach. His Honour sat at the end with Miss Arbuthnott on his right. Beyond was the missionary, trying not to see Holmes or his host.

Altogether few eyes could happily meet. Only Judy and Dr Vincent seemed entirely at ease.

'Offenbach's very red in the face,' Vincent murmured. 'Is there something the matter with him?'

'All that diving, perhaps? Holding his breath. He's always under the water.'

'Was he red on the ship, or is it since he arrived? Does he drink?'

'He drinks viskey.'

'I hope he won't have a stroke.'

'Miss Pollock! What are you whispering about down there with Dr Vincent?'

'We were discussing transplanting trochus, Miss Davidson.'

'Ach!' Offenbach lifted his face from his crab mayonnaise.

'Mr Offenbach!' Janet Holmes exposed her large teeth, known by Dr Vincent as Elegy in a Country Churchyard. 'Now, you're the Expert. Do tell us about the trochus.'

'You vant to know vat? You vant I tell vat?'

Janet showed off her knowledge.

'Well ... tell us ... tell us why is trochus so hard to transplant? So much harder than pearlshell, for instance?'

Offenbach's china-blue eyes did not waver.

'Very well. I explain.' He put down his fork. 'So! You know that there are two sexes, male and female?'

All conversation had stopped. Janet, a good sport, said gaily, 'Yes. I had heard.'

'It is the same mit the trochus. They are multiplying by the fertilization of the egg. You know of the fertilization of the egg, *ja*?'

'Of course.' For all her brightness Janet felt strangely isolated against the background of silence.

'So! Trochus is multiplying by the fertilization of the egg. For example: You are female. I am male. *Ja*?'

'Yes. That's right.'

'So! I am male, you female. I have the spermatazoa, you have the ovum. To reproduce ourselves it is necessary that my spermatazoa your ovum shall fertilize. This you understand?'

48

'Yes yes. I understand.'

'Same mit trochus. In the case of you and me, we have sexual intercourse so my spermatazoa to your ovum is come. But in principle it is same. It is very beautiful,' Offenbach said, going back to his mayonnaise. 'But mit the trochus there are difficulties. It is not so mit humans ... with us is less delicate. I am lying mit you ... *pfft* ... all over. Ovum is fertilized, safely, in your body. *Even temperature!* But mit trochus maybe temperature of the water is not right. Then is disaster....'

'It's wonderful,' said Miss Arbuthnott into the paralysed silence. 'That Pacific peoples may now exchange information ... share each other's knowledge ... experience...'

Miss Davidson waved at the house-boys. Pineapple fritters appeared.

'The Pacific has vastly changed in our lifetime.' Holmes took three fritters. 'In the days of the missions'—Mr Hitchcock stirred—'even as late as pre-war ... a series of little worlds. Now, one great world bound together by common aims. The International Organization has revolutionized....'

'Quite.' His Honour was frowning. Damn Holmes; damn the fellow! Lecturing. Advertising his wares.

Holmes dried up huffily. In the pause Mrs Hitchcock's whisper hissed out.

'Have you seen Nasser?'

'Nasser? Yes, I have seen him,' said Costa obligingly. 'Quite close. One day, at the Gezira Club I was at the next table...'

'Gezira Club!' H.H. remembered war-time junketings. 'Don't tell me they let the gyppos in there now?'

'Nasser is hardly a gyppo,' said his sister.

'What's he like?' pursued Nutkin. 'What was your impression?'

'Very handsome!' Costa assured enthusiastically. 'Dark flashing eyes, you know ... Arabic.'

Nutkin looked doubtful. Costa, perplexed, sensed he had gone too far.

'He's in with Russia!' Nutkin said sharply. 'I don't trust him.'

'Oh no. Nor do I. Nor do I. Not for a minute.'

'You can't trust a single one of them! Not one! They all want war!'

At her mounting aggression Costa struck out for land.

'Only the pope,' he suggested. 'Only he can be trusted. He doesn't want war. He tries always for peace.'

'Are you a Catholic?' Nutkin's voice quivered.

'I? Oh no, no. Not at all.'

'Then your ignorance is the more dangerous. Don't you know, my poor fellow, that Rome works with Moscow?'

Across Dr Vincent, Judy cried cheerfully, 'Oh come, Mrs Hitchcock. That's going too far!'

Marsupial eyes blazed. Cassandra-voiced warnings flooded the company ... Blindness and apathy were the cause of this terrible situation confronting us, that would bring us all to destruction. Kremlin or Vatican ... it made no difference. Antichrist ...'

'Change of life.' murmured Dr Vincent.

'... Catholic or Communist. It's all the same. A gigantic world plot....'

Offenbach surfaced again.

'So! I am Cattolik. Deutch Cattolik. You say I am Communist?'

'I, too!' Miss Arbuthnott leaned forward. 'I am a Catholic convert. Would you suggest, dear Mrs Hitchcock, that I worked for the Kremlin?'

Nutkin's neck had gone red. Leicester said hastily, 'I was reading the other day, that in certain islands—the Ellice, I think—one of the missions ... I believe it was L.M.S. ... operated as a trading company, registed in London.'

'That's right,' said Judy. 'I went to the Ellice once, for the paper....'

Theodore Hitchcock, so long silent, had started to rumble. Fury, seething inside, was about to gush out like a hot spring, but Miss Davidson, crying, 'Excuse me!' ruthlessly cut him off.

'Excuse me, Mr Whiteway!' In her eagerness her beads brushed her fritters. 'Would you kindly repeat what you said?'

'*I?*'

'Yes. You. Would you kindly repeat what you said?'

'I ... Miss Davidson ... I ...'

'... He said that the L.M.S. were registered in London as a trading company....'

'Thank you, Miss Pollock. Mr Whiteway, on what authority do you make this statement?'

Leicester's mouth was dry.

'Oh ... no authority. None at all.'

'I'm extremely interested in your statement, Mr Whiteway. But I should like to hear the references on which you base it. Exactly *where* did you read the charges you have just made?'

'Oh Miss Davidson, I'm not making charges. Any charges at all. I just happened to read somewhere ... that is, I think I did ... that the L.M.S....'

'I did my M.A. thesis on nineteenth-century Pacific missions and I can assure you no such venture came to light during my researches. Had it done ...'

'Perhaps it was after she wrote her thesis.' Dr Vincent's bored whisper was audible.

'... And the whole of the L.M.S. records in London were made available to me...'

'Nevertheless it is true,' Judy said bravely. 'It *was* in the Ellice. It's a fact. They registered for trading there so they could take away copra.'

'Miss Pollock ... if you will permit me, for after all though you have, as you say, been in the Ellice ... I am an authority on this subject....'

Mr Hitchcock broke out. His Shakespearean voice boomed like a storm on the reef.

'It is incredible that this conversation should take place

51

in my presence. I am a man of God. A man of God! A representative of this same London Missionary Society you are all engaged in slandering. Must I sit here and listen to these cheap conjectures? Your Honour, I must ask you permission for my wife and myself to withdraw. Come, my dear!'

Offenbach fought his way out of boredom, heaved himself up.

'It is time too I go. I vill ask to excuse me.'

Miss Davidson had become flustered. Her beads swayed to and fro over her fritters. Her voice touched panic.

'Oh no ... no, not yet. The Queen.'

'The Queen? Koms here?'

'The Queen's health. The port. We must drink. The ladies will drink before they withdraw.... Then we shall leave you gentlemen....'

'Then I go. Tomorrow is much vurk to do.'

Seven ᘓᕐ ᘓᕐ

LIKE most successful Aratoa gatherings the dinner party had widened old breaches—church and state—and created new ones—church and fisheries, church and Pollock, state and Pollock. Those not actively involved in the evening's skirmishes came away with a stimulating irritability towards their fellow guests—Janet Holmes with Offenbach; the Resident with Holmes; Nutkin with Miss Arbuthnott; but they were not unique. Irritation was general at this time of year. When rain and heat came together people found it hard to be civil at all.

Down at the meteorological station, Phyllis Cornick was hating Thelma Jackson. It was too bad that Radio and Met. officers' houses were so close together, so isolated from Aratoa. Daily droppings-in, domestic secrets forcibly shared could only breed dislike. For one thing Phyllis was fed up with Thelma's hair, dyed with that do-it-yourself stuff which never took properly, slid off the roots and came out the colour of cold tea.

She shifted crossly on the edge of Thelma's bath, lit a cigarette and said, 'Have you ever thought of cold water?'

'What are you talking about?' Thelma sounded touchy.

'Cold water; for the hair.'

'Well, what about it?' Thelma suspended the toothbrush with which she was dabbing her parting.

'For washing. You know, it's hot water that makes hair go grey. It dries up the oil in the scalp. Maori women always wash their hair in cold water. And they hardly ever go grey.'

'Oh yes, they do.'

'Not like us. If you gave up washing it in hot water you needn't do this sort of thing.'

'Everyone does it. It's not peculiar to me....'

Phyllis sighed, superior, longsuffering. Boredom descended. She could not be bothered, if people would not make an effort to be agreeable.

'...And frankly, I don't see that we need to copy Maori women in *everything*.'

'Oh, all right. But you said your hair was falling out. I thought it might be the dye.'

'It isn't dye. It's a conditioner; a revitalizer.'

Phyllis yawned. It was too hot and sticky to quarrel. She was tired to death of Thelma, who never read anything, never had an original thought, cared only for gossip and clothes. She herself was used to better; but who else was there? She offered idly, 'They say Leicester Whiteway is always at Ben's house for meals these days.'

Thelma shrugged, spitefully withholding immediate interest. She said Ben was going to work for Native Development.

'Yes, but not for Leicester. He's going to help Offenbach. Offenbach's given him a snorkel.'

Thelma said they made her tired.

Phyllis felt more cheerful. When Thelma was bitchy about the Maoris it meant her husband Kev had been chasing the housegirls. Poor Thelma, you should really feel sorry for her; and the weather was atrocious. Phyllis said encouragingly, 'I don't know why you're so down on the poor Maoris.'

'I'm sick of this sentimental talk about the poor Maoris. They can't do any wrong. It's got now that you just have to have a brown skin for everyone to fall over backwards. Next thing we'll be apologizing for being white. And the Polynesians are terrible snobs about colour. Look how they despise Melanesians; call them *Blacks*. Besides, this Native Development makes me sick. A bunch of phonies, every one of them, out for free rides.'

'I don't think Leicester's a phoney.'

'Oh, but he's *wet*.'

'He's rather sweet. I quite like him and he means well.'

'He's a nonentity.' Thelma twitched her shoulders impatiently. 'Kev says he'll never get anywhere, and he lets that awful Holmes walk all over him.'

'Well, he's pleasant. At least he's polite. I wouldn't want to see him make a fool of himself.'

Words thrown out idly, for something to say; but Thelma, now peering into the looking-glass, quickly said, 'What does that mean, exactly?'

Phyllis shrugged. 'The usual story.'

'What story?'

'I told you, he's always at Ben's place.'

'You mean Temata?'

'I suppose so. Who else?'

'That little bitch!'

'Well, he's young. What can you expect? He hasn't been here all that long.'

'I must admit I hadn't noticed,' Thelma said quite brightly. 'But he wouldn't *marry* her, do you think?'

'I don't know. That Crump woman says her husband says he's crazy about her.'

'Idiot! Someone ought to speak to him. For his own good.'

'You'd need to be careful. One of the men perhaps. I could get George to.'

'Oh, the men! They all stick together. They all think Temata's wonderful.'

'Not when it comes to marrying, surely!'

'You can't *tell* with them. But somebody ought to Do Something. I mean, about the children.'

'The children! I don't suppose he's got any idea!'

'She's clever. You've got to hand it to her.'

'You can't just go up to him in the street and tell him, like that.'

'No, but we could kind of drop a few hints, don't you think? I mean, not about marrying but the children. I mean, anyone could say that quite openly—you know, in all innocence.'

'Risky. I remember once, in Apia, a similar case—'

'I could get up an evening,' said Thelma. 'Ask him round. You and George. The subject could just come up. A slide evening. There's all those we took last leave.'

'The main thing,' said Phyllis. 'Is to do something soon, before it's too late. Someone must get the message through somehow; you'd have to be careful.'

'I frankly don't intend to stand by and watch that little bitch getting *all* her own way,' Thelma pulled off her rubber gloves. 'Not if I can help stop her.'

Eight ✌ ✌

'YOU did not kom!' Offenbach boomed reproachfully. A curious after-speech resonance hummed, like bees, at the back of his nose.

Judy said, 'No. No, I couldn't.'

'Tonight you kom. Der viskey I have. Tonight I vait. I tell you things for your book.'

'What book?'

'Der book you write.'

'Who said I wrote a book?'

Offenbach shrugged.

'Everyone koms to the islands writes a book.'

'Don't tell people. They're terribly touchy because of those Articles.'

'Okay. You kom then. You kom tonight and I do not tell.'

Though he could not afford to dwell on the thought, Holmes was aware that he did not like Constantopoulos.

'It's just that he's foreign,' said Janet, who found that adequate reason.

Her husband could not share her tolerance.

'So awkward. Good Co-op men aren't easy to come by. And this fellow had such excellent references.'

It will be better,' Janet suggested. 'When he settles in. He's already looking less queer since he got into whites.'

Holmes was not comforted. An Egyptian Greek was neither one thing nor the other; not black like Africans nor yet one of us. It was not just the fulsome manner: Costa's personal essence would always triumph over external trappings. Even Colonial whites could not dispel the illusion of brown chalk-stripes, gaudy ties, coloured silk shirts. The bristles on his plump fingers would always sprout round invisible rings, his smile suggest more gold teeth than he had. Oiled hair, scented handkerchiefs, Egyptian cigarettes created an almost tactile aura. Encased like a buddha in incense he smiled, moved, dispensed his favours.

Nevertheless one had to work with the fellow.

'Are you comfortable at the hotel?' Holmes asked as he picked Costa up for his first island tour.

The Co-operatives Officer set a bulging briefcase on the floor.

'Extremely comfortable, thank you.'

He was actually purring. He looked like a satisfied tom-cat. Holmes coughed.

'Cigarette?'

'Thank you. I don't.'

Constantopoulos briefly frowned. *Thank you. I don't.* The English! But at any rate others appreciated him. The feline smile slid back into place.

'This, of course, is only an introductory tour; to show you the villages you'll be working in.'

'I am looking forward to it. I have my speeches prepared.'

'Speeches? There won't be any speeches. You will just meet the leading villagers. I shall say a few words to introduce you and tie up further meetings. We'll be back at the office by midday.' Holmes frowned at the briefcase. Could it be food?

'But there are things I wish to say to the villagers. . . .'

'You can do that later. There's plenty of time.'

'. . . And I have presents. . . .'

'Presents! Constantopoulos, this is work. Not a party. Aporo, we'll get off here. Jacopo's house. And you'd better come with us. It may be useful to you.'

Aporo moodily drew up outside a wooden house, leaden-blue with red trimmings and rusty iron roof. Still sulking over his rhinoceros beetles, he could not see how Co-operatives would help him get to New Zealand.

'Good morning ... good morning ... good morning!' Geared to restrained *bonhomie* Holmes strode up the shell-bordered path. Two solemn islanders, grizzled and stout, rose from verandah chairs.

'Good morning Jacopo; good morning Teresa. I have brought Mr Constantopoulos.'

'You will come in, Mr Holmes. . . . We are ready.'

In the small parlour, chairs were drawn up round a green serge tablecloth. Aporo and his displeasure sank into autumnal Genoa velvet. The Queen, in bright sticky colours, smiled down from the picture-rail.

57

'Ah! What beautiful cushions! What magnificent embroidery! You have done it, madame?'

'You like it?'

'My mother and sisters are skilled in embroidery; but *this* . . .'

'Constantopoulos! If you're ready . . .' said Holmes.

Teresa disappeared with the cushions. The Native Development Officer cleared his throat.

'Now Jacopo; we will outline our programme . . .'

Teresa was back.

'You will take a drink Mr Holmes? You like a cool drink, Mr . . . ?'

'Costa, madame. My name is Costa. Oh, let me help you with the tray.'

'No no. I manage. Oh, thank you. You will drink?'

Lime juice slopped into glasses.

'And what beautiful cakes! You have made them yourself?'

'Constantopoulos! Teresa! If you *please*! We are busy.'

'Yes Mr Holmes. But you will have a drink first; and a cake.'

'Thank you. Now Jacopo, if your house is available for meetings . . .'

'My house is yours, Mr Holmes.'

'. . . Then I'll ask you to call the first meeting. Is that agreeable, Constantopoulos? A general meeting next week!'

'Oh yes yes . . . anytime. I'll be delighted.'

'Mr Constantopoulos has many things to explain about co-operative societies,' Holmes began crossly.

'More cake, Mr Costa?'

'Oh yes, indeed. Thank you, Teresa. Delicious. So fresh.'

'More lime juice?'

'Thank you, thank you. Such a delicate flavour. So cool.'

Jacopo groped into a drawer.

'I will call the meeting, Mr Holmes. I have already the books we shall keep; and the boxes for money. Here . . . you see?'

58

'Splendid. But first you must get the people together. Account books and money-boxes aren't much use without members, are they? Ha-ha.'

'At the meeting will ... Mr Costa explain it all to us?'

'Indeed I shall, Jacopo! Thank you, Teresa—I shouldn't of course but I cannot resist—my figure is ruined already! Have you a family, may I ask?'

'Two girls. And two boys.'

'Two boys! How fortunate!'

'Then we'll call the meeting for next Tuesday. All right, Constantopoulos?'

'Oh yes, yes. Any time. I'll be delighted.'

'Jacopo?'

'Whenever you say, Mr Holmes, I shall arrange it for Mr Costa.'

'I see I am lucky to have you to work with, Jacopo.'

'It is an honour to serve you and Mr Holmes, Mr Costa. Mr Holmes is our saviour. Mr Holmes is saving our people. The people of the Peaceful Islands will always remember Mr Holmes. Before he came we were a Dying Race. Mr Holmes is a father to us. He is our father and mother. . . .'

'Thank you, Jacopo. Well, I think that's all now. We'd better move on ... If you're ready, Constantopoulos?'

In the hall Teresa was waiting.

'For you, Mr Costa. For you.'

'For *me*? But Teresa ... Oh! But no ... I cannot accept! Your beautiful cushions!'

'You must!' Holmes whisper was furious. 'You admired them, so they must give them. It's the custom.'

'But how charming; and how generous ... I did not understand. But I *thank* you. Aporo ... could you please ... in the car ...'

Jacopo's hall, like the Resident's, was filled with cellophane, plastic ribbons, coloured wrappings. Teresa and Jacopo giggled happily at their cigarettes, Turkish Delight, sugar almonds. Holmes's face cracked at the assault of unfamiliar helplessness. Cutting brutally through the flowery *entente* he snatched Costa's arm.

'Come ... we have more calls to make!'

In the car he said bitterly, 'Well, I hope you have learnt that lesson. Do not admire Maori's possessions! And do not kiss Maori women's hands. They are not used to it.'

'But Teresa seemed enchanted. And I have these beautiful cushions for my bedroom.'

'Very likely; but kissing hands is not a local custom.'

Costa smiled.

'Very soon they will get used to it. I think they do not object.'

Presentations were also being made at the Residency.

'Well,' said His Honour. 'That's very nice of you, I must say. Very nice indeed.'

'Oh, it's nothing,' said Judy. 'I have so much stationery.'

'Don't know if I can accept it though. Presents from a lady, hey?'

'Regard it as a present from my employers. After all, it comes from them; and don't forget there's plenty more.'

'Ha-ha. Damned good. Right then, that's fixed.'

He stacked up the boxes of pencils, the notebooks, reams of quarto.

'Can't have too much paper, you know. Expensive stuff. Price going up all the time.'

'It's the writers who suffer. I don't think the public realize.'

'Damn sure they don't. Damn sure. One must do the best for oneself. Could be a shortage any day.'

'I hope you will let me know when your memoirs come out. I should so love to read them.'

'Oh, I shall, I shall ... never fear. Once they're written, of course. I've some pretty good stories, I can tell you.'

'I'm sure you have. You must have seen many changes.'

'Oh, I have, I have. And some pretty queer things, I might add. Not all of them in the past.'

'Really?'

'Not by a long chalk. Since that feller Holmes arrived here, for instance.'

'Ah, *well*!'

'Exactly. Can't stand the feller.'

'He's not easy to get on with.'

'Easy! He's impossible. Quite unsuitable for the islands. Sort of feller thinks niggers begin at Calais, don't you know. And these Experts, so-called. Public money. Tax-payers money!'

'*Our* money.'

'By God, you're right. Our money. Scandalous. Take the knock-down furniture industry, for instance.'

'Furniture? In Aratoa?'

'A scandal. A P.I.D.L. insanity.'

'A furniture industry here?'

'For the outer islands. Experts came. Cost hundreds in fares alone. Tax-payers' money again.'

'I thought the outer islands were atolls. Only coconuts.'

'Didn't discover that till they got here. A P.I.D.L. Expert at Ha'i Koma wrote a paper. It looked well on paper. At the time C.R.A.P.—the French—were getting too much publicity, d'you see; so P.I.D.L. approved this project in a hurry without consulting us. Without bothering to ask if it were feasible. Hah! Three fellers arrived here to set up a factory, train the locals to run it.'

'No!'

'They weren't bad fellers. People liked them. Enjoyed themselves ... plenty of parties and so on. Here for months, travelling round the Group; but no knock-down furniture. No trees, you see.'

'And the Experts?'

'Moved on to Unesco. Doing literacy in Pakistan or Bogota or somewhere. We get Christmas cards every year.'

'Can't believe it.'

'Wouldn't, would you? But it's true. I could write a book, I can tell you!'

'I should like to see the outer islands,' said Judy when she judged enough appreciation had been shown. 'They must be fascinating.'

H.H. shook his head.

'Wrong time of year,' he said cagily. 'No shipping, you know. All gone to Tahiti or Northern Cooks to avoid hurricanes; or to New Zealand for refitting.'

'But when they come back. Couldn't I go in the ship that takes the Experts to Manu? Stay on board and do the round trip?'

'Well, well, I don't know about that.'

'Leicester Whiteway's going to Manu.'

'Whiteway? What's he going for? Joy-riding!'

'Oh no, not Leicester. He's too conscientious. He's going to establish felt needs.'

'Felt needs? What in God's name is that? Nursery toys?'

Judy laughed even harder than when Dr Vincent and Ken Forbes had made the same joke.

'It means getting the people to know they feel they need something.'

'God almighty! God almighty!'

'You work from the inside, you see. You don't just tell people they ought to have things, like Mr Hitchcock tells them they should have the L.M.S. You make them think they thought of it themselves so they can ask for it; then you make them ask for it, without them realizing it's your idea. That's called becoming articulate.'

'God almighty. It's brainwashing! Communist tactics!'

'More like advertising. It's all the rage now. Holmes goes in for it. Mr Holmes, of course does not want me to go round the Group. He'd like to stop me. He doesn't approve of me. We met, you remember, at Ha'i Koma.'

'Oh, he would, would he? Now, you look here, I'm Resident of this Colony, not Mr Holmes. If I say you can go

62

round the Group, you can go! You may tell that to Holmes with my compliments! D'you follow me?'

'Yes,' Judy said. 'How do you feel about carbon? Do you use it at all in your work?'

'Carbon?'

'Carbon paper. You should always make more than one copy. When you send your manuscript off to the publisher you'll want one to keep ... and one for America.'

'America!' H.H. thought of *Life* magazine.

'Your American sales would be fantastic,' said Judy. 'Look at Grimble.'

'Grimble!' said H.H. 'By God, you're right. I never thought of that. Grimble! Made a packet!'

'I'll get you a good stock of carbon,' said Judy. 'And some follow-on paper.'

'If Grimble can do it, there's no reason why I can't. No reason at all.'

Nine ❧ ❧

DO-GOODERS arriving in the islands wake defensive instincts in resident European bosoms. Cynics show deprecating pride; the detached become possessive; the embattled, already engaged in salvage work ... missionaries, doctors, teachers ... mortally affronted; yet chronic boredom weakens resentment, welcomes diversion. If the newcomer is agreeable, carnival briefly reigns. Drink flows; women slash at dress-lengths; picnics, *umukais*, tea, coffee, cocktail, dinner parties are arranged.

All this had been done. The Resident had given his dinner, the Crumps their rort, Kev and Thelma Jackson got up a get-together at the met. station, the Medical Officer and Mrs Vincent invited for Drinks, the Director of Agriculture and Mrs Wilson for Cocktails. Now the Experts were sliding into the local scene, soon to qualify for jealous hostility to the latest arrivals ... a new brace of Fulbrights, a party of Mormons come to build a temple, a linguist on the trail of the glottal stop as used in original Peaceful Islands Maori.

Costa had settled in happily at the hotel. He proposed to buy land and erect a prefabricated house he had seen advertised. Meanwhile Teresa's cushions had been joined by a pink satin bedspread, a negress whose nipples poured gin, a nude dancer holding a lamp. Open-jawed negro and hippopotamus heads, miniature chamber-pots, *bidets* and lavatory pans received ashes. Photographs of family and friends, an ikon on shiny paper hung high on the wall. There was also a female-shaped whiskey-bottle, brass cigarette boxes, red leatherette chairs with chromium frames and black velvet cushions painted with tigers, naked torsoes, slumberous Polynesian heads.

All went well. When hotel meals palled there were always invitations. Drink was plentiful, once you got used to obtaining it by medical certificate, sex available any hour of day or night. Work—visiting village elders, exchanging compliments and protestations of friendship—made no heavy demands. Though nonplussed by their attitude to money, Costa had a rapport with the islanders. There were superficial differences; in Polynesia, speeches, songs, dances, soft drinks and sponge cakes replaced the coffee, compliments, discreet haggling of the Middle East transactions but tempo, attitude to life were much the same.

Offenbach now and then came to the surface of the lagoon, redder than ever. Sometimes he was seen with Ben driving off in a jeep to the north of the island with his kerosene tins of trochus. People at parties said he was a fine worker, a very sound man.

Miss Arbuthnott had left the hotel and set up in a leaf house on the other side of the island. Souvenirs of previous homes provided décor—feather fans, *tapas*, spider shells, photographs—baffled Melanesian faces under nurses' caps, brooding Melanesian mothers with bare breasts, infant Melanesians with stomachs and genitals.

Miss Davidson had provided a housegirl from the Residency. Leicester, finding the peaceful order of the leafhouse, its smells of sponge-cake and hot scones soothing after life with Toa, dropped in more and more often.

Holmes was not at all happy about the Infant Welfare Expert's independent spirit. He did not care for the way she made her plans without reference to him, nor for her leafhouse.

'What is she *doing* round there at Baru? Why doesn't she work from headquarters like everyone else?'

'She's still on her scripts. She likes to live in the villages, with the people, as she did in the French territories. It gives her the feel.'

'The feel! The French! When will she be ready to start production?'

'She says very soon.'

Too many people were working as a law to themselves. The Women's Interests team had gone off to Pinoi and—Holmes felt deliberately—got stranded there till after the hurricane season. Harkness, the glottal-stop expert, had vanished into the mountains and refused to descend. Offenbach, Miss Arbuthnott never consulted him; even Constantopoulos was evasive.

'What's Constantopoulos up to?'

'Oh ... we're working on his posters. And I've photographed his societies. Propaganda, you know, for the outer islands.'

'Photograph! Posters! Propaganda! Well, I hope everyone realizes I expect progress reports in due course. They've got to be in in good time for the Work Committee meeting in June.'

Costa was full of ideas, not always entirely practical. Leicester wondered how understanding of co-operatives aims would be demonstrated by self-conscious figures posed round tables, exercise books displayed open so the camera could see accounts had not been cooked. On the subject of posters there had been quite an argument.

'Here are my drawings for the posters!' Costa had cried, bouncing into the office. 'I am no artist but you will see what I mean. There now! You like it?'

'It's very nice. Very good. What's it for?'

'My dear Leicester! But you can see. It's a Thrift Poster.'

'A thrift poster? What are the beds for?'

'Ah! You see, here it will have the words: DON'T KEEP YOUR MONEY UNDER THE MATTRESS. PUT IT INTO YOUR LOCAL SAVINGS SOCIETY.'

'All that?'

'Yes. Oh yes.'

'It's too much text.'

'It's necessary. So they will understand.'

'But Costa, they don't keep their money under the mattress...'

'Then this will discourage them starting.'

'... and they don't have mattresses.'

'Jacopo has a mattress. I have seen it.'

'And they don't have beds. They sleep on mats. On the floor.'

'I have seen beds.'

'At the hotel. In European houses. In one or two native houses like Jacopo's. Nowhere else. And not in the outer islands ... not on Manu where you are going. The beds must come out.'

'No. They must stay. We shall teach them to sleep in beds, with mattresses.'

'But Costa, you want to use the posters *now*. If people are to take them seriously they must be recognizable ... familiar. They must show life as it is, not as it ought to be.'

'That is negative reasoning. I am surprised at you. The beds will remain. It will be an ideal they will strive for. Everyone shall have a bed. We shall teach them.'

Leicester ran his fingers back through his hair.

'You must ask the Chief.'

'I shall not ask the Chief. I am the Expert. I shall do as I see fit. I am not a slave. You, Leicester, should not allow Holmes to bully you. You are too timid. Ah! I have hurt you! Forgive me!'

'Costa, there are some things you don't understand...'

'I am sorry, forgive me. Look here, let's have a drink, shall we? I have just been to the bond. I have something nice in the Land Rover. Aporo! Bring in the basket!'

'Costa, it's no time for drinking. And not in the office.'

'It is always time for drinking. Here!' He took the basket from Aporo. *Parfait d'Amour.* Made of violets.' He was pouring into a mug. 'Drink it. It will do you good. To show you have forgiven me.'

Leicester sank under the torrent. The sweet sticky liquid lay on his tongue like a polythene film.

'I always keep this in my cocktail cabinet at home. I know what the ladies like! Forgive me, Leicester, I meant no harm. You forgive?'

'Of course; but you must understand...'

'Mmm. Hah! That is a beautiful drink! Perhaps after all my favourite!'

Impossible to resist; all annoying traits outweighed by generosity, warmth of heart. With one exception the women of Aratoa had succumbed, if not to thoughts of romance, to maternal fondness. The general opinion was that he made you feel like a queen.

Miss Arbuthnott's continued resistance was the only flaw in Costa's happiness. A constant reproach to masculine pride, she treated him like one of her stupider breast-feeders.

'She's like a games mistress,' he said. 'A hockey captain. She's not a woman at all. Everyone ... Miss Judy ... Miss Davidson ... Mrs Vincent ... Mrs Hitchcock .. everyone likes me. But not she. She thinks only of babies and milk.'

A fraction of Costa's success with women would have satisfied Leicester. Last night when he called at Ben's on the way home, the princess's father had smiled.

'She gone to her sister. In the mountains.'

'Again?'

'Oh yeah ... yeah. Sister very sick these days. Many children. Very sick.'

Leicester lacked the courage to ask if Temata were avoiding him. The answer might be, 'Why don't you marry her if you want her so much?' He said dismally, 'Will you tell her I came?'

'Okay. I tell her. You stay for *kai*?'

Leicester shook his head, disappointment sharpening awareness of Ben's empty gums, omnipresent chickens, pigs, grimy children. Not tonight; not without Temata.

Since the night of the Resident's dinner he had been embarrassed with Toa. Though she showed no resentment, might have forgotten his outburst, he did not feel absolved. No decent white man lost his temper with animals, servants or natives. Only a cowardly bully attacked those weaker than himself.

Tonight, when she began hovering at the dining-room door he called quickly, 'You needn't wait if you want to go to the pictures. Wash the plates in the morning.'

She giggled.

'Okay, Leicester.' She did not move.

'Well, what is it? Don't you want to go?'

'Yes, yes, I go.'

'Well, then; off you go.'

'But tonight you come with me!'

Oh no. No. No, he couldn't. He said, 'Not tonight, Toa, I haven't finished my dinner.'

'Okay. I wait.'

'But not tonight.'

'Yes yes, tonight you come. Tonight is one picture called *Black Arrow.*'

'That was weeks ago.'

'Yes. Tonight again. Many times. You promised. You said you would come. I wait. I wait for you. I like you see *Black Arrow.*'

Such guileless compelling hospitality defied him to add ungraciousness to his guilt. It was easy expiation, after all; tolerable alternative to solitary drinking among landcrabs and mosquitoes.

'All right; all right. I'll come.'

At the entrance to the cinema a fat bawd supervised a stall with strings of chestnuts, green drinking coconuts, strips of coconut meat for chewing.

'You would like chestnuts?' Toa suggested. 'Or perhaps a coconut to drink?'

Though he would pay for them, her gracious manner made him her guest. She guided him to the head of the noisy queue, smiled at the girl selling tickets.

'For you, Leicester, one-and-six. I pay nothing. This is my sister.'

Inside, the rows of narrow split logs were crowded; children scampered on the sand floor. Toa arranged a soapbox and cushion against the projection-room wall.

'Be seated.'

Chewing a piece of coconut she folded herself up beside him, smiling encouragingly.

Crashes and laughter from the projection room suggested imminent action though crowds still pushed and shuffled through the entrance; then arbitrarily, with a crepitating roar, the programme began.

Upon the screen fell dark moving shadows of patrons stumbling in the aisle; above the crackling sound-track rose urgent shouts to lost friends and relations. Behind Leicester's head a party of free viewers in the projection

69

room bellowed; a beam of white light cut across his face, blinding one eye.

Toa had abandoned him. Crouched forward, she chewed, staring solemnly. An ancient comedy where cars ran backwards, figures moved with epileptic speed failed to amuse. Equally solemn, the audience stared. Only violent fighting and chasing evoked interest.

Interval (renewal of shouted greetings, bodies flocking to the exit for refreshment) preceded the night's main business: *The Black Arrow*; and in small type at the bottom: From a novel by *Robert L. Stevenson*.

How would the Aratoans receive suits of armour, the noble lieges, knightly oaths thundering out on the sweet warm night? Long familiar with the story, they talked and shouted, turned their backs on love scenes, walked about, changed seats. Shouts of encouragement evoked by jousting became angry roars when on the screen a glaring light showed magnified fly-spots, drops of water, scratches on projector lens.

Leicester, automatically noting audience-reaction, knew a brief dismay; but for once it was not he who must struggle in the hot projection room, splicing with shaking hands, with cement that would not set.

Upon the empty screen a group of shadows passed. In the white beam, Temata's face clearly showed.

'You all right?' Toa's eyes were round. 'You feeling sick?'

'No no. I'm all right.' What else to say? Temata had disappeared. What to do but wait till after the film? But what was she doing here? Who was she with? Why did Ben say she was up in the mountains?

The *Black Arrow* recommenced. The sound track exploded, collapsed, revived. The audience expressed delight at tournaments, battles. Hatchets and axes clove and hewed. Aratoa shrieked approval.

'How terrible!' Toa clutched his arm. 'How terrible to see people kill each other. They should not behave like that.'

70

'They are pretending.'

'Oh no, it is real. I see the blood there.'

'All the same they're not really killing each other.'

She showed pity for his simplicity.

'Of course they are. Who could live when they are hit with such an axe? Oh, it is real. I have seen *War over Korea* and I know it is real. Nga'a's cousin in New Zealand went to Korea and fought there and it was real. They killed each other. Airplanes dropped bombs, like the film. Oh yes, it is real.'

Professional indignation briefly replaced Leicester's disturbance.

'The films should be censored!'

Toa looked blank. She said, 'But it is real. I know.'

The lovers came together, merged, their forms obliterated by shadows streaming to the exit. Leicester started up.

'Temata! Temata!' Would she hear? *'Temata!'*

She slowly turned the gleaming head crowned with frangipani. As he saw the blunt golden features, little full mouth, smooth padded eyelids, Leicester felt sick with love. Aware of her effect, Temata raised eyebrows, smiling faintly.

'Temata. I thought you were up in the mountains. Ben said...'

She shrugged.

'Why did he say you were up in the...' But at the gathering blankness of her stare he said humbly, 'May I take you home?'

'I got friends. Not going home.'

'Where are you going?'

'To the beach. It is full moon tonight.'

The beach! The full moon!

'No, Temata ... let me take you home. It's late. Don't go to the beach. You'll be tired.'

She laughed rather loudly.

'Tired? You my father or something? I go to the beach with my friends.'

'But I wanted to talk to you.'

Now she was sulky.

'Some other time.' She petulantly turned away.

Toa, chewing noisily, rose from the floor. Wilted crown, bedraggled dress did not increase her allure. Temata stopped in astonishment.

'Toa! You bring Toa to the cinema?'

'Temata, you don't understand. Toa asked me...'

Toa giggled apologetically.

'Toa!' Incredulity was becoming angry contempt.

'But Temata, Ben said you were up in the...'

'You take your *housegirl* to the cinema! That is a joke!' said the princess without amusement. She glared at them both and ran after her friends.

Leicester said bitterly. 'Toa! Stop giggling!'

She stopped, looking expectant. 'Okay Leicester.'

He sighed. It wasn't her fault.

'Well, thank you for bringing me. You'd better go home now.'

Elevated to status of Other Woman, Toa grew coy.

'You walk with me, Leicester. I'm frightened.'

He shook his head, almost in panic. A flirtation with Toa would be the final outrage.

'Don't try to tell me you're frightened,' he said sternly. 'You go home by yourself every night.'

'But now it is late and I am frightened. Too many ghosts.' She added, 'Temata gone.'

Indignant words rose, were dismissed. What did it matter if he escorted this poor little slut? Temata was now on the beach with her friends, in the moonlight. Beyond that he dared not think.

'All right,' he said resignedly. 'Come on then. Come on; let's go.'

Ten

AT weekends the Europeans played tennis or golf. Few were much good at, even liked games, but one had to do something for exercise. There was also the social side. At the club-house on Saturday the girls brought a Plate and tea was served at four. Sometimes the boys brought beer and often the evening ended with drinks and pot-luck at old So-and-so's.

It was all repeated on Sundays.

On Saturday the Aratoans played basketball or a sort of Samoan cricket. The Guides put their uniforms on and met in a leaf house to tie knots and light fires with one match. They raised three fingers and swore to honour and obey God and the Queen, to help other people at all times, to obey the Guide law. Afterwards, still in uniform, they went to beach or forest and carried on with the boys who were not playing Samoan cricket or basketball.

Miss Davidson, the Guide patron, had been heard to wish they would first take their treffoils off. Nutkin Hitchcock said it was shocking, and it was, but very popular.

On Sunday the natives went to church in their best clothes, the women in white, barefoot, with flower-crowned hats. Church was continuous. Morning and evening, long processions wandered to and from the door; worshippers came and went in shifts, as at the cinema. The Aratoans, being Maoris, enjoyed singing, specially hymns. It gave them a chance to scream and shriek, to harmonize and express the deep lying melancholy said by Experts to dwell in all island peoples.

Between church sessions they played cricket or basketball or fornicated, changing first to old clothes since white spoils in forest or beach. A few delinquents went to the hills to make bush beer on which they got drunk.

73

This was not good enough for Mr Hitchcock. From the pulpit he charged his flock to give up Sunday sport, bush beer, fornication, loudly condemning European tolerance, shooting off arrows of accusation against laxity in High Places. His wife's concern at Girl Guide immorality (in uniform) led her to see their patron as founder and high priestess of the shameless rites. The missionary had called a public meeting to discuss Once and for All the case of Sunday sport. Preceded by a concert, to raise funds for the church roof, followed by voting, for and against, it was expected by the naïve to solve the issue. The cynical hoped it would revitalize old feuds and create new ones.

Social hazards, brilliant manoeuvres complicated life. Miss Davidson contrived to represent Her Majesty at church without seeing God's representative; the Hitchcocks boycotted sporting fixtures, never darkening club-house doors. Occasions when both sides could not avoid encounter, the constant warfare of lesser fry gave needed stimulation to Aratoa society.

Costa, no good at games, enjoyed the club-house gatherings. There was always plenty of home-made cake, women to flatter, hands to kiss. The ladies, full of maternal solicitude, would ask if he were comfortable at the hotel; suffered any *disturbances*? They dared not be more specific, but Costa, assuring them of his comfort, pretended innocence.

'Not really disturbed; but there is a noise I hear every night. Sometimes quite late. Bang—bang—bang; thump—thump—thump. And rattling. Like sticks in tins.'

'Oh, that's practising,' said Phyllis Cornick.

'Practising what? Who is practising?'

'The villagers. Practising Items.'

'What items?'

'Items ... for Mrs Hitchcock's concert.'

'Or the next *tere* party,' said Thelma Jackson.

'I do not understand. What is an item? What is a *tere* party?'

'Oh,' Thelma was disdainful. 'An Item is just an item in a

74

programme you know; native singing or dancing; or drum dances. *Tere* parties are when they get up a crowd and hire a boat and go round the Group visiting friends and relations. The Items are sometimes to raise money for this or to put on when they get there.'

'Sometimes they give Items of native dances at ordinary dances,' Phyllis said. 'They do the same in the Cook Islands.'

'And the rattling?'

'Those are the drums. Kerosene tin drums.'

Thelma and Phyllis had not yet made up their minds about Costa. Each waited for the other to declare so she could take the opposite view. Instinct suggested that he must be watched, but admiring oleaginous eyes were hard to resist. Their husbands Kev and George had never treated them as Costa did. Privately each felt she was being made to feel like a queen; but they were inclined to speak rather tartly as though expecting him to take liberties.

'Who will perform at this concert? You, Miss Davidson?'

'I? Are you crazy, Constantopoulos? What should I do?'

'Sing. Recite poems, perhaps. You have such a splendid voice.'

Miss Davidson, looking angrily pleased, answered 'Rubbish!'

Dolly Vincent said, 'Mr Hitchcock's the one with the voice. He always does Shakespeare.'

Miss Davidson shut up, looking offended.

Aware of tension, Costa said soothingly, 'How industrious you are, Miss Davidson. You remind me of my mother and sisters. Never idle.'

'Don't be a fool, Constantopoulos. I'm the laziest woman on Aratoa.'

'Ah no, you are too modest. You're always busy. Even now you are knitting. So many socks.'

'It's the same sock. I've been at it for years.'

Costa's smile was a poem of courteous disbelief. Phyllis and Thelma exchanged the glance of enemies forced together in common defence. Miss Davidson was so terribly rough. After all, she was supposed to be Aratoa's Official Hostess, sister of the Resident Commissioner, like a Governor's wife almost. Each knew that she could have filled the position with far more grace and distinction; each secretly hated the cloddish spouse who provided no scope for these talents.

Nutkin Hitchcock was working hard on her concert. The programmes were ready for roneoing by the Education Department—so fortunate Theodore was friendly just now with the Director.

'I've put the choir first,' she said. 'They will do the national anthem. Then, Theodore, your opening remarks. Then I thought, *"The Holy City*; or *Jerusalem."* Or would you say *"Bless this House"*?'

'*Bless this House,*' said Theodore, to whom all tunes were the same. 'More variety.'

'Then *Jerusalem* can come later. Then there's the Item from Baru village.'

'Have you seen it?' said Theodore quickly.

'Oh yes. It's quite all right.'

She blushed. She would never forget the terrible night her housegirl's Tahitian cousin did an Item, uncensored. Aratoa would never forget it. Crying *Tamuré-tamuré,* the beautiful creature had wriggled her hips in a frenzied hula, whipped off the *pareu* strip round her chest and rotated each breast, separately, together, inwards, then outwards. The final outrage had been her shameless enjoyment. The men had gone wild; the women had left in protest.

'After that, Theodore, would you do your Soliloquy?'

'If you wish.'

She wrote in; *To be or not to be.* 'Hamlet's Soliloquy.' W. Shakespeare. . . . T. Hitchcock.

'Then there's the schoolchildren's action song.' She wrote, '*Ru's Canoe.*' Closing her eyes she saw white dresses dipping,

76

one behind the other, brown arms paddling ancestor Ru over the ocean to discover Aratoa.

'Then the boys from the school. Their dance. And then interval. How long would you say?'

'Ten minutes.'

'After interval comes my song.' She wrote in 'Butterflies . . . solo. M. Hitchcock. 'Then the Item from Tarorai: *Drum Dance*; and after that the choir again. *Trees. Jerusalem.* I think, Theodore, we really should put *Bless this House* here. It makes a nice finish.'

'As you please, my dear. I'm sure you're right.'

Nutkin wished he really cared about her concert. She said timidly, 'Would you like to recite again before you give Benediction?'

'No. You must keep it short. There's the meeting to follow and we can't keep people out all night.'

Nutkin wondered why the Sunday sport meeting must follow; why it could not be held separately?

'It's the best opportunity to get people together. You know what it's like trying to organize meetings on Aratoa. The pill must be coated. But everyone will be at the concert, even visitors.'

Nutkin supposed that Miss Pollock would come, very likely to jeer. Theodore, turning into Polonius, said all journalists were cynical, hard and unscrupulous. He would not be surprised to hear Miss Pollock was writing subversive articles for her paper. He didn't trust her an inch and advised Nutkin to give her a wide berth. On the other hand a few revealing articles—if written by a responsible hand—on Government would not go amiss.

'Laxity in high places. Immorality being condoned.'

'She has made friends at the Residency. One hears she is much in favour up there.'

'You see?' said Theodore bitterly. 'You cannot trust them.'

'I asked Mr Constantopoulos if he had been *troubled* at the hotel,' said Nutkin in a voice of shame. 'He assured me not.'

'Hard to believe. He probably misunderstood you. The fellow's English is not too good.' Fel-low was very Shakespearean.

'Oh, I believe him. I made my meaning clear. I asked if he'd been approached at night by native women. He said he had heard of incidents but had no trouble himself.'

'I don't trust him either.'

'Oh, but Theodore, he's a gentleman. And he isn't Greek Orthodox ... there's a Huguenot streak. He sounded so *sincere,* telling me how his life of travel had made it hard to keep up attendance at Church.'

'I don't trust him, my dear. I cannot think why you like him.'

His wife said, 'I am sorry for him. He's a gentleman. And he makes one feel like a queen.'

'Why is Constantopoulos buttering up the Hitchcocks?' said His Honour.

'It's part of his policy,' said his sister. 'He butters everyone up.'

'Damned dago. Better not try it here.'

'Oh, but he has. What about the night he came to dinner ... the presents for His Excellency?'

'Tried it on you, I see.'

'Every time we meet. At tennis the other day he said I reminded him of his mother and sisters.'

'His sisters! Damn gyppos! But what's the object? What does he want? What does he get out of it?'

'Hard to say. Perhaps he just wants to be popular. To be liked. Should we have those Fulbrights for dinner this week?'

'No no.... Can't afford it. Too much entertaining this month. Must cut down. Do you think I'm made of money? The fellow's getting round all the women. That madwoman's eating out of his hand. And the Baha'is ... ha-ha ... wonder if she knows that. Ha-ha! He kisses the Baha'is' hands then goes off and kisses Madame Hitchcock's.

Damn good. Clever fellow. Got round you too, I dare say.'

'Not Miss Arbuthnott. She can't stand him.'

'Can't, can't she? Woman's not human. All that talk of breastfeeding. Tell me this ... how did she work in French territories if she doesn't speak French? But he'll get round her too, I've no doubt.'

Eleven 〜◗ 〜◗

FOR weeks Miss Arbuthnott had sat in her leaf house with her scissors-and-paste, adapting her old scripts, composing new ones. Several times Leicester and Aporo had been called in to advise on local idiom. Now she was ready, she said, to spy out the land for filmstrip locations.

'What about food?' she asked when Leicester picked her up at the cottage. 'Should I bring a nose-bag?'

'We'll be back for lunch.' He flinched as she slammed the car door, spreading round and over the frail bucket seat. Eternally mottled, her blue-white legs and feet seemed to fill the car (*My feet swell so frightfully*). On her knees a large basket bulged with papers and charts.

'Right,' she said. 'Off we go. What's the plan of campaign?'

They were to meet Aratoa's policeman on the other side of the island at eight. He was bringing prisoners from the jail to build a set for a filmstrip on housing. Leicester hoped, without conviction, they would not be late.

'Goodoh! Goodoh!'

Her rich fruity voice and admirable diction made the word theatrical. *Bonza* and *Cobber* hovered, awaiting their turn.

A derelict coral house, fern-filled, roof and shutters long since snatched away by a hurricane, was the rendezvous. Neither policeman nor prisoners were visible but towards nine o'clock the gathering crowd hailed a Land Rover full of singing boys. In shorts and yellow flower-crowns, they had brought a guitar and coconut ukeleles. The driver wore a torn coloured shirt, a pink hibiscus behind his ear.

'Good morning,' he said gaily. 'You have asked for people from the jail? I have brought them!'

The prisoners climbed down and stood laughing with the bystanders. They had many friends to greet, much news to exchange. The atmosphere was of relaxed enjoyment.

'Mr Whiteway,' said the policeman when Leicester had introduced Miss Arbuthnott. 'How can we serve you?'

His needs were quite simple, Leicester explained; a small coconut shack, without a roof.

The policeman's gaiety faded. Careworn gravity descended. He cogitated.

'Excuse me, Mr Whiteway, but according to Maori custom this house should have a roof.'

'Of course; but in the pictures the roof would not show. So we shall not need one.'

'But all Maori houses have a roof, Mr Whiteway.'

'I know. But if we have a roof it will be too dark inside to take pictures. My flash—my light for the camera—is not working. It has been damaged, you understand? A new one will come from New Zealand but not till *Marinda* arrives.'

The policeman understood. He pondered, then said, 'Excuse me. Maybe a roof that comes off?'

'Well—that would do very well; but it means much work and the roof would not show in the pictures. It would be a waste of time.'

The policeman plodded on.

'We shall make a roof that lifts off.'

Leicester sighed.

'All right, then; that's settled. If you want me while you're working I shall be here with Miss Arbuthnott taking background pictures.'

He peered into his Rolleiflex. A curious blur filled the groundglass screen. Focusing brought sharpened detail of the policeman's stomach.

'Excuse me, Mr Whiteway ... unfortunately there are no suitable trees here for building a house.'

Leicester put down his camera. Disappointed, the prisoners relaxed their inviting poses.

'It's only a leaf house I want,' he said patiently. 'It doesn't need to be strong.'

'But for poles, you know, Mr Whiteway. There must be poles.'

'Poles? Oh ... poles. Well, all right. Get some poles.'

'Unfortunately, sir, there are no poles. Not here. We must look for them.'

'Look for them.... Will it take long?'

'Oh no, sir, not long'—with a confident smile—'back in a minute.'

'And when you come back, how long will it take you to build the house?'

The policeman gazed mystically at an oracular sun.

'At twelve o'clock it will be done!'

'But good heavens, it's only nine now.'

'Ten o'clock maybe?'

'All right.' Leicester's confidence ebbed as the policeman's grew. 'All right; well, you'd better get started.'

'And then,' the policeman was ponderous again. 'There is the *nikau*. For the roof....'

'*Nikau?*' Leicester gestured impatiently. Coconut trees grew on every side, fallen leaves strewed the grass.

'But you have permission to use these leaves?' pursued the soft insistent voice.

'I'm sure we could use ...'

'Excuse me, Mr Whiteway, but according to Maori custom these trees all belong to someone. It is necessary to have permission before I let the prisoners pick the leaves....'

'Oh!' Desperation threatened Mr Whiteway. 'Let's forget the roof if it's so complicated. I don't need a roof. Just get the work started. It will never be finished.'

'But Mr Whiteway, it must have a roof, to be a Maori house. According to ...'

'All right, all right. Do you know who owns the trees?'

'Yes, Mr Whiteway, they belong to Tangaroa, up near the school.'

'Then please go and ask him. And take your prisoners and get the posts.'

The prisoners reluctantly rose from the grass, still singing. Still playing their ukeleles they drove away.

'Mr Whiteway! Mr Whiteway!' Miss Arbuthnott's voice came from the coral ruin. Round its walls the crowd had increased. Mothers with babies, toddlers, grinning men were straggling out from the village.

'If you used this shell for your set, you need not trouble to build a house. And I could use it afterwards for my strips.' She poked the coral floor with her parasol. 'They could probably sink their wall posts in here ... though it seems so silly ... all this trouble when we already have walls.'

'Coconut walls are part of the story. Anyway it's too late.' Leicester wiped his forehead. 'They've gone for posts; and for permission to pick *nikau* for the roof. They will never forgive me if I stop now.'

'Ah. Ah well. Perhaps they will not come back.'

'Very likely.' He leant weakly against the wall.

The crowd had grown restive when the Land Rover returned but cheered up as poles, crowbars, picks were unloaded, as the prisoners noisily swarmed into the coral shell. While the majority remained round the building, shouting advice, exchanging bawdy pleasantries with the workers, a small section had drawn apart in grave conference. To Leicester's uneasy eye they seemed to be forming into a deputation. Presently, hung round with final instructions, a stout Maori advanced.

'Good morning, Mr Whiteway.'

'Good morning, Tatira.'

Tatira had been to New Zealand, was a man of the world as shown by felt hat and Bonds athletic.

'Excuse me, Mr Whiteway, but what are you doing?'

'We are building a house, Tatira.'

'A house?'

'Yes.'

At this barefaced admission Tatira looked back at his counsellors. Stunned, they signalled helplessness. Tatira started again.

'Excuse me, Mr Whiteway, but there is a house here already.'

'We are building another inside it.'

Tatira took hold of himself.

'Mr Whiteway, you know according to Maori custom everything on this island belongs to someone or other. This coral house belongs to an owner.'

'Yes, Tatira. I know.'

'You see, Mr Whiteway, people can't just come and take things, you know. You see, it is someone's property, this coral house.'

'Tatira, we are working for Government. We will not harm the house. Just building a film set; a little *nikau* hut.'

'But you see, Mr Whiteway, people cannot come and build *nikau* huts like that. It is not allowed. According to Maori custom everyone who owns the land must give permission.'

'But it's not a house to live in. No one is going to live in it.'

'Then what is it for, Mr Whiteway?'

'To take photographs in.'

Tatira stared. Mr Whiteway was clearly insane. He backed away to confer with his advisors. Leicester hopefully moved to the coral shell; but almost at once the felt hat was back.

'Even so, Mr Whiteway, you must still ask the owner. According to . . .'

'But we have asked, Tatira. We asked Tangaroa, this morning. The policeman has asked him.'

'Ah! Tangaroa! But you have not asked me!'

'You?'

'You see, Mr Whiteway, the land belongs also to my old woman. She is the sister of Tangaroa.'

'I see. Very well then, Tatira, we shall ask her permission.'

'But my old woman is dead, Mr Whiteway. She is dead many years.' For a moment he enjoyed Leicester's frustration, then showed mercy. 'However, I am looking after the land for her. You must ask me. You see, Mr Whiteway,' he reminded, 'I have been in New Zealand. I know all these things.'

Apologies offered, face saved, pride salved, honour satisfied, the *nikau* hut offered as reparation, Tatira bowed.

'That is quite all right, Mr Whiteway. You may build a house if you wish.'

The tale was told to the deputation, then again, many times, to the onlookers. The crowd increased, drifted closer, became bolder. Women leaned in the ruined windows, questioning the flowerdecked prisoners, screeching answers across the road to those too lazy to leave their verandahs. Goats and pigs wandered, small children staggered and fell in rubble, figures clambered up Tangaroa's trees, throwing down leaves, aiming nuts at friends. Miss Arbuthnott happily interrogated mothers about breastfeeding. Thankfully Leicester opened his camera, applied himself to his unending quest for reference material.

'Mr Whiteway!' the policeman called from the ruin. 'You will come please to look at the house.'

'Finished?'

'Nearly finished. It is good. Come. You will like it. You see?' he said proudly. 'This is a real Maori house.'

'It is beautiful,' Leicester said after a pause. 'But it is very solid.'

'Oh yes. It is solid. Almost it would stand a hurricane. This is a proper Maori house, like in the Old Time. Walk inside. You will like it.'

Groping in darkness Leicester said, 'I can't see a thing.'

'Yes, it is dark. That is the *nikau* walls and the roof. To make it cool in hot weather, you know.'

'The roof. We can lift it off then?'

'Oh no. It will not come off. Not in a hurricane. It is all tied on with sennit, you see Mr Whiteway. It is very well done. The jail people worked very hard. It is a good house.'

'But ... the roof *must* come off!'

'Oh no, Mr Whiteway. Not in a good Maori house. According to Maori custom everything is tied on. By hand. With sennit, you know. Look, Mr Whiteway—it is properly thatched. Like a real house. And the ridge pole, you see? A proper ridge pole.'

'But my pictures ... how can I take pictures in here?'

'But see Mr Whiteway, there light near the door. See?' His hand moved before Leicester's eyes. 'And then you will have your camera light. . . .'

Leicester exerted enormous control.

'I have told you that I have no light till *Marinda* comes. That I cannot take pictures in the dark.'

'*Marinda*.' The policeman thought deeply. 'Ah. Well, Mr Whiteway, we build you a new house.'

'No no ... that's not necessary.' Leicester almost pleaded. 'Just take the roof off this one. Just lift it off.'

'Take it *off*? But Mr *Whiteway* ...'

'I'm sorry, it will have to come off. I told you right at the start ...'

'But Mr Whiteway, it is a proper roof ... it is all lashed on, with sennit, by hand. Like in the Old Time.'

'They will have to unlash it.'

'But that is impossible, sir. My people from the jail must go back. Only the morning you asked for. Already it is two o'clock. . . .'

When the Land Rover had taken away the happy captives and their deeply-grieved guardian, Miss Arbuthnott left her own researches to comfort Leicester, smoking moodily in his Stygian hut.

'Come come, Mr Whiteway. Don't despair. Your little trouble is not unsurmountable. Shoot your pictures *outside*

85

the hut ... no one will know the difference. You understand? Arrange your people against the outside leaf wall
and it will look just like an interior.'

'Miss Arbuthnott, I've spent a *whole morning* on this. It's
wasted *hours*.'

'I know, I know, it is most provoking. But I have found
one must be philosophical working with islanders. And the
gentleman who owns the land will be delighted to have the
hut. I must say it's delightfully cool.'

'And dark.'

'Ah well.' In the dimlit entrance she sank down among
ferns, digging into her basket. 'Now, for my strips ... we
might as well have a look at the script while we're on the
spot, though I might admit I'm as hungry as a hunter.'

'Lunch will be finished at the hotel,' Leicester said bitterly.

'Never mind. I can give you a bone at my cottage. But
while we're here it's a good chance to see what we'll need.'

She spread her papers in the gloaming, shuffling, sorting,
clucking her tongue. Outside, the crowd waited. Laughter,
scraps of conversation floated in.

'... I thought we should do one in the same vein as your
Mr Wise and Mr Foolish. Not very original, of course, but
adequate. The wise mother and the foolish mother. Mrs
Wise breastfeeds her baby; goes to the clinic; Mrs Foolish—
sit down Mr Whiteway—it's easier to concentrate.'

Leicester shifted uneasily.

'Miss Arbuthnott, we could work this out at your place.'

'... but we really need *two* houses, don't we!' She tapped
her pencil against her teeth. '*Two* houses ... but then—of
course, I could use this leaf house—the outside wall—for
Mrs Wise and the old coral shell for Mrs Foolish. Long shot
here—' she made a scribble ... 'It's perfect!'

A shrill question, raucous answer outside brought bawdy
guffaws from the crowd. Leicester, scarlet, said, 'Miss
Arbuthnott, I really think we should go to the car.'

'All in good time, Mr Whiteway. Oh dash it, I'm going to

call you Leicester. You mustn't mind! You call me Beatrice, or Bea if you'd rather.'

'Thank you. But I think we should go...'

'What *is* the matter? Is something wrong? Sit down. Come now, don't hover.'

'Miss Arbuthnott ... Beatrice,' he mumbled. 'You've been in the islands long enough to know what the people out there think we're *doing*.'

She looked at him blankly. Bravely he said, 'This is Polynesia, you know. In here, in the dark!'

To his relief she leant against the wall, shaking with laughter.

'Oh dear, oh dear. At my age! Is it never too late in the islands? Apparently not. Come then ... let's go to the car.'

Twelve ✌ ✌

'KOM tomorrow night?' Offenbach put his bottle back into the airways bag.

Drinking at the hotel was a sordid affair. Rationing made for meanness. People avoided togetherness, drank privately in their rooms out of toothglasses, kept their bottles locked in the wardrobe. For all her devotion to research Judy found it a joyless pursuit. She said, 'No, really. I can't keep coming here, drinking your whiskey.'

'*Ja.* You kom. I tell you many things, for your book.'

'Please shut up about my book.'

'So. But I tell you, *ja*?'

'Oh yes ... you do. I can't think how you hear things, down on the sea-bed all day.'

'I hear. I listen. I am friendly, you see, mit the autochtones.'

'The ... ?'

'Autochtones. *Indigenes.*'

'Oh, the natives. I suppose Ben tells you things.'

'Oh *ja*. Many things. Now he tells poor Leicester lovs madly Temata, his daughter. He will marry mit her.'

'Surely Leicester wouldn't be such a fool!'

'Temata wishes to marry ... to New Zealand to go. She is pretty.'

'Don't spread that story about. It won't do Leicester any good.'

'Temata is clever. She has many children. She tells to Leicester they are her bruders and sisters.' Offenbach wheezed with delight. The resonance hummed at the back of his nose.

'Little bitch.'

'I sink you marry mit me, Judy, maybe? I vish a vife.'

'Thank you. I don't think I'd do at all.'

'*Ja*. You would make a gut vife for der islands. In the willages you vill gaw ... der language learn. You are not a tea-party kind.'

'Well, hardly. And what should I do while you were under the sea making love to the trochus?'

Offenbach heaved. The bees swarmed wildly.

'So. I make lov mit der trochus! And soon there comes tuna as well.'

'You're transporting tuna?'

'*Nein*. Tuna is here. Now koms men to build a tower.'

'What for?'

'For der tuna to catch.'

Judy shook her head blankly.

'Tomorrow night I have more stories for your book. You vill like them. They vill be good. You vill laugh. You kom.'

'This is Mount Cook,' said Kev Jackson.

A grey fog appeared on the screen.

'Something's wrong,' cried Phyllis Cornick. 'Can you turn it up?'

88

'Ahha! I thought you'd say that. It's meant to be that way. I took it because it's so typical.'

'But you can't see a thing!'

'That's how it was the day we were there. I thought, "So I'll take it". Anyone can photograph Mt Cook in sunlight. No one takes it as it really is on a grey day. That's mist.'

'And what's that? Swaying. In the corner.'

'That's the strap of Kev's camera,' said Thelma.

'Now Leicester ... this will interest you ...'

Why? Why should it interest him just because his job required him to take photographs? Must he forever be victimized by enthusiasts with their boxes of slides? He shifted uneasily. He could not imagine why Thelma had insisted he trail out tonight to the met. Station just to see pictures of New Zealand.

'It's rather nice sometimes,' she had suggested. 'To look at the Old Familiar Places. One gets homesick. And there'll be supper. Phyllis and George Cornick will be popping in. We'll expect you at eight, so don't let us down.'

Strange, how island life affected Europeans. No matter how often they met, how little affection or common interest shared they must persist in this mutually resented exchange of hospitality, like picking at sores. Even he could see Phyllis and Thelma detested each other. Thank God the slides were now over. Lights clicked on. Stiff joints cracked.

Thelma rattled into the corner and whipped the cloth off the table. Generously Phyllis responded.

'Thelma! How marvellous! You must have been cooking for days! It's too good to eat.'

'Help me, Kev. We'll move the table. Over there. Now everyone ... help yourselves. ... Tea? Nescafé? Kwikbru?'

Conversation, planned in advance, began. Cakes, slides, New Zealand scenery, *Sa*-maw, disgusting weather, Aratoa at this time of year, hazards of island life led subtly to the main issue. Phyllis said, 'Did you know that Carruthers—you remember him Leicester—the dentist—was married only six weeks when he found out his wife had a Maori husband?'

89

'I'm not surprised,' said Thelma. 'They say even girls who are fond of a white man have Maori husbands as well.'

'I like the word *husband*,' said George.

Bait taken, the women relaxed.

'And *everyone* warned Carruthers, but he wouldn't listen. No one could tell him anything.'

Kev, cheerfully, spoke out of turn.

'Like all newcomers he thought he knew everything. Eh, Leicester?'

Shock and guilt slopped Kwikbru from Leicester's cup.

'There now! See what you've done, Kev, startling him. Wipe it up. It's my good cloth.'

'Oh. I'm terribly sorry.'

'It's not your fault, Leicester. But it was a real *tragedy*, that one. The old story. Of course, it wasn't really the girl. It was Polynesia—the whole way of life—he fell in love with.'

'She was a pretty girl,' said Kev.

'Oh, they're pretty enough, when they're young. But they don't *last*,' Thelma explained as though Leicester had not yet seen an island girl. 'They get sloppy and fat. They lose their teeth. And of course you can't trust them an inch.'

'Ah now, Thel. Don't be hard on them,' said George. 'After all it's their way of life. Admittedly they lose their looks and all that; but the *other* ... it's their way.'

'You see?' Phyllis shrugged at Thelma. 'Men always defend them.' She added very fairly, 'Of course, all peoples should have the right to live in their own way. It's the white man's mistake for marrying the girls.'

'That's the crux of it. They're all right till you marry them.' Safe from such folly, Kev was wistful.

Thelma said firmly, 'The stupid thing *is* to marry them. They respect a man more when there's a bit of risk.... If he ties himself down they regard him as just one of the family. They expect and demand where before they were grateful.'

Leicester hoarsely suggested a number of white men on Aratoa had Maori wives.

'Yes Leicester, they have,' Phyllis said. 'And they pay for it, sooner or later. I shouldn't like to see *you* with a Maori wife, and that's a fact.'

'Ah well, they're pretty,' Kev said boldly. 'I wouldn't mind having one.'

'You!' said his wife. 'You'd be fed up in a week! You don't imagine she'd look after you properly!'

'Nothing wrong with them in the house. Good cooks; keep the place nice and clean. Washing ... ironing ...'

'If they *want* to. If you're thinking of *our* housegirls,' Thelma said. 'It's because I've trained them and keep on their tail.'

'Well, she could have servants.'

'Servants!' Thelma's scorn was triumphant. 'They can't manage native servants! You'd think a girl might be respected by her own people for getting a white husband; but no! Servants just carry on as they please. They say, 'Who's she to boss me round! She's only so-and-so from my village.'

George said that was true democracy; when he and Phyl were in Apia ...'

'It's all wrong,' Thelma said. 'I mean, after all, these Maori girls are glad enough to have the benefits of our civilization, our way of life ... bicycles, sewing machines, radios and all that. If they're going to accept these things I think they should accept our moral standards as well.'

'You can't change them.'

'No, you can't. None of them. Take Temata, in the post office, for instance.'

Leicester, cake halfway to mouth, successfully commanded himself, pushed the chocolate wedge in. No one now could expect him to speak.

'Temata,' said George Cornick. 'There's a pretty girl. Quiet. Well-behaved.'

'Still waters run deep.'

'That girl has had all the advantages.' Thelma said impressively. 'School in New Zealand. A decent job among Europeans. Treated as one of us. Yet she's no more changed by all we've done for her than a native of Darkest Africa.'

'It's all on the surface,' said Phyllis.

'She's clever.' Thelma was dividing a log with a bird's nest and eggs. 'Now, everyone must have some of this. It took two days to ice. Leicester?'

Head, hands gestured helplessly at stuffed mouth. Birds' nests! At this moment! And how to hear more without showing interest?

'If *clever*'s the word,' Phyllis spoke rather grimly for a lover of natives. 'I should say *crafty*!'

'Oh, come off it, Phyl. She's not as bad as that. You've got your knife into her. She's no worse than the others.'

Phyllis said carefully, for after all this was the speech of the evening: 'No one can say I'm not broad-minded or that I'm prejudiced against Maoris. Colour means nothing to me. As you know, some of my best friends at home are Maoris and when we were in *Sa*-maw—George will tell you—I had many *Sa*-mawn friends. It's not Temata's illegitimate children I object to—for after all everyone has them—but that she pretends they're not hers.'

'Ah, go on. I don't believe all that. That's just gossip.'

'It isn't gossip. They're hers. And you know as well as I do she says they're her little brothers and sisters; or nephews and nieces; or something. . . .' It was clear there was nothing personal. Phyllis was purely concerned with principle.

'Well, they could be. You know how the Maoris swap their kids about. And they can't *all* be hers!'

'One minute she tells you someone gave them to her; then they're her stepmother's; or they're feeding children. Any old thing. But everyone knows they're hers. Or some of them anyway.'

'Who knows?'

'Everyone. She's notorious. She's slept with every man on the island.'

'Hey! Hey! Not everyone. Eh Kev?'

'Present company excepted.' Thelma slipped the bird's nest with eggs on a plate for the kiddies tomorrow. 'We hope! Everyone knows it. But she's clever. She wants a

92

white husband. She wants to get back to New Zealand. Princess!'

'Well, I wish her luck,' said Phyllis. 'Who can she get in this place, now Carruthers has gone!'

George floundered into the conversation again, a labrador splashing home with its trophy.

'There's Leicester! Hey Less, you better look out! Did you know you were the big catch here now?'

Phyllis glared at her husband.

'George! Give him a chance. He's choking. Someone hit his back. It's gone down the wrong way.'

'There's you, Less!' George thumped away. 'How do you feel about that. Eh?'

Breath restored, cake swallowed, Leicester said bravely, 'What a catch *I*'d be!'

'I don't know. She'd be lucky to get you,' Thelma was mysterious.

'From what you girls say, anyone marrying Temata would get quite a family,' Kev suggested.

'That's not exceptional. You always marry the family as well as the girl. All the relations and hangers-on and believe me they run into quite a considerable number. You end up feeding them all.'

'Like that story of Somerset Maugham, about *Sa*-maw: *The Pool*,' said Phyllis the reader.

Leicester made an attempt.

'What about Ken Forbes? He seems happy enough.'

'Now *there*'s a tragedy! Clever man ... made a good living in Sydney ... and look at him now.'

'But he likes the life. He came here on purpose. He's happy.'

'Not as happy as you might think; and mind you, his wife's not even full Maori. She's part European.'

Leicester said stubbornly, 'They seem happy enough.'

'You ask Ken. He'll tell you straight. The worst thing, of course, is the mental side. You can't talk to them. They're like children.'

'Some European women are pretty dumb,' Kev said with feeling.

'It's not a question of dumbness or stupidity,' Phyllis explained exclusively to Leicester. 'Some of them are quite bright; but they don't care about things the way we do. That comes from difference of background, lack of common tradition; different attitude to life ... of looking at things. They don't care, in a way; they're not concerned. It's fair enough, I suppose. Why should they be? It takes all sorts.... But it's a barrier. As a man gets older he wants more than sex and housekeeping. Take Ken's wife, Maria. Only part native; clever; not a bad education; even so, Ken says there are days when he can't get through to her.'

The glibness suggested a gramophone record; the story, so often told, was too familiar. Leicester, revived by indignation, said, 'Perhaps she doesn't *want* him to get through to her. No one ever thinks that. Perhaps the Maoris don't always want us to know what goes on at the back of their minds. Perhaps...'

They laughed, kindly, firmly.

'If you're going to start about the Maori soul, the mystery behind the velvet eyes...' Phyllis said. Leicester thought of Temata's baffling gaze. '...You must know the answer. There's no mystery. It's just empty space.'

'The Maori soul doesn't exist, as we know souls,' Thelma spoke as an expert on souls. 'It's a myth.'

Kev was ready with his favourite story.

'There's a book, by an Expert, telling how to fathom the native mind. This bird's never been in the islands—he lives in New York or Minnesota or somewhere. But he says it's quite easy. He just quotes anthropologists who claim they know how Maoris tick. It's quite easy if you know your references.'

'One of the Fulbrights here had the book,' said George. 'All done in the library, you know. Talk about laugh!'

'Some of the men who've lived with natives for years say they'd like to know what goes on in the native mind. Miller,

94

the trader, had a Polynesian wife twenty-five years, hasn't worked it out yet.'

'Nothing!' Phyllis was emphatic. 'There's nothing there. Teach them a few tricks, they learn like a parrot; but nothing behind it.' She felt enough was enough. To press any further would be inartistic, might even raise suspicion. She said, 'But none of this really affects present company. Tell us, Leicester, what's Offenbach like? No one ever *sees* him.'

Thirteen ❧ ❧

FOR nights Leicester lay staring into the hot darkness, going over the terrible evening at the Jacksons', recalling conversations with Temata, with others concerning Temata, trying to visualize the children, to remember if they really resembled her.

On one of his first visits to Ben's he had asked: 'Do all these children live here?'

Temata had shrugged.

'Oh yes. My little brothers and sisters. My brother's children. My sister's feeding child.'

'Feeding child?'

'Not born by my sister but belongs to my sister. Adopted. Not always here. Sometimes goes to see real mother. Maoris don't have just one parents, like the *popa'as*.'

'And that little girl? She looks like you.'

'She is given to me by my friend. I ask before she is born, so she must be given to me.'

Charming; a charming custom. Innocent, he had not questioned. Why should he? They gave their children away like kittens. And they all looked alike anyway. Who—including parents—could tell whose were whose? Impossible ever to know the truth. But did you *want* to know? Did you want to find out? Was it not better to remain ignorant?

95

Ignorance was well enough if one had no intention of marrying. But marriage ... Surely one ought to know if one were marrying a pure maligned girl or promiscuous harlot; if one were getting a wife, or a wife and large family?

Thank God he had not had to face Temata. Since the night at the cinema she had vanished, taken a holiday, Ben said, gone to her mother's mountain village. Once or twice, in nocturnal agony, Leicester determined to drive there to see her, ask a few skilful questions, but each dawn destroyed courage. He could not face that blank hostile stare. And suppose she were innocent!

Uncertainty nearly drove him to Ben's to survey the children with scientific detachment but such sordid spying was sickening. Besides, Ben would guess. Better to lie in his sticky bed, plagued by wailing mosquitoes, stamping land-crabs. These creatures lived in the garden but rollicked indoors at night, with the clatter of hobnailed boots. They had little vindictive eyes and a great claw for snatching and biting. Leicester feeling even nature against him, would stiffen with fear as they rattled up wire doors, munching and blowing like horses. Crabs, cockroaches, spiders, mynah birds, flies, mosquitoes ... this was called having a house to yourself. Not forgetting Toa, who now brought her son every day; a spearhead, no doubt, for the rest of the family.

He had learnt why his towel was always wet and slimy. Having washed her clothes with his soap in the handbasin, Toa washed Daniel, then the plates, wiping them all with his towel. He had scolded, commanded, pleaded; had bought new towels, but Daniel continued to bath in the basin and there was never more than one towel.

'She takes them, of course,' Phyllis explained. '*Fa'a Sa*maw is the same. Everything for the *aiga,* you know. That means family. To her way of thinking that's right. There's one of you. You need one towel. There's dozens without towels at her place. You must speak to her.'

He spoke.

Toa nodded and smiled, or wept hopelessly so that he felt

a brute. Daniel continued to come and she to spend more time playing with him. Half-chewed scraps of taro and bread lay in the chairs, the furniture bore sticky stains, the refrigerator was permanently full of ants.

'Sack her,' said Thelma and Kev.

'Get rid of her,' said Phyllis and George.

She continued to come, looking hungry. Daniel, grey-faced, had started to cough. Only a brute could eject them.

It was all—like his present plight—the result of innate weakness. A tougher, braver character would have taken a stand ... sacked Toa ... defied the world for Temata; or accepted the white man's philosophy that native girls are as available, easier to handle without marriage. There was so much of this cynical wisdom; so many sardonic comments from traders, old island hands married or living with native girls, snippets of hearsay from envious husbands, gossiping wives; not to mention the fate of Carruthers and earlier hot-headed romantics who had fallen in love with Polynesia.

But such stories and warnings could bear no relation to the gracious princess who had held her own at Ha'i Koma with journalists and cameramen. She was different, even in Aratoa. After the first puritanical shock, the island girls' accessibility had not caused deep concern; it was their way of life, to be taken for granted; but not with Temata. Like a white girl, she must be respected, courted, married or left alone.

Was it possible that while he was respecting her she had been laughing; perhaps even despising him?

He did not believe it; he simply could not. A girl so dignified, so distinguished, even barefoot with hair down her back, could not be the whore those gossips had claimed. It was no more than white women's jealousy—understandable, since how could they compete with the island girls' beauty, youth, warmth of attraction?

Wives were no less malicious than spinsters. The threat was to the whole sex.

Thus he would try to reassure himself. His pattern of

thought was always the same ... uncertainty, misery, doubt, despair; then a somewhat half-hearted attempt to regain faith and perspective.

He was deep in this dubious reasoning when he switched on the lamp to find, not a land-crab, but Temata, halfway across his bedroom floor. She blinked at the light and proceeded towards him.

He addressed her in shocked disbelief.

'What are you doing here?'

Unmoved, she sat down on the bed.

'Put the light out,' she said.

Rehearsed questions, brooded-on-doubts, malicious gossip were forgotten. He said, panicking, 'What is it? Is someone ill? Something wrong?'

'Wrong?'

'Wrong.... Are you in trouble?'

'No trouble.' She reached out and put off the light. 'I stay. Toa gone home. I stay.' She unwrapped her *pareu*.

Leicester's brain split in two. With one half registering this admission of promiscuity, the other rejected it so violently it might never have been. He jumped out of bed, appalled at her lack of discretion.

'Temata ... you mustn't stay here!'

'Not stay? Why not?'

'Because it's all wrong. You must go.'

'Wrong? Why you keep saying *wrong*?'

'Because it is wrong. You shouldn't be here.'

'Why not? You don't want me?'

'Not like this. Not like *this*....'

'Ah. So you do not want me!'

'Oh no ... no ... I don't mean that. But I mean ... not like *this*....'

'Not like this? How you want me then?'

'Temata, you must understand, I do want you, but I respect you too much to let you stay here like this.'

'Respect.' It might have been a rare shell from the reef. Never had she heard so much talk on such an occasion.

'Yes, respect. I don't mean I don't want to sleep with you, but there's so much more to it than that....'

'More?' What more could there be?

'It may be all right for other girls ... the girls at the hotel ... in the villages ... but not for you. Don't you understand? You're too good for this.... And can you imagine what people will say if they knew you came here like this?'

She knew what they'd say; and why shouldn't they? She said impatiently, 'Something wrong with you maybe? You sick?'

'No! Of course not! Of course not!'

Bewilderment turned to suspicion.

'You got someone else coming, hey? Some other girl comes to play with you?'

'No! No! No one else. I love you, I do want to sleep with you ... but I'm not going to take advantage of you. Because I love you and want to protect you.'

It was too absurd, too hard to work out. Shrugging, she fastened her *pareu.*

'Okay. I go.'

Hours later the two halves of Leicester's brain began to fuse. At first, wilfully absorbed in thoughts of foolishness, indiscretion, malicious gossip, he invented explanations for Temata's visit, (should he, by some freak, be questioned), excuses—midnight illnesses, somnambulism, refuge from rapists, but as the other half of his mind sprang from abeyance his thoughts became violent. Fraud! Cheat! Harlot! Liar! Unspeakably shameless! He went through the list, so exciting himself that he presently burst into tears. Sobs closed the gap; his divided mind became one. He knew Temata was a tart; that he loved her. But it was not her fault. How could she be blamed for what was natural to her, to her way of life? She had never lied ... it was just that he had not enquired. Oh, but the children! Yet, even there she had not entirely deceived. They could not all be hers, at her age ... perhaps one or two ... (here he sweated and groaned). But oh, to think of that beautiful creature passed from hand to hand—perhaps flung aside.... Pity, compassion, not censure were her due. Might not love and protection save her? ... Permit her to start afresh? She was a child of nature, untaught. Recalling her blank astonishment he blushed for his naïvety. What could words like *respect* mean to one who had never known chivalry; *discretion* to a way of life utterly frank and free? Any guilt and shame should be on his side for suggesting the need to dissemble.

When the mynah birds started their dawn clamour he had reached no conclusion other than he must keep his mind off the subject if he wished to stay sane. Protective instincts faintly reminded him that attention focused elsewhere might somehow bring salvation.

Fourteen ❧ ❧

'MY husband is writing a paper for the Journal of the Polynesian Society,' said Nutkin.

'How interesting,' Judy said. 'I am sure, Mr Hitchcock, you can tell me about the Old Days ... when the missionaries first came to these islands.'

Theodore glared down his nose.

'Are you writing Articles, may I ask, Miss Pollock, for the Press?'

'Oh no ... not at all. I'm here on holiday. But I'm interested in Pacific history, and my cousins the Vincents told me you knew more than anyone on Aratoa.'

Theodore nodded more graciously, though not entirely convinced, not even sure why this woman had started calling on them. For all her civility he suspected she was there for some purpose; yet temptation was great and each time he could not resist the chance to talk. Even Nutkin, who had suspected her of Leftish tendencies, was being won round.

Theodore now said regally in his Lear voice, 'You may know that the Early Voyagers ... Spaniards, Russians, French ... missed these islands; even the British—though both Cook and Bligh must have sailed very close. When they were finally discovered by English missionaries they were untouched by white men.'

'But who discovered them first? Where did the Peaceful Islanders come from?'

'According to local legend, the voyager Ru, discoverer of Aitutaki in the Cook Islands. Ru's people came in canoes from the East. . . .'

'Like Kon-tiki.'

'Kon-tiki is all you journalists have ever heard of,' Theodore said snappishly. 'Let us keep Heyerdahl's publicity stunts out of it.'

'They have a song about it,' Nutkin said hurriedly. 'You will hear it at the concert. An action song. They sit on the floor as though in a canoe and paddle while they sing.'

'How fascinating.' Judy had heard *Ru's Canoe*. The Peaceful Islanders had sung it at Ha'i Koma and the audience had gone to sleep after the fifteenth verse.

'It is also sung in other islands inhabited by Ru's people,' Theodore resumed the stage. 'However ... since the Group was discovered by ships of peace, our people named it the Peaceful Islands.'

'I thought it was because they were peaceful people. Like Captain Cook naming the Friendly Islands.'

'They were a hot-bed of sin and loose-living!' Theodore could not tolerate interruption. 'The bare breast, you know, and in some villages people were almost stark naked. Fornication was practised as freely and casually as handshaking in other parts of the world.'

His voice trembled indignantly. Judy said, 'Cannibalism?'

'No. They were never cannibals. Unless perhaps for necessity. But very few instances are recorded.'

'In his Articles that American said ... "These old head-hunters now eat corned beef instead of long pig".'

'They never ate long pig and they were never head-hunters!' Theodore thundered. 'It is the Resident's fault for letting that irresponsible idiot into the Colony....'

Mrs Hitchcock raised distressed paws. Judy hastened to soothe.

'What was the spiritual state of the people when the ships of peace came?'

Theodore took himself in hand. Rumbling, he said trucu-lently, 'They were *without love*. They did not love God. Their lives were ruled by fear ... by heathen monstrosities. It was our task to change all this.'

'And they responded?'

'Oh, whole-heartedly!' Nutkin said. 'When one reads the old mission records it brings tears to one's eyes. They tore down their *maraes*, burnt their idols, denounced their gods. To them it was the start of a new life, when God and Jesus Christ came to their islands. The sick were healed, the dark-ness lightened. And Miss Pollock, let me put in a word for my own sex. The missionaries brought their wives. Those intrepid women braved the perils of the reef to come ashore in whale boats, sometimes with babies at the breast.... Not only to stand by their husbands but to teach sewing ... modesty ... chastity ... household arts....'

'The white men performed miracles,' Theodore inter-rupted jealously. 'Imagine the scene! Houses had always been made of leaves; rocks had never been known to burn, but the missionaries set fire to stones and burnt them to powder, mixed it with sand and sea-water and built houses! Ignoring the warnings of their Elders, the natives dug coral from the reef, burnt it for lime, built houses, schools, churches!' His voice had soared; now it came down for greater effect. 'Soon victory was complete. Weeds ... creepers overran the ruined *maraes*.... The people were saved for God!'

He might have done it all with his own hands.

'You make it so real,' Judy said. 'One would think you had been there yourself.'

Theodore bowed and took two more of Nutkin's cakes.

'My husband's a true artist,' Nutkin refilled his cup as though dispensing communion wine. 'And history is his subject. He could have had a great career as a Shakespearean actor if things had been otherwise.'

'I do not regret it,' said Theodore nobly. 'God's work is more rewarding than personal glory.'

'But alas!' Nutkin's voice trembled with loyalty. '*Others* would like to destroy what our people have done. Materialism is rife in the islands ... the old ways scoffed at. ...'

'Oh,' said Judy thoughtlessly. 'But I thought they were all out to restore the old ways ... Native Culture. ...'

Nutkin's eyes remained beady. 'Restore native culture ... that is one thing—I should say *certain aspects* of native culture— But I speak of everyday life. ...'

Theodore interrupted.

'It is fashionable now to decry the achievements of the pioneer missionary. He is blamed for everything—even, one hears, for clothing the naked, for showing the savage how to construct lasting shelter for his wretched body!'

'And this higher education,' said his wife. 'Breeds discontent, dissatisfaction. The natives think only of going to New Zealand ... buying portable wirelesses ... *refrigerators*!'

Judy felt she exaggerated. Few Aratoans went to New Zealand, for all their talk of this promised land; not one native, to her knowledge, had a transistor, even a kerosene fridge; but she said diplomatically, 'Of course, you are perfectly right. But what is the alternative? The world has grown too small. The Pacific is no longer isolated. And if We don't do these things, Someone Else will.'

Nutkin nodded gravely. Approval dodged out behind prejudice and instinctive disapproval. If Miss Pollock were less hoydenish, if her hair were done neatly. ...

'That's what I tell my husband,' she said. 'We have no

choice, the way the world's going. I was saying it only the other day to Mr Constantopoulos. Poor fellow—how he must have suffered. I hear the Turkish atrocities were unspeakable, I dared not ask if he had lost anyone through the terrorists.'

'He comes from Egypt, not Cyprus,' said Theodore crossly. Bored, for the conversation would go to pieces now Nutkin had started her political nonsense, he decided once more one couldn't trust journalists and left the room looking like Polonius.

'How do you find Mr Constantopoulos?'

'Very pleasant. They're all very pleasant. Offenbach...' Judy stopped. Perhaps better not talk of Offenbach, his whiskey, his scandalous gossip; nor did Nutkin wish to talk of him. She had grown pink, remembering His Honour's dinner party, the German's barefaced profession of popery. Judy, feeling her sentence must be given a decent conclusion said, 'Miss Arbuthnott...'

Nutkin's pink became scarlet.

'I'd rather not speak of her, if you don't mind.'

'Miss Arbuthnott? I thought you were friends.'

'Never. Never!' Mrs Hitchcock was tense; but professional discretion gave way to enjoyment of confidable female company. 'From the first I found her too self-assured, too dictatorial; now, one hears *disturbing reports*.'

'Reports? What about?'

'One cannot speak. It would be wrong to accuse without final proof. One can say however that Miss Arbuthnott is a *very strange woman*. Perhaps, as Mr Constantopoulos so generously suggested, one should make allowances. After all, she has lived a very strange life.'

'Constantopoulos? What does he say about her?'

'Mr Constantopoulos is the soul of chivalry, Miss Pollock. I am ashamed to admit he was obliged to take me to task— oh gently of course—for lack of charity. As he pointed out, Miss Arbuthnott has lived many years in Melanesia, alone, always among coloured peoples. It is not natural; unless one has great inner strength there is always the danger of ... of ... there is always a *danger*!'

Judy pressed no further. Fascinating! Costa, making mischief about Miss Arbuthnott. And what was the accusation Mrs Hitchcock clearly longed to confirm? Aratoa life improved every hour. There was no end to its diversity.

Costa often came to sit on Leicester's verandah these nights. He always brought sweets, cigars, impossible drinks. Smooth, urbane, enthroned in his aromatic cloud he murmured, sipped, exuded cosiness. Comforted by his rich fruity voice, almost feminine sympathy, Leicester was tempted to weep on his shoulder, confide private confusions.

For days after her nocturnal visit he had been frightened to face Temata. Co-existent love and distrust had produced a peculiar sensation of guilt. He also suffered vicariously all the shame that he knew in his heart she did not feel. This, with its inference of superiority, was most shameful of all. He went out of his way to avoid her, and at once she began to pursue him ... gently, discreetly, persistently. She would pop out of the post office as he passed, call from her verandah, materialize on the roadside, fresh, scented, flower-crowned. Whatever he thought at other times, in her presence he was an eager jelly, even blind to her now slightly mocking expression.

His attitude to life, to work was affected. Negative thoughts, defeatism he would have scorned were now accepted.

'Sometimes,' he said dejectedly. 'I really wonder if the islanders are ready for us. If we aren't ahead of them.'

Costa sighed, sipped his sticky drink, slapped at a mosquito.

'You are tired, Leicester. You need a holiday. Still, it is difficult sometimes. There are problems.'

'Aren't you happy?' Let Costa hint of unhappiness and Leicester would overflow with his own; but Costa said,

'Socially, life is most enjoyable. And the natives are charming. Still...'

Self-pity banished, Leicester dutifully enquired for the infant societies.

'Oh, very well. Getting on very well. I have made many speeches, you know. We have had meetings. The people are enthusiastic; but there are problems.'

'Yes. Problems.'

'I find, you see, Leicester, that these people produce very little apart from what they need for survival. To have successful co-ops we need a surplus. Something to trade with.'

'The island is fertile enough.'

'The island is fertile, but not developed. Land ownership is confused. People have just a few trees or a small strip of garden. They grow *taro* and *kumaras* for themselves, fish a little, buy corned beef and bread. That is all. They do not care to do more. They are charming, but I ask you, what does one do with them? They don't seem to care about getting on, making money. They don't want to work for normal incentives. What do you offer them?'

'Many have wondered that. An American came here some years ago to start a business but he soon had a nervous breakdown. He could not understand people who had no ambitions and didn't want to be rich or important.'

'It is unusual.'

'They will work, if necessary, to eat, to buy a bicycle ... but they can't understand working just for work's sake; as for saving ... working to make money that you can't spend— Madness. Besides, in most families now there is someone with a job ... a sister or brother or uncle who works as a typist or clerk or in a store or the hospital ... as housegirls or builders or labourers. They can buy what they need. Or they pinch food.'

'In the island of my mother, where I have visited, it is arid, bare, the people are poor; but they work all the time. It is not like here with volcanic soil and beautiful fruits ... it is all dry and...'

106

'Where is this?'

'In the Dodecanese Islands, which perhaps you may have heard of?'

'But this is Polynesia. People do not want to work when they can pick food off the trees.'

'Then we must make them. They must work harder. Produce crops and copra ... tomatoes ... *kumaras....*'

'How? How are you going to make them?'

'How! That is it! That is where we started. What makes them work?'

'Nothing, if they don't want to. Why should they—that's their answer, not mine—if they have what they need?'

'Well, I suppose I must teach them. They will learn. Already some have put money into a savings society. But they are childish, very childish. Last night at the meeting Jacopo asked me to show them the money so they could see it was safe. They ask me to promise I will show it each week. That is childish. Yes, there is much to teach them. And *we* must teach them. If we don't, Someone Else will.'

'I suppose so.' Leicester showed little interest in this possibility. Costa said cautiously, 'How are you getting along with your filmstrips?'

'We are working. We have our problems too.'

'You and Miss Arbuthnott?'

'Yes. Still on her mothercraft strips.'

'Ah, yes. You find her difficult?'

'Not at all. Very pleasant. Very pleasant indeed.'

'You see a great deal of her, no doubt?'

'Oh yes. In our work. And she is most hospitable ... very kind. I've become very fond of her really.'

'So!' said Costa. In the darkness his black eyes were hooded. He drew at his cigar and began to speak; then changed his mind and sat gently whistling through his teeth.

Fifteen 〜 〜

BEATRICE, Leicester felt, was too sweeping about Costa, too censorious.

'You're too hard on him. He's not nearly so bad as you say.'

Miss Arbuthnott, her mind on her work, said, 'It's his *vulgarity* that appals and repels me.'

'But his heart is so warm. And he has no ulterior motives. He just wants people to like him.'

'Very likely.' She leaned forward and shouted in Aporo's ear, 'Stop here, Aporo. Photograph. There's a grave by the road. A child's grave. It's just what I want to complete the strip.'

'Why do you dislike him so much?'

'He stands for everything I dislike. Wait. I'll get the picture. Two shakes.'

The Land Rover rocked as she prised herself out

'But you know,' said Aporo as they drove on. 'That is not a grave.'

'If it isn't a grave, what is it, may I ask? There's a headstone; with an inscription.'

'It's in memory of a *tere* party.'

'What?'

'A memory for a *tere* party from Pinoi. Once they came, five years ago. They have a very good time.'

'Why did you not tell me?'

The New Peaceful Islander shrugged. She had not asked him.

'Sometimes,' her voice was not specially lowered. 'I wonder if the native mind is suited to the responsibilities of instruction and guidance ... if they're ready. The tragedy is, of course, if we don't train them, Someone Else will.'

'I think you misjudge him,' said Leicester.

'Aporo?'

'Costa. Constantopoulos.'

'Why must we talk about him when you know I dislike him?'

'But he's never done you any harm.'

'All that fulsome fawning. So smooth and plump. And those horrid little black eyes, set right in. Like an elephant. He's too Oriental.'

'That's not his fault.'

'He's oily. All those flowery speeches. Turned up at my cottage the other night.'

'Costa?'

'At half-past nine. I was just about to hit the hay. There he was—all smiles. With a bottle. A present, he said. *Parfait d'Amour*. Disgusting stuff. "I know what the ladies like!" '

'What did you say?'

'I said, "What, in this heat?" Besides I can't stand the stuff. Made of roses.'

'Violets.'

'And Turkish Delight, which I hate. All the usual florid compliments. Thought we might talk French together. I sent him packing pretty fast, I can tell you.'

Leicester said rather testily, 'You keep on saying you don't speak French. How did you manage in the New Hebrides?'

'Oh ...' she waved her hands. 'I speak enough for my work. In the villages one need only ask a few key questions. I would ask the women, *"Donnez-vous le sein?"* If they didn't, one showed them the pictures and posters. And of course there were interpreters.'

'Well, that's all it is ...' said Leicester after a thoughtful pause. 'He just wants people to like him.'

'He's slippery. I don't trust him.' She shuddered. The car shook. 'Give him an inch ... the sort of man who would *paw* one. ...'

'Well, I like him!' But her words had directed his thoughts from Costa. Was it possible that beneath her moustache, her martial exterior she was an untouched maiden?

Absurd, with that booming voice, that air of command; yet timid unaware virgins often lurked behind female academics, decisive executives. Was it possible Miss Arbuthnott was frightened of Costa?

'Are you a man-hater?' he said involuntarily.

Her face and throat became burgundy.

'I like the sort of man one can talk to; but I *don't* care much for the sort who, after the second sherreh, starts to get *amorous*.' She added explicitly, 'Ugh!'

'Aporo, where is your cousin?' said Leicester surveying the deserted scene. 'Your cousin and his family? They were to meet us here.'

Aporo put down the camera he was squinting into.

'Today my cousin has gone fishing; but his family comes.'

'Gone fishing? He cannot go fishing! We need him.'

'Today, Miss Arbuthnott, my cousin is gone fishing. But I take his place. I play for you the husband.'

'But that won't do at all. We must have the same man. Leicester, tell him. Explain.'

'It won't do, Aporo. You can't take your cousin's place in the pictures because . . .'

'Yes yes. I take it. He gives me permission.'

'You know perfectly well all our pictures show your cousin as the husband . . . the father . . . all through the story. We can't suddenly change and have someone else. We must have continuity. You know that.'

If Aporo knew he thought it of little importance.

'The wife of my cousin is here. I see her coming now.'

'We must keep calm,' Miss Arbuthnott said resolutely.

'Calm!'

'Yes. Calm. If the cousin is not available we must somehow manage without him.'

'We can't. He's the key of the story. He has to be in this scene.'

'We'll have to shoot round him.'

'We can't.'

'Then we must rewrite the scene. Come Leicester, buck up. When you've worked in the islands as long as I have you won't be so easily cast down.'

Leicester felt entitled to temperament.

'You keep saying that! But every single day there's been something ... weather; technical breakdowns; things getting lost. Look at the number of casts we've had—all unreliable —just to make this simple filmstrip.'

His desperation, utter dejection moved his companion. She took his hand, said encouragingly, 'But it's nearly done now. And it will be very good.'

'My cousin's wife says what do you wish her to do?' Aporo stood like a lion tamer waiting to open the cage.

'We shall photograph her and the baby, since your cousin is not here.'

'But Miss Arbuthnott, I have my cousin's permission ...'

'We know that, Aporo. But we must alter the story. Come dear, where is your baby?'

The cousin's wife bashfully exposed the void in her teeth.

'Tst tst. Such a shame they lose them so early. White bread and sugar. The baby, Aporo; tell her to fetch the baby for the picture.'

Aporo conferred with the wife of his cousin.

'Today she has not brought the baby.'

'Not *brought* it? Why not?'

They conferred again; Aporo said, 'The baby is heavy to carry. Today she has walked from her village.'

'Why did you not fetch her in the Land Rover?'

Aporo's shrug was invisible. Who had asked him?

'Well, you must go now and fetch it at once.'

But the cousin's wife shook her head. She was obstinate.

'Today,' reported Aporo. 'The baby has gone to the house of my cousin's wife's mother. It is far. Soon...' he looked hopeful ... 'the sun will go. It will rain. Then we cannot take pictures.'

'I could murder you all!' said Miss Arbuthnott.

The cousin's wife incuriously glanced. It was beyond her comprehension why rich white women worked; why they rushed about in the heat, getting red in the face; queerest of all, why they trailed round the world alone, without a man, without even one baby.

Aporo tried again.

'There is one woman here in the village has one baby she will lend.'

'Impossible!'

'But Miss Arbuthnott, this is a very good baby. Very good for our hygiene strip. It has scabies. It also has rickets. This will be very important to show.'

'No!'

'There are many women with babies, Miss Arbuthnott. They would lend them if we asked.'

'It's no good. Don't you *understand*, Aporo?'

The high crackling note of frustration roused Leicester from his own sad thoughts. Soothingly he said, 'Don't be upset—it's not worth it. The sun has gone anyway. It's too late to shoot. We must come back tomorrow.'

Sweating angrily, Beatrice shook her fist at Aporo's cousin's wife. She said, 'Drive us to my cottage, Aporo. Come Leicester—we'll at least have tea or a drink.'

'Too-morrow.' The cousin's wife amiably smiled. 'Okay. Too-morrow.'

'Whaddya-know!' Marje Crump asked Dolly Vincent at the freezer. 'They say Miss Arbuthnott's got off with Leicester.'

'Oh nonsense! She's old enough to be his mother.'

'Well, s'what they say. They're always together. Thelma's housegirl's Aporo's cousin. He's always driving them round the island; Leicester's always at her place. The locals say they go off in the bushes.'

Dolly stopped at the door of the freezing chamber.

'Look, I simply can't stand the smell of that meat. I'm

112

going to try for some fish. And you know the Maoris say that about any two people seen together.'

'Getting fish on this island's like getting hen's teeth,' said Marje glumly. She stepped into the frigid mortuary. 'Don't you wait if you want to go on. But you know what they say—where there's smoke there's usually fire. Still, it might take his mind off Temata. Ern reckons he'll be shacked up with her before we know it.'

Costa, collecting his liquor ration at the bond, smiled playfully as Dolly emerged.

'Ah Mrs Vincent, if you weren't such a charming and beautiful lady I should say rude things about your husband.'

'Oh no! What has he done now?'

'Because I cannot buy drink for my friends without his certificate.'

'Oh! But you know it's just to protect the natives.' Recovered from the smell of the meat, her fears of Costa long laid at rest, Dolly smiled and blinked flirtatiously.

Costa advanced a bottle towards her.

'For you!'

'For me? Oh no!'

'*Fior d'Alpini.* See the little flower there inside? You will like it.'

'Oh, but I couldn't. Your ration. I couldn't.'

'I insist. Some Turkish Delight? I keep a supply here in the cool room, you know.'

She was trying to give up sweets, but you simply could not refuse Costa. He was so kind, warmhearted, generous; and his manners ... the way he was handling her now to her car ... she might have been the only woman in the world.

'I can't believe it,' she said. 'Marje Crump says they say Leicester Whiteway is having an affair with Miss Arbuthnott. It's absurd. I can just imagine what Bill will say. Did you hear?'

Costa nodded, silent, grave. Surprised, Dolly said, 'But you don't *believe* it, do you? Not *Leicester*?'

113

'Leicester,' said Costa, 'is a gentleman. But Miss Arbuthnott, you know, is a very strange woman.'

Dolly stopped hopefully.

'Miss Arbuthnott,' said Costa, 'has lived a very strange life.
No husband, no children of her own; always with natives, in
tropical islands. People change; they get strange ideas. Miss
Arbuthnott was for years in Melanesia, you know; in the
French islands of the Condominium.' He shrugged. 'For myself, I adore the French way of life ... the freedom ... the
lack of feeling about colour. I do not criticize. But as you
know, it is not our own way....'

Sixteen 🐦 🐦

WHEN Mr Holmes talked now about Leicester's visit to
Manu his assistant showed gratifying interest. Whiteway, for
all his shortcomings was keen, and that, after all was what
one needed. Mistakes, errors of judgment, Holmes said
generously, could be rectified; one learnt by experience; but
without enthusiasm, knowledge was useless in this game.

Leicester was thankful the cause of his eagerness was not
evident. Manu had assumed features of paradise. Ashamed
of his unworthy motives, he could not control a longing to
escape the scene of his trials, hourly increasing. Frustration
at work, unresolved situation with Temata were now joined
by domestic crisis.

At home, Daniel dominated life. No matter how much his
mother hugged him or sang to him he continued to cough.
Slumped on kitchen floor or propped on sink draining-
board, swathed in one of Leicester's sheets, he sweated,
struggled to breathe, bubbling with each inhalation.
Leicester was appalled. The smooth brown skin had turned
dirty grey, once-plump shiny cheeks hung limp on bird
bones. A pitiful little skeleton peered out through the
wreckage of Daniel's deflated flesh.

Each morning he urged Toa to take the child to hospital. Each evening she offered fresh excuses. Evasive, she clung to the baby, as though Leicester had threatened to drag him away.

'Don't you realize he could die? He's so young. He's very ill. You must see the doctor.'

She looked at him, stricken.

'They'll make him better if you take him to hospital; but now; *today*! You must take him *now*!'

She shook her head, desperate, hunted.

'What's the matter? Are you frightened you'll have to pay? I'll give you money.'

Silent refusal; another fevered grappling. Sighing, Leicester turned away.

Bare feet pattered after him.

'Leicester?'

'Yes?'

'But if I put him in hospital he will die!'

He groaned. No matter what you did or said, all over the Pacific they still believed it. The reason why mothers hid sick babies in the bush; why patients were spirited from wards by anxious families; why many were kept from doctors till too late; the hospital is the death-house, the place where you go to die. Native Development indeed!

'No no. He'll get better there. People get better in hospital, *if they don't leave it too late!*'

But she knew. She had seen too many go in and never come out. He tried to compromise. 'You needn't leave him there. If you go to the dispensary you could get medicine to give him at home.'

How to talk to those eyes, that primitive fear undiluted by knowledge or confidence? Daniel's illness had turned a carefree child to a defenceless animal, driven by foreboding instincts. One could not chat to such dark unnerving forces; but he plodded on, now infected by her panic.

'Be a good girl. You take him to the dispensary. I won't let them keep him. I promise.'

Astonishingly, she was all smiles next morning, though Daniel, bubbling in his sheet, looked no better.

'I went to the hospital. They have given me one pill for Daniel.'

'What did they tell you?'

'They said for Daniel to keep warm, in bed.'

This she interpreted literally, to be effected at once. Before Leicester left for work the verandah bed had been requisitioned. Sheet-swathed, only dark tormented eyes visible above a yashmak, Daniel was packed all round with pillows. Toa's own body contributed extra warmth. All pretence at housework abandoned, she lay like a boa-constrictor round the child, singing to him occasionally, for the most part sleeping heavily. The baby dozed restlessly, waking to choke, to give his terrifying cough.

Coming home from his day with Miss Arbuthnott Leicester found them awake. Daniel breathed heavily in his shroud. Toa crouched on the bed, coaxing him to eat.

'Surely he shouldn't eat with a temperature?'

'He is hungry.'

'But not sardines! Not cold *kumara*! He needs water. Fruit juice.'

'I gave him lime juice. He did not like.' Daniel, opening his mouth for breath, she pushed in the teaspoon. Tired of the unequal struggle he heaved up all he had eaten for some time past.

'Ah,' Toa said reproachfully. 'Now he is sick.'

'Clean it up!' Leicester commanded. 'And for goodness sake take him home. Stay home and nurse him. Understand? Don't come to work till he's better.'

She did not answer, mopping vaguely at the bed. Leicester helped himself to whiskey without ice—the refrigerator was out—and began searching for food.

'Where is my *kai*?'

'No *kai*,' she looked surprised. 'You have *kai* at hotel maybe?'

They had warned him; they had all warned him. It was

his own fault ... he had let her go on too long. Now she was turning him out of his own house to seek food at the hotel, where dinner would be finished, at his own expense, while her child monopolized beds, sheets, attention.... Hungry, angry, frustrated he set off down the road.

Without destination, he needed movement, a physical channel for rage. Surprised, he realized he had stopped outside Temata's house.

'Leicester ... you will come in? Come and have *kai* with us?'

Ben waved and called from his verandah chair.

'Come in, Leicester. Temata is home.'

Temata! At this stage! But he turned and moved towards the house.

Temata, bold as brass, sweet as pie, followed him to the verandah after the meal. Once more, as she flicked back her beautiful hair, stretched her golden arms, he dissolved. Hunger assuaged, anger forgotten, he was ripe for deception.

'This old woman ... you are sleeping with her?'

'Miss Arbuthnott? Are you crazy?'

'People say so. You go with her always. In the bush. In her house.'

'We're working. She's twenty years older than me.'

'She's a woman. You are a man. People say it.'

'Well, they're wrong.'

'Toa. You sleep with her too?'

'Never.'

'You will marry her, maybe? Take her to New Zealand?'

'You're joking!'

'You take her to cinema. She sleep in your house. Her baby sleep there. You give her things for her baby....'

'What things?'

'Towels; sheets. I have seen. *Kai*...'

'I give her nothing. She helps herself. She steals.'

'I think you give to her.'

Why reassure her? Jealousy should be fed, his own value raised; or she should be sent about her business.

'You don't come any more to our house,' said Temata. 'I think you like Toa.'

'Toa's my housegirl. She is poor and has a sick baby....' Temata had babies too; any amount. He stood up suddenly. 'I must go home.'

'You go to sleep with Toa maybe?'

'That's ridiculous.'

'Why you don't send her away? Why she sleeps there each night?'

'I tell you, the baby's sick.'

'I think you send her away, eh? Now. You send her to-night. She's no good. She coughs. No good for you. Bad. Toa has TB. You will get TB and die.'

'She has not got TB.' Strange how her uncertainty evoked this new firmness, almost sense of power. Sensing it, Temata tried harder.

'Oh yes, she had. Before you came. All her family. Her brother a *leper*! You get sick. She blows on your food....'

He escaped with a promise to come for dinner the night before sailing for Manu, to send Toa away.

No capitulation there. Walking home he planned his speech of dismissal. He would give money and food, pack her and Daniel into the car and drive them home. No pleas or arguments; kind, firm, *definite*. They must go!

Though it was after nine, Toa was busy in the sitting-room. She had pushed aside the table and arranged a mattress diagonally across the floor, an effective obstruction to movement. Upon it sat Daniel, in yashmak, padded round with pillows. From a clothesline at throat level hung damp garments Daniel had vomited on, some of Toa's underwear, a floral crêpe dress. Windows were shut, back door wedged tightly with a flat-iron. Considering the curtain between bedroom and sitting-room inadequate protection, she had also shut bedroom windows. She was preparing to seal the front door. The air was fetid.

At Leicester's challenge she looked over her shoulder as at an absurd question.

'The night air. I am keeping it out.'

'You mean to tell me you're sleeping here? In *here*?'

She nodded. 'Oh yes. Too cold on the verandah.'

'But you cannot stay here! You must go home.'

'I stay. It is late. I cannot carry Daniel.'

'I will drive you. *You can't stay here!*'

'I cannot!' she suddenly wailed. 'He will die. He will catch cold in the night air and die. They told me, at the hospital.'

Daniel woke. He cried, fretfully, working to a crescendo of coughs. Toa seized him so passionately that he screamed.

'For God's sake stop him! He'll choke. All right, all right. For tonight. But just for tonight. I mean it! In the morning you will take him home.'

She nodded, appeased. Daniel's paroxysm subsided to a spongey groan.

'In the morning. Okay. Tonight we stay here.' She returned the baby to his mattress.

'Meanwhile,' said Leicester, stepping over the mummified carcase, 'you can open the windows. I cannot sleep with the windows shut.'

She began to wail again.

'The night air! The night air.... He will die!'

He turned away, too tired for anger.

'You can keep them shut in here if you want to smother,' he said. 'But *not in my room.*'

Seventeen ❧ ❧

FOR the last few weeks the hurricane season had been losing its grip on Aratoa. Unpleasant northerlies with their squalls had slowly retreated as the cool south-east trade winds grew stronger. Hope could return, life resume, the claustrophobic sensation of the wet season fade at the thought of renewed communications with the outer world. Soon inter-island ships would creep back from their refuges, smartened with paint, crews refreshed and restored. In the cooler night air the bangs would grow louder, the singing more strident as Aratoans held final rehearsals for *tere* parties.

When Leicester woke he looked out at a clear sky, deep sparkling sea, sunlight no longer filtered through steam. The island was subtly transformed, outlines sharpened, colours deepened, beauty clarified. The faithful trade wind blew steadily, reassuringly. There was a lightening of spirit, a new freedom in breathing.

He had slept little. Each time he dozed he had been woken by coughing; first Toa, then Daniel, then Toa, then Daniel again, the sequence varied by unholy crepitations, asthmatic struggles and gasps. He had thought of Temata's warnings, was convinced she had spoken the truth, saw himself doomed. Once or twice Daniel's gurgling breath so resembled a death rattle that he got up but Toa, fully clothed, swathed in blankets, could not be prised apart from the child. Leicester left them to die and went back to bed in disgust.

Now, buoyed up by the change, by a new sense of perspective, he went cheerfully to work leaving Toa and Daniel in possession. Let them stay where they were, poor tragic waifs. He would soon be free.

'You're booked on *Expire*,' said Holmes. 'She's due in next week. You, Miss Arbuthnott and Constantopoulos. She'll leave you at Manu for several days and pick you up on her way back.'

'Who else is going in *Expire*? Judy Pollock?'

'She is not. There is not enough accommodation. She is going in *Tiare Maori*, a Cook Islanders' schooner. Round the Group.'

'I thought *Tiare Maori* was booked for the *tere* party?'

'She is. Miss Pollock has got in with them somehow; as she

has got permission to visit the Outer Islands. I did not make the arrangements,' he said acidly. 'She has no doubt got round Davidson. If it were left to me she would not go at all.'

Judy was enthusiastic when Leicester met her next day at the bond.

'Buying whiskey for the voyage,' she said. 'What a pity you can't come in *Tiare Maori*. I'm going with the *tere* party.'

Leicester said priggishly that he was going to work.

'Bill says the last European who travelled with a *tere* party died of enlarged liver. He had to join in all the feasts, everywhere they stopped. We'll be away weeks.'

'You'll be more comfortable than in *Expire*.'

'Oh, I know. Ken says *Expire* is falling to pieces. He says last time he travelled in her someone put their foot through the deck and Bill says her wireless isn't working. They say it's a scandal she's registered. She's not seaworthy. They say the captain brings rare shells back for H.H. Not that I should talk about bribes, I suppose.'

Leicester blushed. Shameless! She said impatiently, 'Oh, don't be silly, Leicester. Of course everyone knows. How else was I to see the Outer Islands?'

When Nutkin woke on the day of the concert it seemed God had turned against her. Her smile, entrusted each night to the tumbler, was gone.

'But I *know* they were there when I went to bed,' she lisped piteously, flapping lips concealed beneath trembling paw.

Theodore was so annoyed one might have thought they were his.

'Well, they're not here now. Are you *sure* you put them in the glass?'

'Of course. Or . . . Oh, I don't know really if I put them in; but they were there, by the bed. You must have seen them.'

He reminded her that she only removed them after lights out.

'Well, they were there. But who would take them?'

The servants were questioned.

'Someone,' Nutkin said tensely, 'who would like to ruin my concert tonight. Someone who harbours a grudge against us for our campaign against Sunday sport.'

Towards lunch time, Dr Vincent, called in at last to give sedatives, had an inspiration.

'Look under the mats!' he commanded. 'Look round the garden.'

The mats were lifted. Mrs Hitchcock's smile shone out from a crab hole with a cotton reel and some dead hibiscus flowers.

'I thought for a moment it was subversive activities,' she said mysteriously, clamping them in.

The incident put the island into a holiday mood. Pleasing images were evoked, the land crab likened to a Spanish dancer, clicking Nutkin's smile over its head in the dark. By seven o'clock there was no one who did not feel better for her disaster.

She had faced them all bravely, been cheered when she stood up to sing:

> 'Flay whate butterflays out to seee,
> Flay ... flayhay ... flayyyyy.'

The hall was full. Cigarette smoke, greeting cries, the shuffling feet of seat-changers suggested a night at stadium or music hall. All Aratoa had come, Miss Davidson deputising for His Honour. Offenbach, Judy, the Forbeses, the Vincents, Miss Arbuthnott sat happily together; Leicester, less happily, felt obliged to accompany Holmes and Janet. Costa had caused a sensation in mess jacket, cummerbund, cigar. He swept in with the Baha'is, Misses Manders and Jones, each carrying boxes of sweets, looking flushed and amazed. Inexplicably, he gave the impression of going on to the theatre from a first-class restaurant.

The concert ran without hitch, sensation or shock. When *Ru's Canoe* had dipped and rolled, voyagers spied out the land, paddles been plied, when This House had been blessed and the Queen had been saved, the evening's business began.

Theodore could not have asked for a larger or more attentive house. The platform cleared of all but himself he threw round his challenging look, inhaled and projected his Henry V battle-scene voice.

'This meeting has been called to discuss *once and for all* the question of Sunday sport in Aratoa. There are, as we know, *elements* in this island claiming to see no harm in the practice. That is not the view of the church; but since we live in a democracy the only way to settle the matter is to put it to the vote. I shall therefore commence by stating my case for the abolition of Sunday sport. Open discussion will then be called, after which we shall cast our votes.'

He droned on. Leicester's thoughts wandered. That morning Holmes had called him in.

'Whiteway. I'd like a word about the Savings Group poster design.'

'Yes sir.'

'You realize of course that the posters are for the Peaceful Islands—not for New Zealand suburbs?'

'Yes sir; I...'

'The beds, Whiteway. You've been here nearly six months. Do you have to be told that the Peaceful Islanders sleep on mats? Take the beds out. And cut down the wording. There's far too much text. And another thing, Whiteway. People are talking.'

'Talking sir?'

'About you and Miss Arbuthnott.'

'Sir! That's my work!'

'I know—I know. But the natives say you are always together, in the bushes. Be more discreet in future. You know how they talk. H.H. won't be pleased. If rumours get round to Ha'i Koma...'

'The meeting is now open for discussion!'

Theodore sat down, drank a glass of water, mopped his

face and glared at his flock. At last he said into the silence, 'Come now ... I am sure you all *have* something to say. Judging by what I have heard in the last few months, plenty have opinions to air. Someone must start the ball rolling.'

The shuffling began.

'Well, Tangaroa? You have something to say? Come now, speak up.'

'Mr Hitchcock, I am an old man. I have been born and bred in these islands and my father before me ...'

Theodore nodded graciously.

'... and his father before him. My people have always lived in these islands. When the white men came, the Ships of Peace, my fathers were brought to God by the missionaries. We have always been people of the church. I myself was Deacon for many years...'

'Till sacked for pinching the offertory,' Dr Vincent murmured.

'... My children have been baptised into the church. My grandchildren...'

People moved uneasily. Tangaroa descended, on his mother's side, from a Samoan Talking Chief. Mr Hitchcock looked at his watch.

'Every day in my house we are reading from the Bible. We are talking about the word of God...' Tangaroa paused, looking up at the ceiling. Theodore showed asperity.

'Come, Tangaroa ... Make your point. Others are waiting to speak.'

Tangaroa jumped like a startled sleepwalker. He stared at the missionary, then astoundingly asked, 'Mr Hitchcock, speaking as our shepherd, would you say the Sabbath was made for man, or man for the Sabbath?'

'Hear hear,' said Dr Vincent.

Theodore's folded lips were his only acknowledgement of treachery.

'Do I take it, Tangaroa, that you are in *favour* of Sunday sport?'

124

'Mr Hitchcock ... My people have been church-goers since the first Ships of Peace came to these islands. . . .'

'Quite. Thank you. Perhaps now Simeone will give us his views.'

Tangaroa lingered a moment, then sat down looking baffled.

Simeone sprang up.

'It's not for me to say,' he said eagerly. 'Of course we should not allow sport on the Lord's Day; but what will people *do* if they cannot play basket-ball?'

He sat down. Dr Vincent stood up.

'Of course,' he said. 'It's not for me to say either, but I think they'll go up into the hills and make bush beer and get drunk on it.'

This was applauded.

Theodore shouted 'Silence! This attitude is disgraceful!'

'Say something!' Holmes commanded.

Leicester jumped.

'Me? Never. I couldn't. I have nothing to say.'

'Then I will.' Holmes stood up. 'Mr Chairman,' he said suavely. 'Of course you are right in your preliminary re-marks; but the Peaceful Islanders look to Government to give the lead, to set the example. I take it therefore that abolition of Sunday basketball infers abolition of Sunday tennis and golf for Europeans!'

There was a hostile rumble. Someone said 'Shame!'

'Precisely. I am glad, Mr Holmes, that you see my point. Mrs Vincent?'

'Of course,' Dolly was apologetic, 'it's not for *me* to say but after all, I mean, I know Sunday sport is all wrong and that but I always feel ... I mean, I know people do feel sometimes that they can worship God in his beautiful fresh air just as well as in the four walls of a church. Of course, that's only *my* feeling but I feel that. . . .'

'Mr Chairman!' Miss Manders was struggling up, assisted by Costa, who might have been signalling a bus. 'Mr Chairman,' she fluted when Theodore's attention was caught.

'Speaking as members of the Baha'i faith, Miss Jones and I feel we should like to take this opportunity to support what Mrs Vincent has so beautifully expressed. We do not feel that the Holy Spirit is only to be found within the walls of churches. The kingdom of Gahd is after all within us. . . .'

It was growing hard to hear. The Deacon raised his voice.

'Mr Chairman,' he bellowed. 'I feel we should abolish Sunday sport. My people would be better off quietly at home in the bosom of their family than playing basketball.'

'Nonsense!' Miss Arbuthnott was up. 'Why deprive the poor people of their innocent games? You must excuse me if I remind you that the *Church* does not hold with this puritanical nonsense. Once one has attended Mass, one is free to play games if one wishes. . . .'

Janet Holmes raised her hand.

'I *do* feel,' she said loudly, drowning Nutkin's fuming stutter, 'as my husband points out, that if we expect Peaceful Islanders to give up basketball we should give up tennis and golf. I mean, fair's fair, after all!'

'At which she is no bloody good,' Dr Vincent reminded his wife. 'Now what will Miss Davidson say?'

Miss Davidson was already on her feet.

'Mr Chairman. We can go on all night discussing this matter without getting anywhere. Frankly, I feel it's all quite unnecessary in this day and age. You will no doubt agree that we may take our standard of behaviour from our own Royal Family. May I remind you that His Royal Highness the Duke of Edinburgh plays polo on Sunday? What's good enough for Buckingham Palace is good enough for Aratoa, in my opinion!'

The silence that fell had the quality of a crouching animal. Leicester felt Holmes stirring but Nutkin beat him, moving noisily, clumsily, all but paralysed with rage for Miss Davidson's insolence, for her brother's arrogance allowing those Baha'is into the Colony, for Miss Arbuthnott's shameless proselytizing.

126

'Render unto Caesar what is Caesar's; unto God what is God's!' she cried. 'Too many are led astray by sophisticated reasoning, by decadent example....'

'This is treason,' Dr Vincent suggested. *'Lèse-majesté.'*

'... Since when,' Nutkin was growing shrill, 'since when has the Queen's Representative abused privileges ... joined issue in local politics? Does her Majesty speak in Parliament, advising one side or the other? And while on the subject I should like to draw attention to the deplorable conduct of the Aratoa Girl Guides. Their behaviour has become a byword; their uniforms no more than a means of flaunting themselves for the basest purpose....'

'Try flaunting in a Guide uniform,' Judy said to Ken Forbes.

Miss Davidson was up again, so fast that she seemed not to have sat down. With Nutkin still on her feet they faced each other across the eager crowd.

'While we are quoting from the Bible,' said Miss Davidson, 'I should like to mention that there is also something about purity in the eye of the beholder. To the pure all is pure. My Guides...'

Nutkin's eyes gleamed insanely. She had been through a good deal that day.

'Aratoa is riddled with subversive activities,' she began. 'When those in High Places adopt a policy of complaisance, laxity, cynical disregard for morality...'

Theodore banged his ruler, shouting above the clamour. One could not know where Nutkin might finish when she started on politics.

'We will now have a show of hands! Those in favour of abolishing Sunday sport, say *"Aye"*!'

A ragged silence limped in.

'*Aye?*' said Theodore.

'Aye.' Barely audible, Nutkin and the Deacon raised their hands.

'Against?'

All hands were raised. Voices soared again.

'This is not the last word!' Theodore promised grimly. 'The matter will be referred to a higher authority.'

'What does that mean?' Dolly Vincent felt guilty about her speech. 'The Bishop?'

'It could be God,' said her husband. 'Or perhaps just the Privy Council. It probably means he is going to bring it all up again next month.'

But Theodore's moment was over. No one was listening to him. They had all flocked into the street where they stood talking, reluctant to move, separate, go indoors from the cool serene night.

'Good night ... Good night ...' People passed, called to each other, Costa's cigar smoke floated back with the scent of island flowers. 'Good night, Leicester. Good night Mr Holmes...'

How loud the surf on the reef!

'Oh,' Dolly lifted her face to the sky. 'To feel that breeze ... after all those months....'

Miss Arbuthnott gathered her stole round her shoulders.

'And this time next week we'll be on Manu. Fresh fields and pastures new.'

'Everyone going,' Dolly regretted. 'You; Costa; Leicester; Judy...'

'Others will come, my dear; have no fear,' said her husband. '*Marinda* will shortly be in, full of surprises, no doubt. Come ... let's not stand about here. Let's go home for a drink. Miss Arbuthnott?'

'Thank you, Dr Vincent, but it's early to bed for me!'

'Good night then; good night.'

Slowly the groups broke up, ambled off into the darkness.

Eighteen ❧ ❧

LEICESTER was embarrassed when Miss Arbuthnott waved at him from the roadside. Should he tell her Holmes's comment? And how? To treat the rumour as a joke was hardly chivalrous; besides she'd be gone from Aratoa in the morning.... He drew up.

'I thought you were going to pass me,' she said jovially. 'I was getting ready to hitch up my skirt, show a bit of leg.'

'What's happened? Where's the Land Rover?'

'Aporo's gone off somewhere. I must get home to finish packing.' She swarmed into the car. 'He's quite the stupidest islander I've ever met. The Leader of the Community Development team! The Leader!

'He's inclined to be lazy and complacent. Did you realize that if the language had an *l* his name would be Apollo?'

'I hadn't; but that's all it needs. Look here, Leicester, I'm taking you out of your way. But I'll give you a drink; or dinner perhaps?'

'Thank you.' He regretted his promise to eat at Ben's. Temata would want to know why he had not sacked Toa; he would be disturbed by her beauty, the sight of the children. He said dubiously, 'I can't come to dinner but I could give you a drink on the way.'

'Excellent! I'm in no hurry. Then I'll go on home. And I've never been to your house.'

'No, you haven't.' But what did it matter. Better Beatrice than anyone else if sordid secrets must be revealed.

The mynah birds were at it in the *flamboyant* leaves but neither Toa nor Daniel were visible. Leicester pulled out a verandah chair.

'Sit down, Beatrice. We'll have it out here. I'll go and find Toa.'

The house was stuffy, neglected. Though mattress and

clothes line were gone the sitting-room still smelt of vomit and sweat. He pioneered to the kitchen.

'Toa! Get some glasses for drinks and some ice. I have a visitor.'

Toa turned from the draining-board where Daniel, as usual, was propped.

'*Is* there any ice?' Leicester moved towards the refrigerator.

'I get glasses.' She straightened Daniel against the wall and went reproachfully to the sitting-room.

Leicester was despondently viewing the lukewarm ice tray when Miss Arbuthnott said, 'Can't I help? Please don't go to trouble. Just a small drop of Scotch.'

'Ice; I had hoped we'd have ice, but somehow ... I don't know. I suppose the fridge has gone out again.'

'Let's have a look.' She advanced into the shadowy kitchen, stooped to peer, straightened up, stood transfixed.

'That baby! Where does the baby come from? What's he doing here?'

'That's Daniel. He belongs to my housegirl.'

'What's he eating?' She pounced, prised open Daniel's clammy hand. 'As I thought! Taro! Where's his mother?'

Rigid with primitive fear, Toa stood in the door holding two smeary tumblers.

'*My* baby! *My* baby!' It was the cry of a cow raped of its calf.

'Your baby! You naughty girl! You don't deserve a baby! What are you giving him? Don't you know he shouldn't be eating things like that at his age?'

Toa wrapped her arms round Daniel, adjusting shawls and shrouds.

'... and why is he all wrapped up like that?' Miss Arbuthnott dabbed at the draperies. 'Do you want to smother him?'

'Doctor said Daniel not get cold.' Yet hypnotic subjection already tainted Toa's anguished defiance.

'Nonsense! Take off those wrappings!' Leicester, ice, refrigerator forgotten, Miss Arbuthnott seized the baby.

'Is he breastfed?'

Chin and eyebrows jerked up.

'How old is he?'

'Two years, I think.'

'Ha! You see? The same old story! Half-weaned, I'll be bound. Worn-out useless breast-milk every now and then and when he cries with hunger lumps of taro thrust into his mouth to silence him. No wonder they get sick.'

She had unwrapped the outer layers. Daniel, stupefied, began to stiffen.

'Poor little fellow. There there ... we'll soon fix you up.' Ignoring suspended breath, blackening cheeks, lids squeezed for maximum oral aperture she jogged the child up and down. Shock dropped his jaw; his eyes opened. Unaware, he breathed normally, roar lost forever. Stunned, Toa hovered.

'Now look here, my dear, you must listen to me. You must do what I tell you. He *must* be put on to powdered milk. You *must* wean him *properly*!'

Toa shook her head helplessly.

'You're not only starving the child, you're killing yourself. Look at you ... arms like chicken bones ... hollow cheeks ... lank hair. If I had you both in my charge for a couple of months I'd fix all that.'

Toa said, 'We come with you, maybe? To your house.'

'No dear, not to my house. Alas, I'm going away tomorrow. You must stay here with Mr Whiteway....'

'But Beatrice, she can't stay here. I'm going away myself, don't forget.'

'So you are. Then what happens to these two? Has she money? Another job?'

'I'll give her some money,' Leicester said uneasily. 'She has no job to go to....'

Toa, gazing at Miss Arbuthnott, announced, 'We come with you. You make Daniel better.' She wore the mulish expression with which she had taken over Leicester's living-room.

E*

131

'I wish you could, dear. But I'm going to Manu in the morning.'

'We come. My mother Manu woman. We come.'

'I wonder. I *wonder*! Do you think perhaps, Leicester ... ?'

Oh God, oh God, could it be true?

'Oh yes. I'm sure it could be arranged. I'm sure we could fix it.' Terror of second thoughts caused a rush of words. 'She should go with you. She should. You should go with Miss Arbuthnott, Toa. She could tell you how to look after Daniel and make him well and strong; and you would get well and strong too....'

Toa looked dumbly at her child, at Miss Arbuthnott.

'He would get well and strong? He would grow big and fat?'

'Of course. If we can get permission to take you ...'

Fearing reflection, Leicester said quickly, 'We'll get permission. I'll see the Chief. I'll see H.H. ... Dr Vincent ... I'll get it all arranged. If she has people on Manu there should be no problem. She could go as your housegirl ... perhaps you could train her to help with the babies....'

'That's the ticket! How would you like that, my dear?'

Toa nodded without comprehension. One idea at a time fully stretched her capacity.

'Yes, we come with you and get well and strong.'

Well pleased with her salvage work, Miss Arbuthnott completed her packing and sat down to check through her progress report. All posters adapted, film-strips reshot, flannelgraph figures changed from black Melanesians to smooth Polynesians. Good. It would shortly be dark but if she hurried she could finish before lighting the lamps. She clicked her tongue at a knock on the door.

'Good evening, Miss Arbuthnott.'

Stately, leisured, pontifical, Aporo loomed in the doorway.

'Aporo! What is it?'

'I may come in, Miss Arbuthnott?' He was entering with deliberation. 'I have brought this to show you.'

He drew a scroll from under his arm. 'This is a poster for the lino cutting. Special poster I have designed. For the baby food.'

He unrolled the paper. A large tin of dried milk was revealed, the lettering carefully printed.

'I cut it myself. You see? The name of the milk ... everything. It is good?'

'It's a life-like portrait of a tin of dried milk,' Miss Arbuthnott said. 'But I have enough posters already.'

'But this one, Miss Arbuthnott, I have designed. You will tell Mr Holmes ... you will tell him how good it is?'

'I'm going away in the morning; I shan't have a chance. And at the moment I'm busy. . . .'

'Maybe you will write from Manu and tell him. Then he will send me to New Zealand, to Art School.'

'Yes yes. Well, leave it here, Aporo. I'll do what I can.'

'I'd like you to have a good look at it, Miss Arbuthnott,' Aporo said. 'See how fine are the lines in the letters. These I cut myself.'

'It's too dark to see now,' she said rather sharply. 'I'll look in the morning.'

'Yes, it is too dark. You need the light. I fix it.'

Slowly, deliberately he lit the lamp; then reseating himself, leant back comfortably. His dignified gravity gave a sense of being in audience. He was there to stay.

'Are you not afraid of the dark, Miss Arbuthnott? Are you not afraid, all alone in this cottage?'

'No. Why should I be afraid? No one would hurt me.'

'Oh, I don't mean people. I mean ghosts.'

'Come come, you don't believe in ghosts, Aporo. You're all Christians now. Good Christians don't believe in ghosts.'

'Many people on Aratoa believe in ghosts even if they go to church. Myself, I and my family are Seventh Day Adventists but we believe in ghosts.'

'Can you actually tell me that you've seen a ghost?'

Aporo looked evasive. 'We had a werewolf here. A woman turned into a werewolf.'

'Nonsense! Nonsense! There are no werewolves in the Pacific!'

'Oh yes. On this island. On Aratoa. This woman, she died, you see; then she became a werewolf. She tore people's throats and drank their blood.'

'You've been going to the cinema too much.'

'It is true. Last year it happened, here on Aratoa.'

'Did she attack dead or live people?'

'Mostly dead. They were easier to get at, you know; but sometimes she carried away little children.'

'Little children! And what did Mr Hitchcock have to say about that?'

'The people did not tell Mr Hitchcock. They went up in the mountains where this woman was buried and dug her up.' He paused for effect. *They dug her up and cut off her head! Then they set fire to her!*'

'Fiddlesticks! I don't believe a word of it!'

'It is true. After that, no more werewolves. You see, Miss Arbuthnott, the Peaceful Islands people are very brave. Like in the Old Time. We are not frightened of anything.' He leaned back contentedly.

A shattering screech outside stiffened his body. His face became grey.

'Is that one of your werewolves?' Miss Arbuthnott said callously.

A shower of angry Maori rattled against the window. Aporo rose, sweating slightly.

'I must go,' he said. 'You will excuse me. It is my wife who is coming to find me.' He moved to the door. 'I think maybe she is wanting me.'

'Take your poster,' Miss Arbuthnott called down the path, but her voice evoked only a fresh gush of acrimony. Aporo replied in a low, beaten mumble.

Smiling, she returned to her progress report.

Nineteen ❧ ❧

'YOU are ready to go?' said Ben.

'Yes. At six in the morning.'

'Manu is a rich island. There is much pearl-shell in the lagoon.'

'Manu people have much money,' said Temata. 'They go to New Zealand *first class* always. They have television sets.'

'There's no television in the Colony, Temata.'

'But still they have television sets. And many fine things in their houses. Not like *here*.'

'Aratoa is poor,' said Ben complacently. 'We are a Dying Race.'

They were both talking nonsense but it did not matter. Relieved of Toa and Daniel, soon to escape Aratoa, Leicester felt mellow, uncritical, pleasingly sad. In the light of departure all was charming, beautiful. Outside, the mountains were darkening, greens deepening to purple as the sky paled. Nearby, cheerful village sounds strangely emphasized the underlying sadness, haunting island melancholy. The horizon had retreated, the sea become flatter, solid, a wide bare plain. It glowed, luminous. Blue mists moved across the distance, scattered woodsmoke climbed the quiet air. Soothed by tranquillity, comforted by food, Leicester stood on the verandah, exhaling goodwill.

'Come for a walk?' said Temata.

Beyond the narrow beach bordering the lagoon they lingered on a low sand spit, watching the last of the sunset. Temata had been quiet all evening; no questions about Toa, Miss Arbuthnott; no reproaches about neglect. Gentle, beautiful in white, crowned with flowers, she had embalmed him in her soft dark gaze till now his will lay smothered, expiring in delight.

'I wish you do not go,' she said. 'I am so sad.' Moisture formed in the glowing eyes, oozed down the golden cheeks.

'Don't cry, Temata. I will soon be back.'

'I wish you do not go,' she sobbed. 'Maybe you don't come back. Maybe you find a Manu woman.'

'Oh no! How could you say so! I love you, Temata ... no one else.'

'You do not love me. You sent me away.'

'Only because ... Oh, don't you understand? Because I really love you ... want to marry you....'

Silence. Too late! What had he done? Had she understood? Would she perhaps reject...?

She would not. Tears arrested, she said quickly, 'Okay. I marry you.'

So that's how you got engaged. No speeches, embraces, bended knees. Simply a slip of the tongue, out before you realized. No excitement, on either side, for Temata remained unflatteringly calm; but her mind was well on the subject.

'We shall marry when you come back from Manu?'

Manu, forgotten reprieve! Slightly fortified, he said carefully, 'Not straightaway. First we shall be engaged. You would like to be engaged?'

'Oh yes. I shall have one ring to wear?'

Shamed at his little victory, he assured her. 'Of course. I shall get one from New Zealand. I'll ask my mother to order it.'

'You will send Toa away? Forever? You will tell her to go?'

'Toa is going. Going to Manu with Miss Arbuthnott.'

'So she goes with you on the ship?'

'With Miss Arbuthnott. I shall not see her. They go to Arumai, on the other side of the island.'

After a pause Temata resumed.

'I shall have a house?'

'Yes. You'll have my house. You will look after it for me.'

'How many servants shall I have?' At the prospect she

leant her head on his shoulder. He inhaled her flower-scented hair oil.

'As many as you need.' What did promises matter since this was all part of a dream?

'And we'll go to New Zealand?'

'If we wait till my leave to get married we could go there for a honeymoon.'

As on the night of Temata's visit his mind had split. One personality dealt—not too badly he thought—with the emergency; the other stood by, surprised, ashamed at this rather shabby cleverness.

She wriggled closer.

'I shall be able to buy new dresses there. And then we will live there. In Auckland.'

'Well...'

'You will go back to New Zealand? We shall live there one day?'

Her naïve anxiety fused the two halves in pity. The power of New Zealand suburbia to reduce the exotic to cheapness; bitter Wellington winds turning brown skin grey-blue; coconut ukeleles sounding thin, dismal in the substantial solidity of Mother's house; the eyes, tongues of Mother's friends... He forgot his own plight in compassion.

'It's so cold there, Temata. You'd hate it.'

'But I have been. I have been to Auckland ... to school ...'

'We'll see,' he said. 'After we're married. We'll see.'

She pushed his arm away.

'We go now and tell my family.'

This was no dream state. This was reality, here and now. Deprived of his clever self, the true Leicester fumbled.

'Not now. I must go home and finish packing.'

'But I must tell my family, my friends!' She was displeased.

He summoned his *alter ego* for a last service.

'As you like, Temata; but it's better not to tell people till your ring comes.'

'Why not?'

'Because when you have your ring you can show it ... that's the time to announce the engagement.'

She pondered.

'Maybe people do not believe me till they see my ring?'

'Yes. . . . They believe you more with the ring.'

'How long before my ring comes?'

'I'll go home now and write to my mother. She'll get it soon ... now we have ships again. You tell me what you would like.'

'Diamonds. Many diamonds. They are best.'

'All right, I'll get diamonds. I'll ask my mother to send you a catalogue with pictures. Then you can choose.'

She was pleased. 'Yes. And we shall have a lovely house in New Zealand. And I shall have many nice dresses and a telephone. Perhaps a car for myself.'

'Whatever you like,' he assured her.

One would have thought this the time to sit together, holding hands, kissing, gazing into the future; but Temata, grown restless, was not in the mood for white man's sentimentality. Leicester, fearing further commitment, let her go.

He walked home alone. So Temata was his! The beautiful princess. Best to concentrate on the pleasing aspects of victory, avoid the familiar word echoing in the far corridors of his mind: *Fool! Fool! Fool!*

'I'll think about it tomorrow.' Tonight, the letter to Mother; then he must put it from his mind till he returned from Manu.

But as he walked his trapped dismay subtly faded. In the dusk Aratoa seemed gentler, the villagers less Europeanized. Their voices, cheerful, inquisitive, friendly, from the shadowy trees were those of unspoilt islanders. Tonight, he and they were glad of each other. He as entertainment; they as background. No matter that they were discussing him, perhaps even laughing at him. He walked on, automatically turning over empty shells and coconut husks with his foot while they called their remarks to each other across the deepening green.

Now, in the darkness, white stars coruscated overhead, villagers became disembodied voices, invisible eyes; petals drifted down from trees and all the waxy island flowers gave out their wandering scents.

Twenty ✌ ✌

EXPIRE did not sail at six, as announced. It was nearly midday by the time loading was finished, passengers embarked, crew retrieved from reunions with friends and relations.

On board, Costa, Toa and Daniel surrendered at once to seasickness. Leicester drugged himself and went early to bed. Miss Arbuthnott sat up with the captain explaining the virtues of timely weaning for Melanesians.

Twelve hours later they anchored at the reef north of Manu, where the Experts were to land. Canoes, a whaleboat were out in welcome, to land cargo.

'It does not look to me like an atoll,' Beatrice Arbuthnott peered disbelievingly across the placid reef. 'I thought atolls were rings of land round lagoons. This is not a lagoon, it's an open sea.'

'Your *motu*, Arumai, over there,' the captain pointed ahead to a pudding-shaped islet. 'This, Mr Whiteway's.'

Leicester looked dejectedly at Manu's main island, a long dark smudge on the right. It gave little encouragement to a seeker of felt needs.

'I must say yours looks rather bleak. Ours at least is picturesque.' She went below to call Toa.

A still-green phosphorescent Costa, informed that the captain had a mistress and children in the village, would stay there all day. Beatrice, drafting her stupefied charges on deck, added she would be sorted out after lunch, if Leicester liked to come ashore then.

They went over the side with a good deal of flurry. The whaleboat, low in the water, flanked, followed by loaded canoes, lumbered through the reef passage to the distant *motu*.

Leicester, some hours later, found the beach piled with Holmes's familiar ammunition ... tinned milk, film cans, projectors, portable screens, tape recorders, batteries, boxes of books, cases of food. Beatrice and Costa, already in their houses, were adapting to their new setting. The former, sleeves rolled up, drove the still anti-hystemined Toa to action. In the shade, Daniel drew gluttonously on a bottle of reconstituted milk. Costa, supplied by local women with rainbow-cake and lemonade, reclined in a wooden chair under a breadfruit tree while villagers staggered up the sand with his luggage.

A silent crowd watched carefully as boxes and crates were moved. Struck by their uncharacteristic reserve, Leicester recalled the Chief's brave words:

'*A great community development project conducted by islanders for the benefit of islanders, under an island leader!*'

'What do the islanders think of it?' Leicester had asked.

'They welcome it. One would not embark on such a venture without the full and voluntary support of the natives. They await it eagerly.'

He sought now for signs of this eager awaiting. Had it not been absurd one might have said the people looked nervous.

A hovering old man in a faded *pareu* approached.

'Excuse me sir, you are from the government?'

'Yes. That is ... I am from Aratoa.'

'Excuse me, sir. Please can you tell me what is all these boxes? Is it Americans? People say it is Americans coming to make atom bombs like at Bikini. The people say we will all be blown ...' He stopped, his empty jaw quivering.

'Oh no ... nothing like that. No atom bombs. The things are for Arumai—for the people.'

'For us? The government sends these boxes for us?'

'There are things in them for . . .' for what, in God's name? . . . 'for work.'

Incredulous, the old man whispered, 'For work?'

'The government in Aratoa sends these things so the new people staying here . . . Mr Costa . . . Miss Arbuthnott . . . will be able to do their work with the people of Arumai.'

The old man had turned slightly grey. He pondered, whispered with bystanders; approached again.

'Sir,' he said humbly. 'What is it the government wishes to do to us?'

'*This*,' said Beatrice, 'is a perfect example of what Holmes calls enthusiastic voluntary co-operation and support of the natives! He will write it up thus in his report to P.I.D.L.'

'You can't blame the Chief for that old man. He's hardly typical . . . I think he's not all there.'

'Perhaps. But Holmes is still impossible. An odious little man. However, one just has to plug on, despite him. After all, it's the mothers and babies we must think of.'

Leicester looked round at the nephews and nieces, native babies, black breastfeeding mothers already installed, at the embroidered doyleys and cushions, feather-trimmed fans and shells full of flowers.

'You've made it just like home already. I'm going to miss you on Aratoa.'

'I too. You should get married, dear boy. You're lonely. You need a nice little wife to look after you.'

A wife! Oh God! If only he could confide . . . seek advice . . .

'I'm going to give you advice, not about marrying of course. . . . You should not let Holmes push you about. He's a bully. He gives in if one stands firm enough. No need to blush and protest. Your loyalty does you credit, but it's misplaced.'

'He works so hard. He's terribly keen.'

'Of course he is. He wants to be successful. And you know why! He wants a nice fat job with Unesco, for his old age. If

he can present a glowing account of his work here he might
have a chance of getting one. The eyes of every international
busybody in the world are focused on the Peaceful Islands
these days.'

'I don't think he . . .'

'Don't be so naïve, Leicester. Do you really believe he
came out of retirement just for the Peaceful Islanders? He
would like to end up in Paris, no doubt, at the Secretariat,
on a handsome salary. Flying to conferences and seminars,
giving Expert advice. When he goes to the next Session he
will read a report based on your work, and mine and others
like us, and he will take all the credit. And you will go back
to your Wellington job, or to school teaching. But there . . . I
should not embarrass you. But I feel you should not let him
push you about.'

Costa, though comfortably installed, supplied with
women, cake, *Parfait d'Amour*, was gloomy.

'The truth is I do not want to stay here with Miss Arbuthnott. The thought of weeks alone with only that Englishwoman is too bad. Too bad.'

'You will be very busy,' Leicester suggested, but Costa
said, 'It is too bad for me, for my morale. Everyone else likes
me. Only she is hostile.'

'She's not really hostile. She's very kind.'

'She has always made it clear she despises me. And this I
find hard—from her, who has no right to despise me.'

'You will make other friends on the island.'

'That is not the point. Why should this woman consider
herself too good for me, when she is, after all no better than
a whore!'

'Costa! You're mad!'

'I am not mad. I have heard the gossip. I have heard how
she chases you, for instance.'

'You don't expect me to believe you take that seriously?
The Maoris say that sort of thing about everyone. You know
it's not true.'

'Perhaps. Per*haps*. But there are others of which I do not

142

know it's untrue. All right then, laugh. It is all over Aratoa that she was caught, red-handed, with Aporo.'

'Aporo!'

'Yes. Aporo. And by his wife. Caught, mark you. Red-handed. In her cottage. The night before we sailed. All Aratoa is talking of it. Even the *Expire*'s captain knew it.'

'Who told you?'

'Offenbach told me. Ben told him. Aporo's wife is mad with jealousy. She has caught Aporo at that woman's cottage. The girls at the hotel . . . everyone knows it already.'

'It's absurd. It's typical Maori gossip.'

'You may think so. But it's true. Everyone's laughing now at Aporo. His wife will make his life hell. If this woman had not left Aratoa, very likely there would be a tragedy by now.'

'You know it's ridiculous.'

'I know this woman has no husband; lives always with blacks. And this is the one I must be penned up with; a whore who makes plain she despises me!'

As they walked to the beach in the dusk Leicester tried reassurance, pointing out it would not be for long.

Costa said dramatically, 'I have a feeling of impending tragedy. It's the vibrations. I'm like that. I *feel* things. My mother too. Goodbye,' he embraced Leicester as the canoe slid in to the shore. 'You at any rate have always been good to me.'

Twenty-one

AT dawn *Expire* entered the reef passage to anchor in Manu lagoon.

A reception committee was on board immediately. Leicester looked sleepily at the expectant figures.

'I am David, Native Magistrate of Manu. Welcome to our island.'

'Welcome,' murmured the committee. '*Kia orana.*'

Leicester bowed. Everyone bowed.

'*Expire* will come no closer in, Mr Whiteway. I have brought the whaleboat. You are ready to come ashore?'

Ready or not, they intended to take him. Nor was their hospitality to be brushed aside. As they smoothly traversed the lagoon David listed attractions offering.

'While you are on Manu, Mr Whiteway, you will sleep in our house. My wife and I will be honoured. We have prepared for you.'

'Thank you, David.'

'Mr Whiteway, at our house you would like a drink to refresh you?'

'Thank you.'

'You would like whiskey? Beer? Rum? Oh yes, we have plenty, Mr Whiteway. You may choose what you like.'

'I should like tea, thank you, David. It's too early for alcohol.'

'Oh, not on Manu, Mr Whiteway. We drink alcohol any time on Manu.'

They did, did they? What would Holmes think of that? And what would he say when he heard of the whiskey crates coming ashore in the whaleboat; the beach strewn with nightsoil, the bottles, cans, coconut husks full of water?

'Does the District Officer come here often?'

'Oh no. I look after Manu. I am in charge. Manu is very rich. Now, here is my house. This is my wife and family.'

The shy pretty girl with the care-worn face dropped her head meekly, withdrew with her cluster of children. Proudly David led the way into a jungle of orange *moquette*, pea-green verandah chairs, geometric linoleum. A household of substance.

'Be seated, Mr Whiteway. My wife brings the tea. You like my house?'

'It is very fine.'

'It cost much money. A real European house. It cost much, bringing the timber, the iron. No one else has such a house on Manu.'

144

David expanded, helping himself from a garish cocktail cabinet.

'Now Mr Whiteway, what can I do for you? What is your wish?'

Leicester thankfully set aside the stratified horror of rainbow cake, the weak oleaginous tea, with its queer brackish flavour of atoll water. There were people he wanted to see. The schoolmaster; the Assistant Medical Practitioner. He would like to meet Father Pieter, the Dutch priest....

'Ah. That is easy. No hurry. I bring them here to you. We have a few drinks ... you discuss your business pleasantly ... Father Pieter—' a shrug—'you do not need to see him. What is it you wish to ask these people?'

Leicester said reprovingly that he preferred separate interviews; that he needed to establish what materials should be sent from Aratoa ... if those already sent had been useful....

'Materials?'

'Posters. Films. A projector....'

'Ah yes. That is right. I remember. Well, the people do not like the films you are sending, Mr Whiteway. They prefer cowboy pictures, you know. What you call westerns.'

'But the films were not sent for entertainment! They were for teaching how to make pit latrines; improve coconuts...'

'They were rather boring, you know, Mr Whiteway. After the first time the people would not come to see them. Next time, you send us some westerns, eh? Besides, we cannot make pit latrines here—we cannot dig into the coral; and no one bothers about coconuts. We have the lagoon. Why should we make copra when we can earn much money diving for pearlshell?'

'You will not always have the lagoon. One day it will be closed; you will have no pearlshell, no diving, no money. Then you will be sorry you do not make copra.'

David said, 'Maybe.' Polynesian courtesy became tinged with arrogance as whiskey consumption increased.

'Thank you for the tea,' Leicester said. 'I should like now

to see Tata, your A.M.P. if you'll tell me where to find him.'

'Tata? He will come here. I will send. Tonight. After dinner, maybe.'

Leicester rose. 'I would rather go to him, thank you.'

The shutter descending on David's face suggested Temata in one of her moods.

'Okay. He is at the dispensary. My son Nga'a will show you. It is not far.'

For all its pearlshell, Manu was a slum; dirty, strewn with dead coconut leaves, empty whiskey crates; the makeshift houses without gardens or flowers. The slovenly women peering from doorways had ulcerous, filarial legs, the grimy children ringworm and sores. Even nature reflected the atmosphere of indifference. Withered coconuts leaned in exhaustion over a beach made uglier by low tide; morose frigate birds drooped on ragged perches, flies gluttoned on putrid garbage. Outside the village a ruined church gaped. Among the coral rubble a small figure in white scrambled nimbly in silent rage.

'Is that Father Pieter?'

Nga'a nodded, jerking his head to urge Leicester along.

In a grove of bedraggled trees a wooden hut flung back heat from its tin roof.

'Tata,' said Nga'a. He smiled and scuttled off.

'Welcome, Mr Whiteway,' said Tata, Assistant Medical Practitioner for Manu. 'We are honoured to have you.' He waved lethargically to a hard chair and sank back into his dream.

His torpor was infectious. In the heat of the dispensary Leicester's eyelids drooped. It would be pleasant to let this sleeping dog lie; but conscientiously forcing a note of enthusiasm he went through his list of enticements ... films, filmstrips, flannelgraphs, posters, booklets in the vernacular ... ?

Tata shook his head. He said, 'Nothing.'

'No illnesses?' Leicester persuaded. 'No pests? No bad habits that could be corrected by education?'

'Nothing.'

Nothing? But he couldn't want nothing! What about his felt needs? What about the sights just seen in the village? And what would the Chief have to say if Leicester returned empty-handed from such a rich field? He pondered; then said experimentally, 'You are lucky. The A.M.P.s on the other islands send to us for help all the time. But of course they have problems ... TB, leprosy, filariasis, dysentery.... Your life must be very easy. Much easier than poor Elias on Pinoi. He works terribly hard.'

The somnolent Tata stirred. He looked slightly put out.

'I also work very hard. I am very busy. I never take holiday!'

'But it's very bad on Pinoi. Very bad. In Aratoa we feel sorry for Elias. He is a very good A.M.P.'

'It is very bad here!' said Tata indignantly. 'I work harder than Elias. The babies die. They are always dying. The mothers do not feed them properly. They get dysentery.'

'But not so bad as on Pinoi. There they have terrible dysentery. So many flies spreading disease; but Elias works hard teaching the people not to leave rubbish about.'

'Our flies are very bad indeed! Much worse than Pinoi. They also come from rubbish and from *latrines as well!*'

Leicester showed little interest, absorbed in Pinoi's troubles.

'On Pinoi the people won't use the latrines. They use the beach.'

'They use the beach here, all the time!'

'...and Elias has to fight TB and leprosy. That is something you don't have to worry about. We send so many materials to Elias...'

'We have leprosy too!' Tata was triumphant. 'The other day I found a woman who has the face of a lion. That is a sign of leprosy. And we also have much TB and our filariasis is *worse* than Pinoi's...'

'The Pinoi teeth,' began Leicester, 'are all decayed...' but Tata interrupted, saying snappishly that teeth on Manu were terrible, that it was unfair everything went to Pinoi which was only a little island where they had no money, no pearlshell, only copra. Manu was much bigger and richer and why...?

Leicester was relentless.

'Because Pinoi *needs* them, *asks* for them, *uses* them. Besides you have had posters and films ... we have sent you many things....'

Tata shrugged. His energy was exhausted. He was sliding down into his chair again.

'David keeps the films. They are no good. People don't want to pay to see films like that. They like cowboys ... *War over Korea*....'

'Pay? Who pays?'

'The people. To see the picture-show David is giving. Three shillings, we pay. And the films are no good. The people are disappointed. They are not pleased.'

'How often does David have a cinema?'

'When films come. But people don't go any more.'

'And the posters?'

'Posters?'

'Five posters, in Peaceful Islands Maori.'

'Oh yes. The posters. Long ago.'

'Not long ago. Two months ago. Where are they? Didn't you use them?'

'Oh no. We did not use them. They are quite safe. I put them away myself. I cannot quite remember where but I know they're quite safe.'

Leicester said rather sharply, 'But they were *meant* to be used ... that's what they're for. To be pinned up where people can see them. Why didn't you put them up—here, in the dispensary? In the post office? The school? In the villages?'

Tata searched his memory. It was all so long ago. He said hopefully, 'There were no tacks. At the time we had no small

148

nails. We could not put up the posters because we could not find the tacks. So I put them away. I cannot say where; but I know they are safe.'

David next morning denied the film shows, claiming Tata a liar, a half-wit, a drunkard.

'He is drunk all the time. Why you think he's so stupid? He has a hangover. All this week he is drunk.'

The Native Magistrate did not look very well himself. The Manu notables, called in after dinner to greet Mr Whiteway, had made a night of it. After Leicester retired, drunken shouts and laughter kept him awake, men staggered past his verandah bed to vomit on the steps. Bodies fell, glasses shattered, furniture scraped the floor. Waking fitfully, he heard distant shouts, the crash of a building and wondered if all Manu were celebrating. The party continued till dawn, when the guests collapsed in sleep. Leicester woke unfreshed. Sodden bodies strewing the way to the bath-house disgusted and angered; a warm brackish shower increased discomfort. He thought, with approval, of the Articles in *Life* Magazine.

It was not a favourable time to reprimand David. He was relieved when the Native Magistrate's wife led in a tall melancholy young man with a folded black umbrella.

'You are Mr Whiteway?' said the newcomer earnestly. 'Ah! Thank God! I am Joseph, Headmaster of the school. I wish to talk to you, sir. I wish to show you my schoolhouse. It is a scandal! I have written to Mr Holmes ...'

'I remember.' Leicester felt better. Joseph was clearly brimming with needs.

'Mr Whiteway, there is no time to lose. It is important to do something. You must tell them in Aratoa ... The lavs ...'

'The ... ?'

'The lavs. The W.C.s. It is a scandal. My school is also a scandal. You will come now and see it?'

Leicester gestured at his half-eaten breakfast ... slimy

149

fried egg, cake, tinned grapefruit; but one had to eat something.

'I will wait.' Joseph sat solemnly, hands on the crook of umbrella, meditating on his wrongs.

'You will tell them in Aratoa, that I must have a new school,' he began as they walked to the village. 'For years I have waited and waited and now at last . . .'

Leicester stopped, bewildered.

'Where's the church?'

'Church? Oh . . . it's gone. And, Mr Whiteway, have you seen the beach? It is disgraceful! The people will not use . . .'

'*Gone?* How do you mean Gone? Gone where?'

'Last night they pulled it down, Mr Whiteway.'

'Pulled it *down?*' Did Manu revels extend to this?

'Oh yes. For Father Pieter. He wants a new church. He is trying to pull down the old one by himself, so the people help him; but see . . . There!' he stopped. 'See, Mr Whiteway! *That's* what I want for my school!'

On the end of a catwalk a large sentry-box poised above the lagoon.

'What a splendid latrine!' Joseph said lovingly. 'It has room for four people. Clean; comfortable; convenient. But the lav at my school . . . it is appalling. It has no roof. It is falling down, Mr Whiteway! *Collapsing!*'

'Can't it be mended?'

Joseph barked bitterly.

'No money. We have no money. You will tell them in Aratoa that we have *no money!*'

'But this is a very rich island. The people have plenty of money.'

'They do not give to the school, Mr Whiteway. They give nothing. They spend on drinking; on bicycles; sewing machines. They go for trips round the Group . . . to New Zealand . . . Tahiti . . . always first class. They do not care about the school. Here it is. You see? It is small and hot and old-fashioned. The children are waiting to welcome you.'

When the children had groaned their dirge about Ancestor Ru, danced with grass skirts over cotton dresses, sung popular songs with local words, clapped courteously at his expected oration, opened mouths to show rotted teeth, pulled up sleeves to show sores, presented heads to show lice, Leicester and Joseph got down to business. Results were confused. Joseph's sights were focused on solid constructions, not visual aids.

'Posters? Can you use posters?'

'Yes, Mr Whiteway. Now, the school buildings. We must have ...'

'What on? What subjects do you need most?'

'Well, Mr Whiteway, the lavs ...'

'I mean posters, not buildings. I'll pass on your requests, Joseph, but I'm not in charge of buildings, you know. It's not my department ... that's Public Works. Now, what posters?'

'Posters!' Joseph pondered. He said finally, 'We must have posters to say DON'T USE CRABHOLES. You see, Mr Whiteway, the people will not use the lagoon lavs at night. It is too far away. They are frightened in the dark because of the ghosts. So they use the crabholes near the houses. This is very bad for health, Mr Whiteway. It brings flies. If you will tell them in Aratoa to send money and timber we could build the new lavs ourselves, near the village.... And you have written down about my schoolhouse? What you have seen? You will tell them I must have a new building? Oh thank God, you have come, Mr Whiteway. Thank God you have come!'

Father Pieter lived in a wooden box by the lagoon. Scraggy coconuts, pebble garden gave an impression of heat and sterility. There was no sign of life.

'He is perhaps sleeping,' said Joseph nervously. 'He does not like to be disturbed. He will be angry.'

The box rumbled. Stockinged feet thudded. The door opened suddenly upon a bearded kewpie glowering in

151

crumpled white gown. Above pink celluloid cheeks, white hair rose in a disordered question mark.

'So! Who is dis?'

Joseph turned to Leicester, bowed, backed away.

'Father Pieter. I'm from Aratoa. Leicester Whiteway. May we come in?'

It was no longer plural. Joseph was fast retreating.

'I hope I'm not disturbing you....'

'I vos slipping!' the little priest said indignantly. 'Kom in.'

The hut was full of sleep, stale breathed-out air, imprisoned heat, sweat, smell of feet.

'Sit.'

Leicester obeyed.

'I vos slipping. I am tired. All night I vurk; dis morning, vurking. Lifting stones. Dis my rest time.'

'I am sorry ... but I wanted to talk .... to ask ... Father Pieter, I wondered if there was some way we could help you?'

'Ve? Who is ve?'

'Mr Holmes ... Native Development Department in Aratoa. We...'

'Ah! So! You are from dis people in Aratoa!'

'And I wondered, if we could help you—in some way—in your work...?'

'You vant to help? In vot vay you vill help?'

'Well ... I thought ... filmstrips perhaps. Posters. Flannel-graphs...'

'Vot is dis? Flannelgrifs?'

'Well ... flannelgraphs ... they're very simple ... easy to use. No need for elaborate equipment. It's really quite an old medium but it's being used a lot in Fundamental Education now, specially in more isolated areas. Unesco has found...'

Father Pieter smote his knee.

'Flannel! Posters! Vot I vant dis for? Dis is toys! I vant something useful!'

'Oh, but these simple media *are* useful, Father Pieter. They're instructional—for adults as well as children. Some quite remarkable work has been done with them in Iran, for instance ... *bilhazaria* ...'

'You say you vant to help? Send money! Vurkmen to build my church! Send agriculture men to show how to plant coconuts. Send doctors ... nurses to make injections for leprosy ... TB ... yaws. Dat's vot ve vant here! Not filmstrips! Not flannel!'

'Oh, there will be Experts coming,' Leicester assured. 'But at the same time we must educate. For the future. People must understand, if the Experts' work is to do lasting good.'

'Experts! Tell me, Mr Vitevay. How long you been in the islands?'

'Nearly six months.'

'And before ... You are living in the Pacific?'

'In New Zealand.'

'Ah. You vurked vif de Maoris.'

'Well no, not exactly. Actually, I was in the Education Office at Department of Island Territories. In—Wellington.'

'So! So you kom now to give me advice!'

'Oh no ... not at all. I came, out of admiration for your work. And of course to see if we could help....'

'De government does not help. It does nodding. Never nodding. All, I do myself. By myself; vith dese hands alone. I *vurk*. Not sit in office writing reports. I vurk like a labourer. In Holland I am a peasant. I alvays vurk. Send here some labourers, doctors, farmers ... not people for talking!'

'They will, they will come,' Leicester repeated valiantly. 'A Community Development Team is being trained ...'

'Community Development! Vot is dat? More *Experts*?'

'Yes, well ... but natives ... trained ...'

'Natives! Cha! Vot dey know? Nodding. Ve vant doctors ... nurses ... labourers.'

His obsessions were no less violent than Joseph's. 'You people ... *vasting* time. Vasting time. Train natives! Vot you know about de natives? Thirty years I am in dese islands ... not yet I understand der natives. But more I understand dan Experts ... me, a peasant, from the Nederlands. Dese natives I can make vurk ... only I. Lazy, idle ... but *I* make them vurk. Last night they pull my church for me ...'

'Oh yes ... I heard ... I saw ... I wondered ...'

'You saw! I tell you. All dese months I vant my church down. Vant a new church. No one ... no one help me ... people ... government ... no one. No one give me money. So. I do not ask. I do not teach or show de flannelgrifs. I vurk. I *vurk*! Alone ... mine two hands. I pull de church ... Stones I move. Each day, I go; I pull; I move.

'Der natives are lazy but dey are proud. Dey feel ashamed. Dey see me ... I am old ... I am not big. Last night dey come and pull de church for me. And why? Because I make them ashamed. Now you will tell your Experts vot I tell you, if you please, and kom not more on Manu with de filmstrips. Doctors, nurses, farmers send ... vurkmen, labourers, money send. Not flannel. Not de toys for children!'

Twenty-two ᪉ ᪉

'BUT it's your job to *make* them want help!' said Holmes. 'That's what you're here for.'

'I did my best. Joseph said he'd try posters. Tata ...'

'You can't stop there! Establishment of felt needs is just the beginning. You must go on from there to build up a climate of acceptance.'

'Tata accepts; but he doesn't use ...'

'He must be made to; but from *within*. Interest imposed by us, by outside agencies is useless. The need, the interest must come from within.'

Leicester thought of Tata's face and was not encouraged. The Chief's irritation was not unreasonable. There is nothing more maddening than a subordinate newcomer back from an area one has not seen oneself. Whiteway, no doubt unconsciously, had assumed an air of possessiveness about Manu; had even suggested he, Holmes, should press the Resident to amend legislation for controlling the island's drinking.

'Father Pieter just flatly rejected my offer, but he said ...'

'You had no business wasing time on that ignorant, fanatical, reactionary peasant. You were sent to interview those in government service!'

'But sir, he does work for the people. And he understands them. He gets them to do what he wants.'

'Are you suggesting we could learn from him, perhaps? Should model our techniques on him?'

'Of course not, sir. I only thought ...'

Withdrawal, apology scarcely appeased. The Chief, fiery-coloured, announced Manu must wait for the Community Development team. Meanwhile he must admit he was rather surprised and disappointed at Leicester's poor harvest. A lot of time wasted in talking ... a few posters ...

'But Chief, they do want things ... I mean real things....'

'*Real* things?'

Leicester's own words had stopped him. What a slip! What a *thought*! He mumbled abjectly, 'Schoolhouse ... latrines...'

'That is not our department. That is Public Works. Health. I think you're well aware that we have our hands full with our own work without taking on that of other departments?'

'It was just that I thought ... you see, sir, even Father Pieter could be won round if we could get what he needs from Government...'

'Won round? And why should we win him round?'

'Well, sir, I thought...'

'I think, Whiteway, you will perhaps—I may be wrong—agree that I know best who is to be "won round" as you put it? That I know best what is needed for Manu? That I am, after all, in charge of this project?'

Aratoa life had moved on during Leicester's absence.

Toa had been replaced by a childless, edentulous whale who cooked and stole with competence. The Baha'is, who had made a convert, were now in Miss Arbuthnott's leaf house with a harmonium. Phyllis and Thelma were having a coolness.

Miss Davidson and Mrs Hitchcock had surprisingly been united by the scandalous stories sweeping the island about Miss Arbuthnott. Though believing that all men are brothers and the colour of one's skin makes no difference, there were, after all, limits. Nutkin had, for the moment, ceased attacking the Guides, who continued to fornicate in their trefoils. The Aratoans still, after cricket and basketball, went to the hills to make bush beer on which they got drunk.

Harkness, the linguist, back from the mountains, had offended Mr Hitchcock, criticizing the Mission Press, which he claimed used apostrophes to denote glottal stops. The Women's Interests team had been recalled from Pinoi, and all three months pregnant, were now up in the mountains trying, unsuccessfully, to persuade local women to organize themselves into clubs. *Marinda* had called, bringing several strange men who sat about heavily on the hotel verandah.

'Who are they?' Leicester asked.

'Boy,' said Ern Crump. 'They're the tuna people. Offenbach sent for them.'

'What are they going to do?'

'Build a tower; for spotting tuna. On the other side of the island. There's going to be a cannery there too ... big project ahead ... catching and canning right on the spot. There's a Nip here too ... haven't you seen him?'

'A Japanese?'

"Sright. Honourable canning expert. He's over the other
156

side of the island. Making notes ... taking pictures to send home about landing sites for when the Yellow Peril comes.'

'But is there tuna there?'

'Offenbach reckons there is. The natives say the Nips have been poaching round here for months. That's always a sign. Mind you, this bird's polite enough, hissing and bowing, but frankly I think H.H.'s gone round the bend letting coloured types into the Group. I mean, I know it doesn't do to keep up old feelings but when I think what those yellow bastards done to our boys I could castrate this Sukiyaki, that's for sure. Good thing he keeps out of the way. No one ever sees him. He doesn't come into town.'

Nor did Offenbach appear. He had left the hotel, set up camp on the other side of the island. For all its newcomers, Leicester felt Aratoa deserted.

There was, of course, Temata.

Anticipating a crisis, he found anticlimax as well as relief. The engagement had not been publicised. Temata did not renew suggestions of announcement, prepared, apparently, to await the ring. Pleasant but evasive, she was disturbing and baffling. Though she came for walks in the twilight, Leicester never knew when he would find her at home. If he went to pick her up after work she was annoyed. There was always some story about sick relations, family crises. She would disappear inexplicably, evading questions. The little brothers and sisters stared, giggled, ran when he asked where she was; and Ben always said, 'She'll be back soon. Just gone to my sister;' or 'To the cinema;' or 'Visiting friends in the mountains.'

Even Ben seemed different. His old attitude of cheerful but subtly respectful comradeship was now informed with complacence, even a trace of patronage. He talked a great deal of his 'work' with Offenbach, in the tones of a serious scientist, spent much time at the fisheries camp. Bewildered, uneasy, Leicester sniffed faintly a curious scent of betrayal, even treachery.

'Temata ... Do you love me?'

'Oh yes, of course.' But she wriggled away. 'Not here on the beach, Leicester. People are laughing at us.'

'I never see you now. We never have a minute together.'

She shrugged. 'My mother's sister very sick. I am all the time at her house. She has many children. I must look after them.'

Many children.

'How ... how are your little brothers and sisters?'

'They are well.'

'We must have a talk; about ...'

'Yes?'

'About things,' he said cravenly.

She looked moody.

'You lecture me, Leicester?'

'Oh no. No, not at all. Of course not. Of course not.'

There was no point in going on with it. He knew he would never get satisfaction. Better leave it alone; try to forget uneasiness in work.

Twenty-three ₪ ₪

WINTER was now well established. The trade wind blew steadily, the sun shone through crystal air. The noisy red trees had long been green; the frangipani were dropping their blossoms, but *tiare Maori*, Queen of the Night scented the island. After sunset people were known to wear cardigans. It was said that blankets were used at night.

Everybody felt better. Cooler weather renewed energy for tennis, golf, social life, warfare. Feuds and vendettas took on fresh life, gossip surpassed itself as imagination revived from summer lassitude.

Holmes was edgy. He complained that Costa and Miss

Arbuthnott did not keep in touch enough, that he didn't know what they were up to, there was no excuse now that shipping was normal again. There had been little news from Manu, apart from an occasional radio demanding filmstrips, projectors or tinned milk; no progress reports, no information, though the Experts had been there over two months.

The Chief suffered other annoyances. Every mail brought sheaves of pamphlets from rival organizations: booklets on infant feeding from the South Pacific Health Service in Suva; South Pacific Commission technical papers on *Coral as a Building Material; Treatment against decay and fire of grasses and Palmyra leaves used for thatching roofs*. The first Holmes interpreted as an oblique attack on Miss Arbuthnott's appointment, the second on his use of timber and iron in the housing project. On the whole, he objected less to the South Pacific Commission than the others, their philosophy being action through inaction. More disturbing was W.H.O., who were offering to send a team to Pinoi and Hinoa to inject for yaws.

'Damned impertinence! That's P.I.D.L. territory!'

'But we haven't got the facilities,' Leicester reminded. 'Dr Vincent says it would be a godsend.'

'He would. Anything to save himself trouble.'

Dr Vincent had been jovially vulgar.

'Injecting for yaws? Jolly good. The more backsides they can inject the merrier.'

'But it's our territory!'

'Ah well. We must just turn the other cheek!' Vincent had wept with delight at his own wit.

Leicester had not noticed the passage of time, absorbed in work, baffled by Temata's continuing patience. The catalogue from a Wellington jeweller had been gravely studied, the sparkling circle picked out and ordered. Now he had best put it out of his mind, enjoy his uneasy reprieve.

There were other disturbing thoughts; the haunting

image of Joseph's mournful face, the memory of his implicit trust. Was he waiting, still hopeful, on Manu for news of his schoolhouse, his lagoon privies? Leicester had not the heart to tell him, had postponed writing, hoping perhaps ... What? Hoping what? Why not face the truth and admit Holmes would never help Joseph, beyond his own departmental province.

This was a shocking thought; but there were worse. These days Leicester found himself fearfully facing, guiltily dismissing all sorts of treason stirred by Father Pieter's honest rage, by the Chief's attitude to the priest. Why must one see both sides? Why could one not be a bigot, a proper bastard? He could see the Chief's point, but after all that old man was also working for the natives. He dug and planted, and weeded, tended the sick, tried to help the weak. He had given his life to the Peaceful Islanders; they were his children, not an impersonal project. Difficult, even unpleasant, but undeniably sincere. Could it be—shameful thought— rivalry? Competition? Surely not; surely not! The Chief too was dedicated, in his own fashion. *In his own fashion!* Leicester blushed.

Holmes himself seemed set to destroy his own image in his assistant's mind. Announcing he would go alone to the Work Committee meeting next month at Ha'i Koma, he had rejected all protests and pleas on grounds of economy. False! Completely false! Leicester knew there was plenty of money; his fare was provided for in the estimates. It was his place, his right to go. What was behind it? Had rumours about Temata, even Beatrice been used against him; reported to Ha'i Koma? He began to suspect plots, feel himself victimized; thought enviously of Costa and Beatrice on Arumai, of their peaceful atoll existence, their cut-and-dried undemanding work. He could never sit back, never afford to relax. The Aratoans were so slow with felt needs. It was no good waiting for them to come forward and ask; you must constantly think up new ways of giving them what they did not know they wanted.

Aporo, grafting an earnest expression upon his habitual complacency, had begun to put on airs. Leicester suspected he enjoyed, was perhaps helping foster the rumour about himself and Beatrice. In the office he was painfully smug.

'There is trouble,' he announced, 'with the Use More Soap poster we tried out in Baru village.'

'What sort of trouble? How could there be trouble with soap?'

'Well, you remember you asked what I thought about it, and I told you...'

'I remember.'

'I told you, Leicester, what would happen. You showed a fat baby and a sick baby covered with sores. The poster said SOAP MAKES THE DIFFERENCE. I warned you...'

'Well, what's the matter?'

'I *told* you the mothers would think it meant they must give their babies soap to eat. Now, you see, they're complaining it makes them sick—they do not like the taste. The babies are vomiting bubbles. They scream. They get diarrhoea. The mothers say white bread and taro are better and cheaper...'

'Well, get them in and change them!' Leicester felt he sounded like Holmes.

'I have,' said Aporo. He added, also with a good imitation of Holmes, 'You have to remember the literalness of the native mind, Leicester.'

With unusual spite Leicester sent him to the mountains with a kerosene filmstrip projector that had already blown up several villagers.

Struggling with his Progress Report, Leicester had put down his pen to check through a sentence when sleep overcame him.

His words began to swim: 'After interval we showed some strips on New Guinea... historical curiosities... tree-dwellings, people with penis-sheaths and nose perforations. The

161

village audience were rather restless, even a little bored and irritated. There were the usual Polynesian disparaging comments about blacks...'

'Whiteway!'

Holmes, trembling, stood in the door. Leicester jumped guiltily, wide awake.

'Sir! Are you all right?'

The little man seemed unable to move.

'Chief! What is it? What's happened? Are you ill?'

'Look at this!' The telegram quivered. 'Read it!'

This was fury, not grief.

'Please accept notice of resignation effective immediately stop Grateful earliest outward passage MARINDA stop Discuss suggested substitute arrival Aratoa Wednesday Arbuthnott.'

'Resignation!'

'The woman's mad! Mad! Four months ... barely four months since she came and now she proposes to leave! Leave us high and dry, just as the programme is getting under way.'

'She must be ill.'

'Ill! Women like that are never ill. Strong as oxen. No ... it's something else. *There's something behind it,* mark my words!'

'There couldn't be. She must be ill; or trouble at home. Family sickness ... a death perhaps....'

His bewilderment inflamed the Chief.

'She has no family! No home! Don't try to find excuses. It's treachery; and I know what's behind it. I can guess what it means!'

'Behind it?'

'It's the French at the back of it. You mark my words! The *French!*'

'The French?'

'The French. C.R.A.P. They want her back. They've probably offered her higher pay.'

'But why should they want her back? She finished her work for them.'

'Hah! They'd give a lot to know what goes on in our territories. They're aware how much could be learnt from our techniques and methods. What have they ever done? A few metal bands round the trees in Tahiti to keep rats from the coconuts....'

'Sir, that's not fair. They...'

'Don't defend them to *me*! To wreck a great multiple project in development such as we're implementing here ... to find out our ideas ... future action ... would be quite an achievement.'

'But sir ... there's no secrecy in our work. It's discussed at the Sessions!'

'The *inside* workings are never discussed at the Sessions. Only at Work Committees, which C.R.A.P. does not attend.'

'But sir, it's not like nuclear tests...'

It was no time for reason. Holmes was prepared to bite any hand indicating it.

'Do you think C.R.A.P. really want us to make a success of this project? When my report is read at the Session do you really think they'll be overjoyed at our success? You watch. ... This defection is only the first. Watch Constantopoulos! Watch Offenbach! Just see if I'm not right. Just wait and see if we don't hear of others resigning.'

Leicester searched his conscience for his own defection.

'She'll have to give an account of herself,' Holmes was quieter but more menacing. 'Send a radio saying *Resignation rejected.*'

On Wednesday, as stated, Miss Arbuthnott arrived, packed and ready to sail. Meeting *Expire*, Leicester was struck by her changed appearance; but though pale and rather drawn she was cheerful, showing neither guilt nor remorse. Holmes was not mentioned.

'I'll be at the hotel till *Marinda* comes in. It's not worth setting up house.'

F*

'And Toa?'

'Excellent. Has put on weight ... cheered up no end. Daniel's flourishing. Toa's been helping me weigh the babies at the Clinic. No thanks, I won't. I've given it up.'

'But you were a chain smoker.'

'Yes I was. But I've gone off them somehow. Well ... let's have it! What about Holmes?'

'If you'd come to the office.... When you're ready.'

'Crawss?'

'He's not very happy.'

'No, I don't suppose he is. Oh well. Let's get it over.'

The interview, which was long, ended in a draw.

'Greek meets Greek,' Miss Arbuthnott said when Leicester called at the hotel. 'He tried to threaten me.'

'What's happening?'

'Neither side will give way an inch. When he said he'd report me to H.H. for insubordination I pointed out I was no longer under his authority. Then he said I should be refused my passage home. This, of course, is promised in my contract.'

'What did you say?'

'I remained calm. I suggested we go together to see the Resident; to put our cases before him. We're to go in the morning.'

She had also given up drinking, but was generous to her guest.

'Have another,' she repeated each time Leicester rose to go 'Stay and have dinner.'

Could it be that she did not want to be alone? He left late, slightly drunk and drove to Ben's.

Temata was not at home. No one knew where she was.

'Cinema,' Ben suggested obligingly. There was no cinema that night. Leicester fancied they looked at him mockingly. Confused, frustrated, he went home and fell asleep in his clothes.

Miss Arbuthnott, pale, puffy, composed, with the air of one with right on her side, said sternly, 'I haven't seen Holmes yet. He left a message with Aporo to say he'd soon be back. I've been waiting three-quarters of an hour; but if he is hoping I will tire and give up he will be disappointed.'

Half an hour later, still calm, with greater firmness she said reasonably, 'I shan't wait any longer. I shall go ahead and see Davidson by myself.'

Flushed, rather breathless, Holmes entered suddenly.

'I had given you up!' Miss Arbuthnott was crisp. 'I am on my way to headquarters without you.'

The chief paused, breathed hard, gestured to his office.

'A moment, Miss Arbuthnott. Just come in here for a moment, if you would.'

Standing firm, she regarded him coolly. 'We have an appointment. We are already very late.'

His colour deepened.

'I should like a word with you first.'

She considered, shrugged, entered. The door closed.

A murmur from Holmes; a short sharp bark from Miss Arbuthnott. The door opened violently.

'Outrageous! I have never encountered such despicable behaviour. Anywhere! Ever! In my life!'

She charged through the outer office and disappeared towards headquarters.

Holmes's glimpsed face suggested a seizure. Aporo bulged with curiosity. Uneasily Leicester tried to concentrate on his report. A few minutes later the Chief strode through the outer office and drove away.

Beatrice did not return, nor come to lunch at the hotel. She was not in her room; but during the afternoon Leicester received a note:

'I am going to fight this out to the end if it means taking them to Court. While I waited for him this morning *in all good faith* he went to Davidson and presented his version of the case and persuaded H.H. to refuse my passage home.'

Aporo, in and out every half-hour, brought changing

rumours. Miss Arbuthnott was with Dr Vincent; Holmes was with H.H.; Miss Arbuthnott was with H.H.; Mr Holmes was with Dr Vincent; Dr Vincent was with H.H.

At four-thirty Leicester crossed to the hotel for tea. The roar of voices suggested revolution rather than cocktail party.

'She's going to sue them for breach of contract!' 'She claimed she was eligible on health grounds!' 'It's in her bloody contract. Repatriation in case of illness.' 'Vincent's only too pleased to give a certificate. He'll do anything to have a jab at Holmes and H.H.'

Leicester grasped the Radio Officer's arm.

'What is it? What's happened? Who?'

'Miss Arbuthnott, of course.' George was delirious with joy. 'She's raised quite a stink.'

'Good on her!' said Ern Crump. 'That bastard Holmes has bloody well asked for it.'

'He went behind her back....'

'Yes yes, I know that. But what happened then?'

'She went to Vincent and got a certificate. He said in view of her age ... or kidneys or something ... that she must go at once to where she could get specialist treatment.'

'So she's really sick after all?'

'Sick!' said Ern Crump. 'Sick ... if you could call it sick.' And at Leicester's blank expression, 'Don't you know?'

'Know what?'

'Jesus, he doesn't know! She's pregnant.'

'Pregnant as blazes. That's why she's quitting.' George sloshed his tea with excitement. 'What do you think of that!'

'I don't believe it.'

'That's what Phyl said. But it's true.'

'It can't be!'

'It is. She's not making any mystery about it.'

'It's an act. An act, to get a certificate. To get back at Holmes.'

'You ask Vincent. It's true, boy, I tell you.'

166

'But how could she? I mean ... she's too *old*, for one thing!'

'Ha ha!' said Ern. 'How about Sarah! In the Bible, eh? She was sixty.'

Twenty-four ❧ ❧

JUDY POLLOCK, bouncing ashore from her schooner, full of traveller's tales, found no one prepared to listen. Only one subject interested Aratoa ... Who? Who? *Who?*

'But do they *really* believe it's Aporo?'

'Mrs Hitchcock does,' said Dolly Vincent. 'At first it was all rather gay, you know. People made absurd suggestions ... H.H.; Mr Holmes (that was Bill); an immaculate conception and so on; then Aporo's name began to circulate.'

'But does anyone believe it *possible*?'

'I think they'd like to,' said Dr Vincent. 'It would be a wonderful lift for the old place. From the way they're now lowering their voices ... glancing sideways ... I suspect they're beginning to believe it.'

'But who could have started the rumour? Aporo?'

'Mrs Hitchcock, of course. She believes it.'

'But *why*?'

'She loathes Miss A. Disliked her from the start. She's a Catholic, you see; and then she spoke out at the Sunday Sport meeting. And Mrs Hitchcock's got a bit of a crush on Costa....'

'Oh nonsense, Bill. But Costa was always taking tea there. And he was planting weird ideas in people's minds about Miss A. long before this. He hinted all sorts of things to me once at the freezer.'

Judy said she had heard a rumour on Hinoa about Aporo being caught by his wife with Miss Arbuthnott. Dr Vincent

reminded them hell had no fury like a woman with meno-
pause. That Mrs Hitchcock!

'But Bill, she's always been queer. Remember Sputnik and
the innerspring mattress?'

'Yes yes. Years ago, when Sputnik was going round, giving
out signals Mrs Hitchcock picked them up on her innerspring mattress.'

'She distinctly heard *beep-beep-beep* from her mattress.
She's always been queer.'

'What about Aporo?'

'Oh, he's gloating on it. Fatter and more complacent than
ever.'

No matter how angrily Leicester fought it, the rumour
persisted. Lowered voices, downcast eyes continued. Holmes
was curt and irritable; Dr Vincent, happy enough to talk,
had nothing to tell beyond what all knew.

Aratoa's new preoccupation was How to Face Miss
Arbuthnott; how to keep from one's eyes the burning en-
quiry? Pretend one never considered the subject? Believe
she had done it unaided? But it was easier than expected,
for Beatrice herself appeared unconcerned. Uncrushed by
notoriety, proudly triumphant, she confronted Aratoa
blandly.

'I did not mean to broadcast it, of course,' she told
Leicester. 'But when those devils forced my hand I didn't
care. I was only keeping it quiet for their sakes . . . not for my
own. After all, *I* have nothing to be ashamed of.'

Direct references to her condition brought smothering
discomfort. Leicester, plagued by grotesque images, unspeakable probabilities, mumbled, 'You're glad?'

'Glad? Of course I'm glad. What else should I be? What I
never thought could happen has now come about. After
years of making do with other people's children. How could
I be anything than glad?'

So great was his curiosity that it took the form of fearing

she might volunteer the embarrassing details all Aratoa craved; but she said nothing more, beyond stern references to Infant Welfare's future.

'I had intended to do all I could to help with replacements. I meant to—if possible—get hold of a suitable woman I know in New Zealand, even to give her some specialized training, free, gratis, for nothing. Now I shan't bother. I shall get out the first possible moment. The only things I regret leaving are you, Leicester, and my mothers and babies.'

'How will you ... manage? What will you do?'

'I shall be all right. I have a nice little nest egg. And later, of course, I shall resume my work. Perhaps with the New Zealand Maoris. Perhaps Melanesia. I shall manage.'

She would manage, without doubt; but what of the project? The mothers and babies to whom, she had inferred, her life was dedicated? Of course, one was on her side; of course she had been rottenly treated; of course one was fond of her, glad for her sake she was happy, but ... But was it not rather shocking that she could so off-handedly discard her life's work, abandon her breastfeeders with no more than a regretful sentence? Of course it was natural, but how *could* she? She, so devoted, so single-minded towards her work? How could she completely lose interest the moment her personal life intruded?

But she could; and she had.

Holmes, pulling himself together, commanded Leicester to go at once to Manu and sort out Miss Arbuthnott's leavings. He was to bring back Toa, and, the Chief said tersely, see what Constantopoulos was up to.

The orders were received thankfully. Leicester itched to escape Aratoa. Temata's ring, coruscating with diamonds, had arrived from New Zealand, committing him to a lifetime of debt; nor had Mother's comments consoled.

'I hope,' she had written, 'the girl you have ordered this for is worthy. I feel the cost is exorbitant and fear you may have been led astray. No really nice girl would demand such a showy engagement ring nor involve her future husband in such expense. I await with interest the photographs you spoke of. I find it a little embarrassing that I cannot show my friends my future daughter-in-law's portrait.'

'Oh God!' In asking her not to announce the engagement he had overlooked dear personal friends who would not of course breathe a word. By now it would be all over Wellington; probably his old colleagues in Island Territories knew. Soon it would leak back to the Peaceful Islands.

Temata's pleasure in the ring was transitory. She tried it on, smiled, arched her neck, held out her hand to sparkle the diamonds.

'It's okay,' she said.

'You're pleased?'

'Oh sure; sure;' but she grew annoyed when he sought stronger signs of pleasure.

'Okay, Leicester. Okay, I like it. You want me to cut off my hand for you, maybe?'

She had changed. She was harder. She had never talked like that before. He said dejectedly, 'Well, now you have your ring to show you can tell people.' But, rejecting appeasement, Temata frowned.

'Maybe. Maybe I wait a while. Too much sickness in our family just now.'

There was irony for you. He who had dreaded the announcement, now resented her lack of interest. Should he be more aloof? Try to make her jealous? Alas! She never saw his aloofness; humility annoyed her; questions brought always the same reply: 'My mother's sister. Maybe die. Very sick. Very sad. Many children to feed.'

The mother's sister: postponed engagement ... broken appointments ... evaded meetings ... sullen moods, all laid at her door. And nothing he could do about it.

Miss Arbuthnott had departed in a furnace of excitement. A week of farewell parties culminated in a tearful farewell on the quay. She left her liquor ration to Leicester and a bundle of papers known as My Lectures, the fruits of her years in the islands.

'Do as you will with them. I have other copies. Use them for my successor, if there's to be one. They're the basis of my work. And you have my *Feed Your Baby* books as well.'

Then she was gone, a kind of *Marie Celeste*—for none expected to learn her secret—and at once forgotten in the next scandal.

'Can you believe it?' People asked each other. 'It's incredible!'

'I could have told them,' said the clever ones.

'Hundreds of pounds in air fares alone. Tax-payers' money.'

'It's the knock-down furniture over again.'

'The tower is half-*built*! And they've started the factory foundations!'

'So there's no tuna there after all!' Dr Vincent roared it out at the tennis club, at golf, at morning tea. 'No bloody tuna at all!'

'Why didn't they find out before?'

'Don't ask me. They know everything. They're the Experts. Offenbach's going to need some good answers. H.H. has sent for him.'

'He'll get round H.H. A bucket of *pau'a* or some shells from the reef. . . .'

'Oh, the *expense*! It's disgraceful. When you think what could have been done with the money.'

'I thought Offenbach was an Expert!'

'Well, he's been shown up here by Honourable Nippo-san. I'd like to see Holmes with that oriental bastard. That's one boy he won't be able to bully.'

'Don't *ask* me!' Holmes barked at Leicester. 'It's Offenbach's fault. He's in charge.'

'Is it definite?'

'Of course it's definite. The natives say *now* there has

never been tuna ... they say *now* that they always knew it; but no one spoke up. *They say no one asked them!'*

'What will happen?'

'Offenbach saw H.H. He says he would like to resign. Resign! I ask you. He should be sacked; thrown out in disgrace.'

'Is he leaving?'

'Not if I have any say in it. He'll stay on and see it through.'

'But if there's no tuna ... ?'

'There's the rest of the fisheries project. Do you propose we should abandon it just because of this?'

Twenty-five ஒ ஒ

COSTA was on the beach when Leicester landed on Arumai. He looked abstracted, had lost weight.

'Yes, I am thinner.' Strangely he made no suggestion that this was due to amorous excesses. 'I've lost a lot in the last few weeks.' He fell into a moody silence.

'And how's everything?'

'It's all right. And with you?'

'Well ... it's a long story.'

'How's Miss Arbuthnott? All well with her?'

'You haven't heard?'

'Heard? What should I hear, on this desert island?'

'That she's gone.'

'Gone?'

'Yes. Left Aratoa. Didn't you know?'

'No. I didn't. But she's coming back? This is a holiday?'

'I don't think so. In fact I know it isn't. She's gone for good.'

Costa looked stunned; then he spoke very quickly.

'Where has she gone? Why isn't she coming back?'

At the end of Leicester's story they walked silently from the beach.

'Did you know ... about the baby?'

'Yes. I knew about that.' Costa's voice was tight. 'Here is my house. Please come in.'

Heat, flamboyant oleographs, feather fans, whiskey bottles. Costa waved to a wooden garden chair.

'Please sit down. We will have a drink.'

'Not for me, thanks. It's too early.'

Shrugging, Costa swallowed a whiskey, poured out another.

'Costa, is anything wrong?'

'Wrong? Why should it be? Did you eat breakfast on the ship?'

'Yes. Have you ... ?'

'To tell the truth I've rather given up breakfast. I don't seem to feel like it any more. It must be the heat.'

The glass in his hand quivered. Should even so dark a man be quite so blue round the chin after one night? Had he given up shaving as well?

'Costa! *Is* something wrong? Something worrying you? You could tell me....'

'No.' Costa was angry. 'Why should there be? Why should you ask such foolish questions? What could be wrong?'

Co-op funds, perhaps; a little embezzlement....

'If you think maybe I've been pinching the co-op funds, think again. You know how much they come to on Arumai? Four pounds eight and six!'

'Oh Costa ... I'd never *dream* ...'

'No. Well, I'll tell them to make you some tea. Then maybe you take a shower?'

At Miss Arbuthnott's cottage the sound of the ukelele had not changed but a different Toa greeted him.

'Yes, I am well; and Daniel is also well. Miss Arbuthnott is a good woman. She gives us plenty of *kai*. We are both fat.'

'But now you must come back. Miss Arbuthnott has left Aratoa. Gone to New Zealand.'

Toa shrugged. She said complacently, 'I stay here. I have many relations here. My mother a Manu woman. Arumai people like me. I weigh babies very well.'

'We'll discuss this again; later. You'd better take me now to the clinic.'

At the Baby Centre decay had set in. Spiders spun round scales, landcrabs made free with mats, mould flourished on posters, weeds in the garden, rats in the thatched roof. Leicester's flannelgraph figures were stuck together; the blanket for mounting them, did he but know it, was on Toa's bed. Her talent for weighing babies did not extend to servicing or running repairs.

It was all so foreseeable he wondered why he had come all this way. His report could have been accurately written on Aratoa. Counting tins of dried milk, he instructed Toa to clear out the livestock, brush off the mould. Her reluctance suggested she had risen above menial work. She showed him exercise books in which infant weights soared and sank like fever charts, reminding him of her skill at this demanding art. Arumai could not afford to lose her.

'All the same you'll have to come back. Mr Holmes wants to see you.'

This false incitement failed to impress. She shrugged again. She had never thought much of Mr Holmes.

'Aratoa no good. I stay here. Daniel likes it here.'

At dinner that night it was hard making conversation with Costa.

'Did you show any filmstrips?'

'No.'

'Why not, Costa? We sent all those strips you asked for ... *Co-ops in Fiji* ...'

'The Arumai natives do not like them. They despise the Fijians. They say, "That's all right for those blacks, but not for us. We are Polynesians." '

174

'If anyone tells me the Peaceful Islanders have no pride! They're as snobbish about colour and race as Tongans and Samoans!'

'That is true,' Costa was apathetic. He had not shaved since morning.

'But the Gilbertese aren't black. You have strips about Gilbertese co-ops. . . . You have English strips!'

'The people here do not care for the Rochdale Pioneers. Besides, the projector blew up. We all got a fright. Now no one will use it.'

'What about your savings groups?'

Again the dejected shrug.

'They thought they would save for a boat ... buy a schooner for exporting cargo ... when they have something to export, of course. But so far we have £4/8/6; and I think the idea of the boat is really for picnics and *tere* parties round the Group.'

'Costa,' said Leicester after another long silence. 'Something is wrong. You're ill, or worried. You're not yourself. You're not happy. For weeks you've been sending us wires, asking for books, posters, films, filmstrips ... everything. Now you don't seem to care. Have you forgotten how you used to say you were going to have every Peaceful Islander sleeping in a bed with a mattress. . . ?'

There were other changes not to be mentioned—the deplorable meal; Costa's unshaven face; *Parfait d'Amour* in pretty glasses replaced by whiskey in greasy tumblers.

Costa pondered. He made an effort. Without much conviction he put on his Colonial Service voice.

'Look here, old man. The truth of the matter is...' he took a drink ... 'the truth, old boy, is that I've *had* co-ops.'

'Had?'

'That's it. I've had them.'

'Does that mean ... do you mean that you've *had* them? Had enough? Had too much?'

'Exactly. I've had enough. Too much, in fact; much too much.'

'But ... In what way, Costa? What way? I mean, what are you going to ...'

Half-expected, came the terrible answer.

'Well, old boy, I'm tossing it in.'

'Tossing it in! And what does that mean? You don't mean you're *leaving*?'

The hysterical shrillness penetrated. Costa, looking surprised, said, 'Yes. That's it. I'm leaving.'

'It's a joke! You don't mean it! A joke.'

'Oh yes, I do. It isn't a joke.'

'You've gone crazy. You've gone round the bend. You're having a nervous breakdown.'

'I probably am having a nervous breakdown. I have every reason to have a nervous breakdown. But I'm still not joking.'

'You can't be serious. You can't mean it.'

'Can't I? Why can't I? Why not?'

Why not? That was the terrible part; but Leicester fought on.

'You've only just come. You've hardly started.'

Costa shrugged.

'And all that stuff you sent for ... all those posters and strips. All your plans. Your prefabricated house. What about that?'

'I've changed my mind, that's all.'

There was silence. Costa lit a new cigarette from the last one, emptied his tumbler.

'What is it, Costa? It's no good pretending. What is wrong?'

'Nothing's wrong.' Costa's voice proclaimed things could hardly be worse. He reached for the bottle, but Leicester seized it, holding it out of reach.

'Pull yourself together. What's going on here? What's been happening?'

Colonial Service control gave way to Mediterranean sensibility. Tears streamed down to the plump charcoal chin.

'Happening? Happening? You may well ask. Ah, it's too much for me; too much!'

'What's too much? The people? The work? What's gone wrong?'

'Not the work. It's a personal matter.' Sniffing, Costa padded his pockets. Leicester offered a handkerchief.

'Bad news? Family troubles?'

'Yes. No. In fact, I do happen to have lost a relation, but it is not that. On the contrary, he has left me a legacy. No, no, it's not that. But I find I must leave.'

'But why? Can't you just take a holiday ... sick leave?'

'*Poh-poh-poh.*' Costa mopped, fanned, felt better. 'No. I must leave altogether; leave the Colony. And at once. At once!'

'Don't tell me you're sick too?'

'No. Not sick. But I've had a shock. A bad shock. Not physically sick but for some weeks now *emotionally* frightfully disturbed. A *crise des nerfs.* Now comes this shock. This decides me that I must go.'

'Costa,' Leicester was abrupt. 'Are you being straight with me? Are you telling the truth?'

The black olives slid.

'Of course.'

'It wouldn't be that you've been offered another job?'

'No.'

'That another organization perhaps has made you a better offer?'

'Organization? What other organization, for example?'

'Well ... the French, perhaps. C.R.A.P.?'

'C.R.A.P. The *French*? Offering for me? For Co-operatives Officer? Now it's you who is unbalanced. Whoever heard of the French promoting co-operatives?'

'Then if it isn't that, what in God's name is it?'

'I just want to leave. To retire. I can do that if I choose, I suppose? It's a free country.'

'Your contract ...'

'I will settle all that.'

'It's hard to believe this isn't a joke. Miss Arbuthnott has left; Offenbach also wants to leave. If you leave too, what of the projects? The Chief?'

'I did not know about Offenbach. It's not my business what he does. I'm sorry, but it's just bad luck for Holmes. Miss Arbuthnott ... Why should I suffer because of this woman?'

'You don't have to *suffer* because of her. All I'm asking you is to reconsider your plans.'

'No. You don't understand.'

'I understand that *I* have to break the news to the Chief. And I doubt if I can do it. I think it will kill him.'

'*Poh-poh-poh.*'

'I know you don't like him; but you must admit he's sincere about work. He thinks of nothing but this project. It's unfair that everyone lets him down.'

Costa was not listening.

'I'll tell him myself, if you're frightened. I'll tell him. What's it got to do with him, anyway? It's my life ... my private life.'

'But it *has* got to do with him. He's your boss.'

'Not any more. I've resigned.'

'You'll never get another job if you break this contract.'

'I could not care less. I am finishing with this sort of work anyway. My cousin in Egypt has left me a legacy. I want to get on. There's no money in this game and you know it. I'm going to buy a seafood restaurant, a fruit emporium. I have to think of the future.'

'Why didn't you think of it before you came here?'

'It was different then. I was alone. A bachelor gay.'

'A bachelor? Are you married then? Is that what it is? Have you married here ... married an Arumai woman? Have you ...' Leicester felt hysterical ... 'married Toa?'

'Don't be absurd. Toa! Or any Arumai woman. There's no need to *marry* them. But I'm going to marry. That's why I must leave.'

'But you don't have to give up your job because of that.

You can just go on leave. For goodness sake, Costa, don't make it worse than it is. You could bring your fiancée to Aratoa and marry her here.'

Costa burst into tears again.

'You don't understand! It's my son. I must have my son. My son! My boy! Do you think I would give him up like that?'

'Calm yourself, Costa! Put down that bottle. Now, tell me. Just pull yourself together and explain.'

Leicester put his handkerchief back into the shaking hand, a cigarette between the trembling lips. Costa blew, sniffed, dabbed, sighed, shivered, inhaled and blew out smoke.

'All right. I'll explain. If I don't go at once I may be unable to get possession of my son.'

'What son? I didn't know you had a son. I didn't know you were married.'

'I am not. Not yet. But I shall be. Don't you see, I must marry quickly to secure possession!'

'Ah. Now I understand. Someone is pregnant and you want to acknowledge this child. But Costa...'

'Acknowledge?' Costa shrilled like a woman. 'What a word! I am *proud* ... proud of my son. He will bear my name, support me in old age ... give me grandchildren ... close my eyes in death. He will carry my name ... He is my immortality!'

'... And the girl is not here. She's in Egypt?'

'Ah! Stupid! You have understood nothing!'

'Wherever she is,' Leicester was suddenly tired of it all, 'get her here. Marry her....'

Costa's cry came from the heart.

'But she won't marry me! She wants the child all for herself!'

A phantom moved through the mists of Leicester's confusion.

'*Where* did you say she was?'

'I don't know. You know as much as I do.'

'I . . . ?'

'You said Australia . . . New Zealand . . .'

'*Are you telling me Miss Arbuthnott's the mother of your child?*'

'Of course. Of course I am. Who else?'

'No no! I can't believe it! Can't believe it!'

'Can't you? Well, it's true.'

'But it can't be! *Can't* be!'

'Why not? What's so strange?'

'Too many shocks,' Leicester said weakly. 'I can't take it in. Miss Arbuthnott.' But how? But *how*, even allowing for Mediterranean male pride in conquest? 'You never got on together. You didn't *like* each other!'

'It wasn't a question of liking. . . . We got used to each other, you know, living here. These things happen to the best of us. Alcohol helps, I suppose.'

'Beatrice! Miss Arbuthnott!'

'Now do you understand my plight? She's just gone off. She's double-crossed me. She said she was going to Aratoa to see the doctor. She never mentioned leaving the Group. And it's my son she's gone off with. *My son!*'

What Colonial Service regulation covered such primitive force? Costa's passionate attitude to breeding, his oriental conviction the child was male startled, intimidated. Feeble, ashamed, feeling effete, Leicester struggled to do his duty.

'I still can't see why everything has to be thrown away. Lots of people get married, have babies without wrecking their careers.'

'But you don't under*stand*!' The table bounced under Costa's fist. 'It's not just a question of marrying. I told you. She *won't* marry me. I asked. I begged. I implored!'

'Why? Why not? She must be made to see reason.'

Costa was silent. Pride still stung at the memory of Miss Arbuthnott's rejection: '*No, really, Constantopoulos; I mean, after all . . . I don't somehow see us married.*' Nothing, not the fruit emporium, the sea-food restaurant could persuade that great fawn-coloured woman who had used him and cheated him A snob; a snob! She thought him not good enough for her; yet his child was good enough. He let out a cry of despair.

'She wanted my child for herself. I obliged her. I gave her the child and she double-crossed me!'

'Strange that she doesn't mind it having no father.'

'No father?' Costa swelled up like a frog. '*I* am his father!'

'I mean, no husband.'

'She is crafty; deceitful. She has all these babies in her work. She will say he is adopted. My son! To be denied his own father!'

Towards midnight Leicester struggled from his chair.

'I am going to bed. I must be up early. Once more ... can I persuade you to change your mind? To stay on ... or come back? Can I persuade you not to resign?'

But he knew he was wasting his time. Costa, sunk in alcohol and despair could not even reply.

Twenty-six 🌿 🌿

THE interview with Holmes was as terrible as anticipated. The little man went white, then purple. Rigidity, bulging veins suggested sudden death; but presently he grew strangely quiet.

'We must persuade him.'

'He won't be persuaded.'

'Then we'll sue him.'

'That won't frighten him. He's got plenty of money.'

'We'll break him! We'll wreck his career!'

'He doesn't care about that either.' Leicester mentioned the legacy, the fruit emporium, the seafood restaurant.

Holmes was silent.

'What are we going to do?' asked Leicester at last.

'Leave me!' said Holmes.

'If there's anything I can do ...'

'Thank you. For the moment I must think.'

'Sir...' Leicester was fearful. 'What happened about the fisheries?'

The Chief re-purpled.

'Must you pester me now? At this moment. Has *every*one gone insane?'

In the outer office Aporo whispered, 'Mr Constantopoulos is leaving?'

'You shouldn't listen!'

'I heard through the door. Mr Holmes shouts very loud. Mr Offenbach is leaving too. Soon there will be no one at all.'

'That's no reason to look pleased.'

'Then the Peaceful Islanders will be the Experts. My people will lead the projects.'

'Very likely,' said Leicester, wandering away to the hotel for lunch.

It was no time for togetherness, but Thelma and Kev wouldn't take No. Phyllis and George were there, and Judy, an Ancient Mariner with tale still untold. No other topic could compete with the drama of Native Development.

'But whatever you may feel personally,' Leicester cried at last. 'You must admit the Chief is sincere about work ... difficult sometimes to work with, perhaps, but only because he wants the best. Perfectionists are always difficult.'

Plagued with doubts, shocked disapproval of Holmes's behaviour to Beatrice, shamed at his own traitorous thoughts, he had spent the evening defending the Chief. Now, excited by argument, beer, guilt, his protests were growing wilder. The others, even Phyllis, were shouting; giving honest opinions. It was a vulgar evening.

'But he *isn't* sincere,' Judy retorted. 'He's self-seeking. If he really cared about the islanders he would try to help Joseph get his schoolhouse instead of just sending him posters; but school buildings are not in Holmes's department. If he helped Joseph the credit would go to Public Works, not Native Development. And if he helped Father Pieter get his doctors and nurses and planters instead of abusing him all over Aratoa, the credit would go to Department of Health or Agriculture.'

'I can't think why you defend him,' George said. 'Bumptious, self-seeking little bastard.'

Thelma confided she couldn't stand little men; they were always aggressive.

Leicester said, 'Aggression is the only way he can get what he wants. If he were, well, like me for instance, we'd never get anywhere.'

The company cried their disagreement. Kev said the whole bloody project—assuming it had any use at all—would be better in Leicester's hands. Phyllis told him he had an inferiority complex; George said Leicester would make a bloody good Director. He didn't throw his weight about.

'People *like* you,' said Thelma. 'You may not be very *dynamic*, but they like you. They'd do things for you because you don't push them around.'

Well-meant attempts to encourage, but useless, said Leicester. He knew too well his own failings. No courage, no guts. No confidence, even in his own anger. Too likely to see the other side's point of view in the midst of an argument; always betrayed at the moment of crisis by the thought he might be mistaken, by his hatred of rows, people shouting, banging the table. His hopeless lack of decision; his fatal habit of letting others trample on him, push him about, double-cross him. Not aggressive enough. Something wrong with his adrenal glands. A no-hoper.

'The trouble with you, Leicester,' Judy said, 'is you think too much of yourself. If you thought more about helping the islanders and less about your shortcomings...' Leicester looked at her in amazement, '...and there's so much to do, so much really needed.'

Leicester said indignantly, 'A good deal of work has already been done ... permanent, worthwhile work. Everyone forgets that. No one makes allowances for the time it takes to show results.'

'Ah, go on,' said Kev, who was now very drunk. 'Who cares about Native Culture? What the hell does it matter about glottal stops? You don't call that *work*! It's all a racket.'

'If people really cared they'd be doing something about Manu drinking, for instance,' said Thel, as though deeply concerned. 'I mean ... it's disgraceful.'

'Ah, what's the use, anyway?' cried George. 'Why not leave the bloody natives in peace? They're all right as they are. They'll do me.'

'We can't leave them ...'

'Hah!' said Kev. 'If we don't do it, Someone Else will, eh?'

'The Peaceful Island Maori,' said Phyllis, 'is like a sponge. He appears to absorb, but squeeze him, it all runs out! Compared to the *Sa*-mawn ...'

'It's that sort of talk that has made him a Dying Race....'

'Dying! They're breeding like rabbits!'

'A racket! A bleeding racket. Experts. Trips round the world. Trips to Ha'i Koma. *Ha'i Koma!* How'd you like that for a name?'

'It may be a racket,' Judy shouted. 'It may be a racket but sometimes you can make use of rackets ... good use. You don't have to *believe* in them—you can see through them but use them to good purpose.... This Native Development racket could be used to good purpose, if it was in the right hands.... You're too starry-eyed, Leicester. You're too idealistic ... and you're wasting your time being loyal to Holmes. He'll wriggle out of the mess somehow, leaving you holding the baby.'

'He'll have to wriggle fast,' Phyllis said. 'He hasn't got long before he goes to Ha'i Koma.'

Judy's scream became piercing.

'Ha'i Koma! He'll be sailing in *Marinda* with Costa and Offenbach! All together! Not speaking!'

'What's he going to tell P.I.D.L.?' George demanded. 'He'll have to cook up some likely tale.'

'He will. He'll manage it,' Judy assured him. 'He'll cook up something.'

Holmes had cooked. Leicester, in mild shock, listened.

'We'll carry on as we are. We have funds till the end of the year.'

'But Chief, who will take over the projects?'

'To start with, you'll take over Co-ops.'

'But Chief...'

'...passing them later to Aporo.'

'*Aporo?*'

'He will need some little training—you'll see to that. But he already has a grasp of the subject. He went to meetings with Constantopoulos....'

Leicester dwelt on Aporo's power to grasp. He said. 'Chief. I can't train him if I don't know anything about Co-ops myself.'

Holmes waved impatiently. 'Well, find out from Constantopoulos. Get his manuals ... papers and so on before he leaves. Study them.'

'I thought Aporo was to lead Community Development?'

'Later; we'll come to that later. Now, Infant Welfare.... The girl, Toa, can take over.'

'Oh no sir, not Toa. Not *Toa!*'

'Why not?'

'She's almost half-witted. Stupid, lazy. Quite irresponsible. I know, sir, she was my housegirl. Besides, she won't come back from Manu.'

'I've wired, ordering her back. She'll take over Infant Welfare. When she comes you'll brief her.'

'*I* will?'

'You have Miss Arbuthnott's material; her lectures and notes. Look here, Whiteway, it may all seem very strange and unorthodox but I assure you I don't mean to have this

185

whole project ruined because a couple of unprincipled people act in an immoral and irresponsible manner.'

'Yes sir. And Fisheries? Is Offenbach staying?'

'We are not dependent on Offenbach. For the moment Hasuke will carry on. He will hand over to Ben.'

It was beyond argument, even protest. If Holmes meant to put the Resident in charge of Fisheries nothing would deter him.

'As for you, Whiteway, you'll take over from me when I leave for Ha'i Koma.'

'Yes sir.'

'You'll get the new people into shape ... start them off as soon as you can. Meanwhile, let me have your Progress Report as soon as possible so I can complete my own for the W.C.'

Leicester's consumption of whiskey had increased. The Report completed—a lugubrious chronicle of confusions face-lifted to convey progress and cheer—he now struggled nightly with the Rochdale Pioneers, Costa's handful of Co-op booklets at village level and Miss Arbuthnott's lists of weaning foods, recipes for simple powdered-milk puddings and directions for care of the breasts in pregnancy.

Costa, installed at the hotel, besieging the post office with daily telegrams to Miss Arbuthnott in Auckland, had no help to give.

'Don't ask me, old boy. I've resigned.'

Toa had not returned. She had intimated through Costa that if Holmes wanted to see her he must go to Manu.

Aporo, swollen with importance, reminded him daily of his coming advancement. Ben, who he now saw rarely, had grown very smug, spoke with condescension of his work with Hasuke, his future glory. Leicester had given up calling at the house. Temata, still wearing his ring, was never there. The family's amiable contempt was too much to support. For the moment he viewed his crushing burden of work with dejected gratitude.

Costa had become Aratoa's sweetheart. His popularity was in proportion to dislike for Holmes. All the world loves a lover. The romance was compared to Rossellini and Bergman on Stromboli. His absurd anxiety about his child, his conviction about its sex, his abandonment were endearing. Everyone sided with him against Miss Arbuthnott, against Holmes, who refused to meet him. The Baha'is entertained him at their cottage with tea and harmonium; Mrs Hitchcock had long motherly talks with him, behind her husband's back, and proclaimed that Miss Arbuthnott had seduced him, that he had fallen through loneliness, craving for family life. Miss Davidson jovially offered to knit bootees.

Universal sympathy, an answer (though negative) from Miss Arbuthnott, so improved his spirits that he could go, with saddened dignity, to farewell parties. He went also to parties for Holmes and Offenbach. Though none liked Holmes and few knew Offenbach they were excuses for entertainment. The fact that Holmes was not speaking to either former officers gave extra spice.

Twenty-seven ✌ ✌

WHEN Aratoa woke, two days before *Marinda* was due, a strange ship lay outside the reef. By breakfast she was in the lagoon, the streets loud with eager American voices.

'A millionaire ship'; 'A millionaire cruise'; 'Every passenger is a millionaire.' 'One woman has a suite just for luggage....'

The Americans were lavish, offering their bar, shop, cinema, swimming pool, band, dance floor. Aratoa responded with native dances; private dinners; island tours; an *umukai* at the Residency. Before midday Ken's Kurio

Shoppe was empty. Judy Pollock regretted to clamouring customers that stocks were exhausted.

'No matter. We'll go to the market,' the visitors said.

'What market?' Called in at dawn to help, Judy had not left the building all day.

'Why, the native market down by the port. They told us there'd be more stuff coming in after lunch. Maybe it's in already.'

On the green by the freezer, village women were trading bunches of hibiscus, *tiare Maori*, leaf baskets, fruit wrapped in banana leaves. A few conch, clam and spider shells, plaited leaf hats remained. Costa, transformed, was in charge.

'What's going on?' said Judy.

Costa rolled his eyes, fanned himself.

'*Poh-poh-poh!* If only we'd known they were coming. If we'd had some notice! But never mind.... Yes, Tangaroa; bring them in here. Thank you, thank you, Tatira. Over there. Never mind. We'll manage. Yes ... the mats *here*, the baskets *here*....'

'What is all this?'

'Oh, such a rush! Thank goodness they've gone on board for their lunch. But they'll be back and we must be ready for them.'

'Costa! Where did you get this stuff?'

Costa smiled proudly.

'*I* organized it. I did it all. I sent children to the reef for big shells, to the beach for small ones ... you see, the women are threading them into *eis* and necklaces. How quickly they work! And others are making more leaf hats, leaf baskets...'

'But this lot off Tangaroa's lorry! These mats and baskets?'

'That's from the handcraft class. I bought it all. The tourists want proper baskets ... *tapas* ... mats...'

'You've missed your vocation. But what will Government say? *Holmes?*'

'Why should they say anything? I have paid for it all. The

people who sold to me are quite happy; the tourists are happy; everyone's happy. Why should Government complain because I, and no one else, saw the potential?'

'I don't know. But I feel they might. For that very reason.'

'I am not under their control. I am a free agent. There is no law to stop me; or if there is, all this will be over before it's dug out and deciphered.'

At four o'clock, leaving his office, Leicester met Costa, enraptured, in a deserted battlefield.

'Dear boy, I've made a fortune!'

'But where did you get it all? It couldn't all be from the handcrafts class!'

'Oh no. That all went very early. When we ran out of handcrafts and shells we canvassed the villages,' Costa explained. Working through former lights-of-love he had raided native houses. Mats were pulled from floors, *tapas* from walls, *tivaivais*, embroidered pillows from beds, grass dancing skirts—reintroduced by Native Development—from school children. Even the hectic daubs of the primary art class were brought out and sold as primitives. Coarse food-carrying baskets had been cleaned up and thrown in with odd coconut ukeleles and guitars. Now all was sold, all houses cleaned out, all gardens stripped, all schoolrooms emptied. Pawpaws, reserved by the natives for pigs, were selling at 3/6 each, packets of fruit wrapped in banana leaves for 10/-, leaf-crowns for 5/-.

'They wanted *kava*, of course. Most of these tourists have been to Fiji or Samoa. They expected *kava* ceremonies. But we did what we could with bush beer.'

'Costa! You didn't sell that! It's illegal! It's illegal to make it.'

'There was plenty up in the mountains. Kerosene-tins full. We sold it all. Island Sherbert.'

'Did they drink it?'

'Did they what! They're sleeping it off now. That's why it's so quiet. I hope they wake in time for the *umukai*.'

'They may never wake again! You could kill them. They

could be paralysed; blinded. It's poison. You know what's in it, don't you? Fermented orange juice, coconut milk, *methylated spirits*!'

'Oh, they'll be all right,' Costa said carelessly. 'Americans are tough. They're used to that sort of thing. During prohibition, you know.'

With shouts, laughter, cries of encouragement a motor scooter racketted into the square. Temata, hair streaming, in Tahiti sundress from the ship's shop, straddled the Vespa, helpless with laughter.

'Ah! Pretty!' said Costa. 'Pretty girl.'

Leicester spoke involuntarily.

'What's she doing with that scooter?'

'It's hers,' said a young man standing by. 'Hers. From Tahiti.'

'Hers? She couldn't afford...'

'She don't buy it!' The youth was amused. 'It's a present.'

'I wonder,' said Costa, 'who bought it?'

Leicester, blushing at the enquiring eyes said, 'Her father perhaps. He's got a good job now in Fisheries.' The young man rocked derisively.

'Her father? *Ben?*' He was entranced at the thought.

Humiliated, Leicester drove home. The young man knew; knew Temata was wearing his ring; knew who had paid for the Vespa. The natives knew everything. They knew and they were laughing at him. Temata was laughing at him. Changing for the Residency *umukai* his humiliation turned to anger. The worm was going to turn. For once they were not going to laugh; for once Temata would not make a fool of him. He would have it out with her tonight ... find out what she was up to.

Apart from those tourists lying paralysed in their cabins, everyone was at the *umukai*. Trees in the Residency gardens glowed with fairy-lights; guitars, ukeleles moaned; kerosene-tin drums rattled. Dressed to kill, Aratoa paraded the lawns

190

with the visitors. A deceptive atmosphere of harmony prevailed as old enemies misdirected bows, smiles in the dim light; but it was not too dark for Leicester's eyes, sharpened by rage and alcohol, to see Temata, wearing another new dress. Pearl-shell *croissants-de-lune* dangled from ears to shoulders, pearl-shell *tiare Tahiti* gleamed on wrist and neck. On her hand flashed the ring he was still paying off.

'By God!' He drank another whiskey, glaring round miserably. 'If I knew who it was I'd wring his neck.'

'Hullo, Leicester. Enjoying yourself?'

Judy Pollock, in white, crowned with *tiare Maori*.

'Hi Leicester! Hi, Less! How are you, boy?' Kev and George, their women, for once united, got up like figures of fun. 'Boy, we've been on board! What a ship! This is Sparks.'

Sparks was sure happy to meet Mr Whiteway, Miss Pollock, mam.

The Baha'is swept past with a gaggle of elderly female compatriots. Costa, like a dog drafting sheep, manœuvred a party of lady tourists towards the feast. Then came the Davidsons with the Hitchcocks, the Vincents, the Captain with his V.I.P. millionaires.

'Can't see Holmes,' Judy said. 'Is he here?'

'I don't know.' Leicester hated them all, so cheerful and carefree; so indifferent to his sufferings.

'Well, we better move on,' Ern cried. 'We'll keep a place if you're coming.'

'You go on. I'll be there in a minute.'

It was dark now; blue, scented island night. The coloured lights in a splendid tamarisk gleamed down on Temata, giggling, whispering among Maori girls. Insane to take questions, reproaches, demands into that lions' den. Ignore her; show you don't care, seek her out later; yet, by God, they were looking at him; they were *laughing* at him, by God!

Temata glared as he strode up, seized her arm.

'I want to speak to you!'

He had not meant to sound so aggressive. Jerking her

arm away she shrilled, 'Who you think you're talking to?'

Village shrews, scratching eyes, pulling out hair! Not Temata, oh never Temata! She was different, whatever she'd done.

'Well, I want to speak to you!' That was not at all what he had meant to say.

'You're drunk! How dare you talk to me this way!'

'I want to speak to you, Temata. . . .'

Nothing outrages the sober more than drunken dogged-ness. Temata screamed, 'Well I don't want to talk to you! You go away. Leave me alone!' She jerked her arm again; his diamonds sparkled.

'Well, you're going to. You're still engaged to me, don't forget. I have a right to know what's going on.'

Her movements became more abrupt, almost violent. The *croissants-de-lune* clattered like angry castanets.

'You have no right! I'm not engaged to you!'

'You're wearing my ring.'

'Your ring!' But this could not be Temata! He fumbled to understand. This was another woman, savage, jeering, hateful; not the Ha'i Koma princess, gentle, educated, like a European girl. Too difficult to work it out. Blankly he said, 'My ring. You said you liked it. What's so funny?' And who were those Maori bitches, listening, giggling, enjoying . . .

'Your silly ring!'

'Well, if it's so silly you can give it back!' How alcohol betrayed, brought out childish meannesses!

'I do not give it back!' Temata said clearly. 'And I do not marry you! I marry someone else!'

'You're still engaged to me!' Alcohol also brought stub-bornness.

'I do not marry you if you are the only man on Aratoa. *I hate you!*'

It was the venom, not the words. . . . Temata, with the insolent vulgarity of hostile Polynesians now listed her com-plaints . . . meanness; not enough presents; unfulfilled promises; waste of her time; boring talk; indefinite marriage

192

plans. . . . She concluded with references to his lack of man-hood, enterprise, virility, possible physical deficiency. . . .

He tried not to listen, tried to shut out the cackling audience, but could not exclude the last high-pitched words.

'I'm going to marry someone else and leave Aratoa. Now! Soon! Not *sometime* like you said. Not *maybe*! Tomorrow I marry; after tomorrow I go! What do you think of that?'

He broke through the nightmare to say stiffly, 'May I ask who you're marrying?'

Sweet triumph overcame her desire to confound. She swaggered. 'I'm going to marry Mr Offenbach, the Fisheries Expert!'

He stared, an enquiring idiot, while Temata, swaying hips, rattling earrings waited impatiently.

'You understand?' she demanded at last. 'You understand what I say? I marry Mr Offenbach. All fixed! *In the church*. Tomorrow!'

He laughed.

'Offenbach? *Offenbach?* It's impossible!'

'What's impossible. What are you laughing at? Plenty of men want to marry me! You think you're the only one?'

'But how . . . but how . . .' Offenbach, who spent his time at the bottom of the lagoon. 'But he's *old*!'

'He is rich. Richer than you. He gives me many presents. More than you. He takes care of me properly. Not just talk. Go away. I don't want to talk to you.'

High insolent laughter followed as he turned away.

A white form glimmered beside him.

'Sit down,' Judy said.

'Thank you.' There was nothing else to do. 'Yes. Thank you.'

Hard to know if the trembling came from whiskey or shock.

'Would you like a drink?'

'No. No, thank you. I've had enough. More than enough.'

'You seem perfectly sober.'

He was too, quite suddenly; sober and sick.

'I suppose everyone heard?'

'No. Only me. I'm sorry, I couldn't help it. She rather shouted. . . .'

'A figure of fun!' he said bitterly.

'Don't be silly. You're not the first man to fall in love with an island girl.'

'But *Offenbach!*'

Judy said, 'He must have surfaced more than we realized; unless she went down to the sea-bed to meet him.' She saw Offenbach, redfaced, puffing, rising from the depths. She began to laugh. 'He told me he wanted a wife. So much gossip about other people, but not a word about himself. He's made a fool of us all.'

'That's where she's been all the time! Over there at the fishing camp. It's Ben. I bet Ben arranged it. The scheming old devil!'

'I think you'd better accept that Temata arranged it. However painful.'

'Painful! You don't think I mind?'

'I did think you might. For a while.'

'I couldn't care less,' Leicester said, tears welling. He felt very talkative. 'It wasn't Temata I loved. It was Polynesia. I fell in love with Polynesia. She was only a symbol.'

'Ah.' She might never have heard the words before. 'Then it's a lucky escape.'

'You can say that again.' Tears were now on his cheeks, nose, throat. 'I think perhaps I'll go home. I don't feel very well.'

'No *umukai?*'

'As a matter of fact I'm rather tired; and I had a few drinks before I came. I'd like to get to bed.'

'Of course. Could I run you home perhaps? Bill's car is here.'

'Thanks. I can manage.'

He heaved himself up, looked at her with tired defiance, dimly discerning sympathy.

'Thanks very much. Well . . . so long.'

'So long, Leicester. See you tomorrow maybe.'
Proudly he weaved away into the darkness.

Twenty-eight ❧ ❧

THERE was disappointment but relief when *Marinda* sailed away with her jumble of passengers ... Holmes, for Ha'i Koma, stiff with displeasure; Costa, in tears; Offenbach, silently scarlet; Temata, sulky, despite her new wedding ring. The millionaires left the day before, all cabins crowded with Costa's merchandise, all hospital beds full of bush beer casualties.

Aratoa had reeled from the *umukai* to farewell the sabotaged cruise ship, then lain in a mass hangover twenty-four hours. It was too much to see another ship off so soon and when she pulled out, anticlimax, irritation descended.

'It all comes at *once*!' Thelma complained. 'Why can't things be spread out.'

'That's Aratoa. A feast or a famine,' said Phyllis. 'But at least we didn't have to go to the wedding.'

'Oh, the wedding! You can have that.'

'They say it cost a fortune.'

'Old fool. Serve him right. He'll find out.'

'So will she! Mark my words! I give it three months. Then she'll be back ... without him!'

They wondered how Temata would find life in a small Rhenish town.

'Funny thing, he has a farm. A vineyard, he says.'

'I don't think he ever knew anything about fish.'

'Oh, he did. About trochus, anyway.'

'Well, I feel sorry for him. Poor old fool. They say he's sixty.'

'She's nineteen.'

Leicester, still nursing himself tenderly after the whiskey

and Temata's betrayal, found the farewells a strain. It was difficult to avoid Temata without slighting Offenbach; attendance on Holmes clashed with Costa's emotional claims. Not that Costa lacked well-wishers. Every woman on Aratoa had come to farewell him ... the girls from the hotel, the Baha'is, Miss Davidson, Mrs Hitchcock, Jacopo's wife Teresa ... all were there. Holmes looked lonely, even pathetic with only the Elegy in a Country Churchyard. Leicester felt he should be more cheerful, encouraging, but could manage no more than a pallid smile. Even now, each time he turned his head he feared it might fall off; each time he spoke, dreaded he might burst into tears.

He stood with the Holmeses, trying to reduce the long last minutes with short sentences.

'I've left you a copy of my report,' said Holmes.

'Yes, sir.'

'You can go through it at your leisure.'

'Yes, sir. I'll do it at once.'

'You'll be all right.'

'Oh, of course, sir. And then you won't be away all that long.'

Janet Holmes glanced at him, then at her husband. Holmes said, 'Three weeks; unless I'm delayed.'

'Delayed?'

'Well, you know how it is; something might crop up. Or I might stop off somewhere on the way ... Fiji, perhaps; even Apia. If there's anything worth inspecting in other territories this is the best time to do it.'

'Oh yes, of course.'

Silence caught up with them. It had all been said several times over. Outside work, Leicester had nothing to say to his Chief; yet another hour must pass before they left. Janet seemed uneasy. Did she want to be alone with her husband?

'Well, goodbye, Whiteway,' Holmes suddenly said dismissingly. 'Best of luck.'

Thankfully making for Costa's cabin he ran into Offenbach and the bride.

'So! Vell, I go. I go. Back to Chairmany now at last.'

'Bon voyage,' Leicester edged past, eyes turned down.

'No. You kom now and drink to our health, Mr Vitevay. To der bride, *ja*? I have viskey....'

'Thank you. I must find my friends.'

'Costa? Costa vill vait. Kom now.... Ve are parting for ever, perhaps. You vill kom.'

'Oh, Leicester!' Judy Pollock swooped down the corridor. 'Do hurry up. We're all waiting. Hullo Temata ... hullo Heinrich ... Hurry up Leicester, they're looking for you.'

'Who?' he asked meekly, as she led him away. 'Who's looking for me?'

'No one. You didn't want to drink with *them*, did you?'

'Oh no. Oh ... thank you. *She's still wearing my ring!*'

'Ah well ... You'll have to write that one off. Come on, we'll go to Costa's cabin. Everyone's there, drinking *Parfait d'Amour*.'

The cabin was crowded; people stood in the corridor shouting. Costa, embowered in flowers and fruit, smiled like a prima donna.

'He's a terrible crook but you cannot dislike him,' Judy said.

Shaggy, bilious, sentimental, they all went ashore and waved. Costa cried, the ship departed, people walked down the pier complaining how everything happened at once.

'May I drive you home?' Leicester asked Janet Holmes, but she, flushing, said Thank you, she had her car and must get home to the Littlies.

'Everyone's going,' said Judy. 'I'll be gone soon.'

'Soon?'

'My holiday's over. I have to go back to work.'

'I suppose so,' said Leicester uncertainly. He felt depressed. 'Can I give you a lift?'

'Thanks, but I'm going to the freezer for Dolly.'

There was really no more to say, no reason to linger, but

they stood. Once Judy seemed about to speak but in the end, smiling pleasantly, rather awkwardly they drifted apart.

An audience who, like the Work Committee members, had never seen, were unlikely to visit the Peaceful Islands, could find Holmes's Progress Report impressive.

Its fictions convinced against all factual knowledge. Leicester read giddily, seeking to recognize his own confused efforts in the list of achievements ... recordings of old songs and dances; revival of handcrafts, of indigenous culture; establishment of women's interests, visual aids, broadcast programmes organized; health, co-ops, fisheries, infant welfare.... A note of hysteria, even desperation seeped from the blatant untruths, rising to suicidal defiance:

'The ultimate aim of the Project has always been self-determination for the Peaceful Islands. Our work has been not mere provision of services and facilities but to train islanders to take over and run such themselves.

'Realization of this aim would now seem in sight. It might be said that we are rapidly doing ourselves out of our job. No less than three fully-trained Peaceful Islanders have taken over from project officers, who, however, will still keep a watchful eye on proceedings ... while acting henceforth in an advisory capacity.'

How, in God's name, did the Chief think he could get away with that? How long before the truth got about? In no time the story of Costa and Miss Arbuthnott would be in the folk-lore of every Pacific island; the dining-out repertory of every international busybody. This was after-the-deluge behaviour. He saw Holmes, eyes screwed tight, on a cliff, preparing to leap; felt pity, protective anxiety in his scandalized horror.

Aratoa had criticized, censured, disapproved; even he himself had had unworthy doubts; but here, in black and white, was proof of the Chief's dedication. A man who thus risked his whole future for the sake of the project, the islanders, must be credited with sincerity. Blameless, since his officers had betrayed him for their own selfish ends, he offered himself in martyrdom for the cause.

But the report was lunacy. Leicester gave up brooding on Temata, began dreaming that P.I.D.L. observers had come to investigate. Apprehensively he regarded Judy Pollock, visiting Fulbrights, even temple-building Mormons who might carry the truth to the world. What would C.R.A.P. say? How the French would laugh that this dreary Anglo-Saxon venture should be wrecked by *l'amour*. And the Resident Commissioner, who had now had time to study his copy ... why did he not send for Leicester; comment on the Report? What was he planning?

Suspense, uncertainty, now part of existence, were relieved only by irritations. Toa, sullenly back from Manu, resisted all efforts at training. Aporo clamoured for it unceasingly, came at all hours to discuss accounting or Tolpuddle Martyrs. The need to keep one jump ahead with knowledge was exhausting. Insomnia, alternating with nightmares, began to leave its signature on Leicester's face and behaviour. Phyllis and Thelma regretted hopefully that he was in for a breakdown.

'It's Temata, of course. He's pining. If only he could see what a lucky escape he's had.'

They watched him as a trainer a hopeful champion. He was, at this stage, their only diversion. Aratoa had sunk into shocking dullness. If nothing happened soon to relieve it they'd have to quarrel.

'It's quiet,' said Dolly Vincent. 'Should I give a party?'

'Who for?' Even Dr Vincent was dispirited. 'Those same bloody faces?'

Nothing helped, even the news that Mr Hitchcock was about to revive the Sunday Sport issue; that Miss Davidson had spoken her mind to Nutkin about the Arbuthnott rumours. People began counting months to their leave, anticipating all the joys of home that had sent them to live in the islands. The Aratoans, unconcerned, carried on with

199

their aimless pursuits, their cheerful impersonation of a Dying Race.

Twenty-nine ❧ ❧

WHEN the Resident Commissioner sent for Leicester he knew it was about the Report. Crossing the square to headquarters he sought the best way to defend his Chief.

His Honour seemed even more nervous than he, more cadaverous, longnosed and boney than ever. It was one of his Yes-yes, Come-come days, when he nearly went mad thinking about retirement, pensions, memoirs.

'Well well; sit down, Whiteway.'

His teeth, rather loose, very grey, clacked as he spoke, but God knew he could not afford others.

'You sent for me, sir.' It was a line in a play.

'Yes yes, I sent for you.' The white jointy fingers waved. 'You may smoke if you like. Thanks, I don't. Gave it up long ago. Can't afford it.'

Leicester put back his cigarettes, feeling callously extravagant. The white spider-legs fluttered about, curling around pencils, pushing the blotter.

'Hmhm. Well, Whiteway, I sent for you. As you see.'

'Yes sir.'

'Excuse me a minute, will you? Something under my plate, I believe. Ah, that's better! Got your own teeth, Whiteway?'

'Yes sir.'

'Ah well. Different in my day. My advice to young fellers joining the Pacific service—Get rid of teeth and appendix. Only cause trouble in remote areas. Never know when they'll play up.'

'No sir.'

'Now then, where were we?'

'You sent for me, sir.'

'Yes yes, of course. Where's the damn thing?'

'I have a copy here, sir.'

'What's this? What copy?'

'The Report, sir. I brought my copy. You may use it ...'

'Report? What report?'

'Mr Holmes's, sir. Native Development Progress Report. For the Work Committee. Isn't that why you sent for me, sir?'

'Good God, no! Report! Haven't read the damn thing. Lot of twaddle. Don't know where it is, Whiteway ... somewhere about, I daresay. Your pigeon, not mine. No sir, I did not send for you because of Mr Holmes's paperasserie; I sent for you because I have news. *News*, Whiteway. News from Ha'i Koma!'

Leicester shut his eyes briefly. So! It had come.

'Where is the damn thing?' H.H. shuffled unconvincingly among the papers, but the telegram, shrieking its head off, could not be avoided. 'Hah! I received this extraordinary missive last night from Ha'i Koma!'

If God would make it quick, final, merciful!

'From Holmes, sir. From Holmes! That little *cock-sparrow*!'

Leicester's eyelids flew open.

'Read that, Whiteway! See what you make of it!'

'I don't understand, sir. ...'

'Nor did I. Nor did I, I assure you. Go on ... Take it ... Read the damn thing.' He returned to his teeth.

'What does it mean, sir?'

'It means what it says, I presume, my dear fellow. That Mr Holmes is leaving us. Leaving us, high and dry. For, presumably, a better job!'

'Oh no, sir!'

'Oh yes. Oh yes, *indeed*, Whiteway!'

'But it can't ...'

'It can; it does. And he is. I sent for his wife. She confessed, with reluctance I must admit, that her husband has been planning this move for some time. That when he sailed for Ha'i Koma he did not expect to return.'

Spelling out words, slowly, as though full comprehension could be thus postponed, Leicester barely heard His Honour.

'A well-kept secret, Whiteway, I agree. It appears the new appointment was not fully confirmed when he left here, so nothing was said. Apparently now it's in order for us to know.'

'But C.R.A.P. sir! To go to C.R.A.P.! Unesco ... or the Caribbean Commission I could perhaps understand ... even the S.P.C. But C.R.A.P.! He doesn't even speak French.'

'But look at the pay, Whiteway! Three times what P.I.D.L. gives.'

'Oh no, sir. I can't believe he'd go just for the money!'

'For what else, may I ask? For love of the French? He's crafty, you know Whiteway. Crafty. Only with C.R.A.P. could he do it this way. They know all about him, you see; you might say it's no more than switching departments. With Unesco or one of the others he couldn't have kept it a secret ... there'd be references ... enquiries ... all that. They do, after all, have standards, of a sort.'

Leicester could not speak. His Honour had begun to enjoy himself.

'Yes yes. C.R.A.P. Hah! When I think of his righteous horror at that charming feller, Constantopoulos. And his vituperative attacks on the mothercraft woman; the way he betrayed her ...'

'Is there nothing we can do, sir?'

'I doubt it. I suspect he would not have sent this wire if there were.'

'But his family?'

'They will join him. Mrs Holmes desires to sail in the next *Marinda*. We cannot hold them hostages.'

Leicester put his face into his hands. His Honour looked startled.

'Come come, Whiteway, you must try to rally. It's a shock

... I admit I was quite bowled over at first; but twelve hours of reflection have helped me considerably. To be honest, I would not have him back now at any price. It's a blessing in disguise.'

'It's the shock, sir. I never thought...'

'Well, none of us did.'

'No sir, I mean I never thought ... for *money*! I thought he was dedicated.'

'Ah well, we live and learn. The thing now is to replace him.' He stabbed suddenly down between teeth and cheek, manoeuvring his plate. Relieved, he said, 'I've decided to ask you to carry on.'

'Of course, sir. I'll stay till you get someone else.'

'No no. Not someone else. We don't want outsiders. Take over the job altogether.'

This being no more bizarre than Holmes's telegram, Leicester said limply, 'Oh no, sir.'

'Yes. I'm putting you in as Director, in Holmes's place.'

'I'm sorry sir, but I couldn't.'

'You couldn't? What does that mean?'

'I couldn't, sir. Honestly. I'm sorry, but it's impossible.'

H.H. looked testy. 'Now, don't make snap decisions, Whiteway. Take your time. Think it over.'

'In any case sir, P.I.D.L. would want to make the appointment.'

'Nonsense. They'll be delighted. Save them no end of trouble. Besides, my dear fellow, you forget you're Colonial Service. I can throw out their blasted project tomorrow, start a new one, with you in charge, and as P.I.D.L. is well aware, there's plenty of others only waiting a chance to move in. That crowd in Suva; the S.P.C. ... they'd be in here like lightning.'

'Would it make so much difference who came?'

'Difference? Come come, Whiteway, that's not like you. If P.I.D.L. had to find someone else, imagine the interruption ... delay ... chaos!'

Leicester thought of the present chaos, wondered at the

Resident's concern with delay, dwelt with new cynicism on the revelations, awkward questions, exposures implicit in change.

'Think of the people!' said H.H.

The people! Why? At this stage?

'... the natives. Must think of them. Fond of them, you know. One's children.'

Twaddle. Sentimental traditional twaddle. Leicester said coldly, 'What did you have in mind, sir? What could be done, now that Holmes has made his report?'

'I tell you I haven't read the damn report. What's it got to do with it?'

Leicester told him. H.H. said, 'Well, well ... But Ha'i Koma won't see anything queer in all that. They don't know anything about the girl Toa—Ben—Aporo. They have no call to question, investigate. It won't affect funds. They're approved. Won't come up again till next Session. Project's approved for five years, you know Whiteway. Only automatic review of funds at the Session ... of work in hand at Work Committee meetings. Holmes hasn't told them work's *stopped*. Just lied about progress. Plenty of money in kitty.'

'But those people can't do the *work*, sir, no matter what funds are available.'

'No matter; no matter. Don't use these people. Use others. Call the projects what you like and use the funds where they're really needed.'

How did you answer such proposals from the Resident Commissioner of a British Colony?

Left behind by H.H.'s hurtling mind, Leicester stumbled against ugly words: False pretences. Embezzlement.

'Now look here, Whiteway ... there's a lot to be done in this Group more important than digging up defunct songs and dances or trying to make people wear *tapa*. There's a good many genuine needs and that's where the money should go ... filariasis control ... TB ... work on leprosy ... yaws. I mean work, not just sticking up posters. Have a word with Vincent about it. With decent funds one could do

204

a lot, working through the A.M.P.s ... We have some damn good A.M.P.s in the outer islands....' Leicester thought of Tata .. 'Might as well use them. Infant Welfare ... Well, that's worth keeping. You could get someone from the hospital staff ... use the village nurses. Agriculture ... Wilson has a few fellers there trained enough to do some good. Urgent job on rhinoceros beetle ... rat control ... planting coconuts...'

Leicester's mind was moving ponderously.

'You mean, just go on using the money without telling P.I.D.L. what you're doing?'

'Well, you could put it like that....'

At least he was not proposing to pocket it himself.

'...Why do we have to have Experts? Cost the earth. Air fares alone run into hundreds. All these fellers with their glottal stops ... tuna towers. Why can't the Medical Officer, the Agriculture Officer and their staff do the job, hey?'

Desperation brought bluntness.

'Sir! You can't get away with it. They'll find out. When the estimates go in for the next year. Unless the Reports are complete lies.'

'Tst tst. You don't understand, my dear fellow. No need to put in a progress report for six months. Six months before the next Work Committee meeting, before the next Session. You could do a lot in the time with proper funds. P.I.D.L. won't complain if you put in a report of good work. Damn it all, sir, the Director is surely entitled to change the programme to fit the work. Hey?'

'But sir, the money is granted for certain purposes ... approved projects. One can't just spend it all as one pleases without at least *consulting* them!'

'Rubbish! Never consult international organizations. Don't tell 'em anything. Never ask permission. If you ask, they'll refuse. Have to. Do it, then ask if you like. Once it's done they won't care. They don't care, you know, but they feel they're expected to make a fuss if you give them a chance. You mark my words, Whiteway. Present them with a report showing progress and they'll take all the credit; try to tell you it was their own idea.'

Leicester said, 'What about Holmes's Community Development team?'

'Forget about it. Lot of rubbish from the start. Use the money for something better. That Dutch feller over on Manu has done more on his own than any team of Holmes's could even try. Besides ... there's a District Officer ... Native Magistrates ...'

Leicester thought of David; of the District Officer and his Ph.D. He said rather bitterly, 'Miss Arbuthnott said the Chief only thought of Community Development so he could write it up and get a Unesco job. I didn't believe her.'

'Well, now he can do it at C.R.A.P.'s expense. Ha-ha. That'll teach him. So that's fixed, hey Whiteway? You'll take over ... work in with the people we already have ... use the funds for real necessity....'

'No sir, I can't!'

'If you're worrying about your salary, you'll get the same as Holmes. No problem about your appointment. They'll be relieved to have someone on the spot who knows the work. Save all that trouble y'know ... I tell you, my boy, they don't want to be worried. They just want results to show their taxpayers.'

'All the same, sir, I'm sorry. I couldn't. I don't want ... There's all sorts of reasons....'

'Don't give me your answer now. Bad time. Think it over. Give you till tomorrow ... can't manage longer.'

'I don't ...'

'Looking rather peaky, lately, Whiteway. Take a day off. Give you more time to think. Well now, that's all for the moment. Try and let me know in the morning. Perhaps, if you've time, you could draft out some recommendations. Must get to work ... get results soon as possible ... before any more of these journalist fellers start spreading stories.'

'No sir, I ...' Journalists? *Journalists?* Leicester tried to infuse contempt into his refusal. 'No sir, thank you. I must decline the honour.'

The Resident was not listening.

'Sleep on it. You'll see it differently in the morning. Think of the islanders. Think of their welfare.'

Thirty ⁍ ⁍

'WHEN we got to Hinoa,' Judy continued hopefully, 'the reef was rough. The captain said . . .'

'There goes Leicester!' Ern Crump said. 'In a trance. *Hi, Less!*'

'What's the sudden interest in Leicester? Do you or don't you want to hear what I'm telling you?'

'In a trance, a perpetual trance,' Ern complained. 'Sort of bugger stands about pulling the blind up and down. Oh sure, sure, Judy. Go ahead. Only I wondered what he was going to do. You heard about Holmes?'

'What about him?'

'He's quitting.'

'I don't believe you.'

''Strue. Joe, in the Post Office. Said a telegram came for H.H. giving notice. Going to work for C.R.A.P.'

'Well, I still don't believe you.'

'You ask Joe. Besides, H.H. had Leicester up there this morning offering him the job.'

'Who told you that?'

'Our housegirl's boy-friend—John—works at headquarters. Heard them talking.'

'It's like the gestapo.'

'Yeah, things get around. Imagine old Less, head of the show. But John says he won't take it.'

'Why not?'

Ern shrugged. 'Fed up, I guess; and you know what he's

like. Not enough of a bastard really. No opinion of himself. So go on about Hinoa.'

'Some other time. I'm just going to have a word with Leicester....'

'You bloody well aren't! No one knows anything—understand? This is top secret.'

'Miss Pollock! Miss Pollock! Wait for me!'

Nutkin scuttled out of the freezer building as though chased by the Pope himself.

'Oh, Miss Pollock ... I did want to speak to you ... so out of breath ... to ask your support ...'

'I'm sorry, Mrs Hitchcock,' Judy said thankfully, 'but I shan't be here for the meeting ... I'll be going in the next *Marinda*.'

'Yes, the meeting ... no, but not that meeting, another one. Not Sunday sport—I mean yes of course we must go on campaigning against it but this is another meeting. Oh dear!' Her paws flapped. 'This is a *new* meeting. About Mr Whiteway!'

'A *meeting*?'

'Oh my dear Miss Pollock, such dreadful things happening. Dear Mr Whiteway wants to leave us. Leave Native Development. We mustn't let him. Imagine, if that work is abandoned ... imagine what will happen. They'll be in here, like a shot. Creeping down, through Indonesia. Only a few hours flying time.'

'I don't think the Indonesians will invade Aratoa if Leicester goes. Besides I thought it was a secret that he was leaving?'

'Oh yes, he doesn't know we know. But you see we must stop him. I am getting up a petition ... Education are typing it out ... I shall call for your signature, after lunch ... and I thought a meeting of protest ...'

'I didn't realize you thought so highly of him; of Native Development.'

'Oh Miss Pollock, one needs must.... We must have a bastion. A defence line. Imagine, for instance, if the L.M.S. withdrew from these islands! In no time they'd be swarming with Sacred Heart nuns, Marist priests. It's the same with Mr Whiteway's work. If we abandon the natives, Others will come with their offers of help; and with the present situation in High Places one fears that any smooth-tongued proposal of help would be accepted, no matter from what camp!'

'Who's going to present the petition to Leicester?'

'Well, I had asked my husband, but he's not available at the moment. I wondered if ... I feel you and he are about of an age ... I really don't know, Miss Pollock, *who* to ask ... unless you'd be so very kind ... ?'

'I'll think it over,' said Judy. 'I'll let you know after lunch.'

There was a queer feeling in the air. It was like playing a guessing game in which all but oneself knew the secret word. No one spoke outright but the atmosphere was saturated with hints. At the office Aporo's bulging eyes made work impossible.

'Mr Holmes not coming back?' he demanded, suggestively adding, 'You leaving too, maybe Leicester?'

Morning-tea conversation had become suddenly concentrated on the islanders' welfare. Creaking with discretion, Dr Vincent began a roundabout discourse on methods of filariasis control. Wilson, Director of Agriculture, who rarely recognized Leicester's existence, had occasion to mention, at length, plans for coconut replanting in the outer islands. Humphries, Director of Education, expressed a keen interest in Joseph's village school.

Did they really think he didn't see through them? Did they really believe they could convince him of Santa Claus? Nothing would make him change his mind; no amount of dangled carrots win him round. He was leaving Aratoa, finished for ever with phonies and self-seekers. He would

209

start afresh somewhere else and try to forget it all.

Aporo's discretion had worn thin by lunchtime. A new ambition now replaced thoughts of New Zealand Art School.

'You will stay and train me, so I can take over when you go? Then I shall be Director and lead My People.'

That at least was honest; as was poor Mrs Hitchcock, who meeting him in the square, distractedly revealed that she knew all.

'Oh, but you must stay, Mr Whiteway! Indeed you must! It's your duty. If you don't, if all this fails we know what will happen. We *must* carry on. You know as well as I that if We don't develop these islands, Others will! They're only waiting their chance to get in here. It's your duty to stay!'

Not that it mattered if people knew. His resignation could not remain secret. He was no longer interested in how they had heard, nor that rumour might reach H.H. before his official reply.

'I'm going home, Aporo,' he said at two o'clock. 'You carry on here.' He left quickly before further questioning could begin.

'I don't think I'll bother to sign,' said Thelma. It was one of her days. Kev had been playing up.

'I do think,' Phyllis said. 'That it's Leicester's *duty* to stay!'

'They're all the same. Only think of themselves.'

'I thought he was *different* ... I thought he was *dedicated....*'

'I told you months ago he had no guts.'

'If he stayed on...' Phyllis said thoughtfully. 'There must be lots of part-time jobs in Native Development ... Teaching, I mean ... sewing ... literature...'

'Cooking!' Thelma said more brightly.

'They can cook.'

'They can't ice! Have you ever seen *any*thing here but

sponges? Can you honestly tell me the Peaceful Islands Maori women know how to ice a log, for instance?'

'A part-time job would be handy. And it's not as though I had no *background*. . . .'

'She said she'd be here at three o'clock for our signatures. Judy Pollock's going to take it to him.'

'Will you sign for Kev? I might as well sign for George.'

'Of course. Though they couldn't care less if he stays or goes. But if he *does* stay . . . with the kiddies at school . . .'

'Because they want you to stay,' Judy said. 'That's why.'

Leicester put down the document with its assorted names and said, 'It's very touching but I don't suppose there's a single disinterested signature there.'

'Now Leicester, don't be difficult. Poor Mrs Hitchcock has turned herself inside out to collect them.'

'Look at them . . . apart from Mrs Hitchcock and her insane reasons . . . Vincent . . . he'd like me to stay on and do his work; Wilson, the same; Humphries, the same; Aporo— wants me to stay on and train him, then get out and let him run the department. I don't see H.H.'s name here but I know he wants me to stay, so the project won't collapse and journalists won't write about him in the papers and get him sacked.'

'It's not like you to be cynical, Leicester.'

'Not like me? What *is* "like me"? What do people see me as . . . a piece of plasticine to be pushed into any shape opportunists choose? You know perfectly well that all those people who signed want me to stay on to save their faces or do their work . . . to shift responsibility or pass the buck. And what about the natives? They haven't signed . . . I don't mean Aporo and Ben and Jacopo who need me to finish training them for their jobs. I mean the village people. Has anyone asked what they think?'

'Of course not. Would you expect them to be asked?'

'It wouldn't make any difference anyway. They'd just say

what they thought we wanted them to say. You'd never know what they thought. If they think at all!'

Surprisingly Judy said, 'I know everyone else says you ought to stay but personally I think you'd be a fool if you did.'

'It's time I thought about myself,' he said. He felt slightly let-down. 'Like the others ... Every single one of them you can mention was only concerned with personal interests ... dropped the job the minute it got in the way ... Holmes, Costa, Beatrice, Offenbach; Temata, H.H., Toa, Aporo; P.I.D.L. with its behind-the-scenes political motives. Even Father Pieter is out for himself in a tangled-up way ... with his bloody-minded determination to show up the government, his pride in doing everything singlehanded.'

'Don't think I'm trying to persuade you,' Judy said. 'I think the whole thing stinks ... I always did ... you know my opinion of Native Development. It just seems a pity the chance can't be used to do some real good.'

'What real good?'

'You know what good ... all the things that are needed will never get done now. When you go, P.I.D.L. will find a retired bus-driver and train him and he'll go on with the Morris dances and native culture.'

'I couldn't stay on here, even if I wanted to. I couldn't go on working for a Resident Commissioner I don't respect, or an organization I don't believe in. Whatever else I haven't got, at least I've got a few principles.'

'You needn't bark at me; I'm not trying to persuade you. It's just that I don't see what believing in them has to do with it. I mean, the money works just the same whether you believe in them or not ... it does the job building schools or planting coconuts. . . .'

'I know your views. You believe that even if you can see through a racket there's nothing wrong with being in it if you think the end justifies the means.'

'If Mrs Hitchcock heard you say that she'd have me run off the island. Well Leicester, I won't hold you up any longer. I just said I'd deliver the petition. When will you be leaving? Perhaps we'll be going together. I'm booked in the next *Marinda*.'

A trap-door opened. Leicester fell through into misery. Thus expressed, so calmly taken for granted, his departure might be over and done with.

'Well, I'll see you before then. I hope you find a nice job in Wellington. Will you go back to the department?'

'I don't know. I haven't thought about it yet.' The prospect of Wellington was beyond thought.

'You need a break, after all your work here. It's sickening to see it all going to waste ... Thrown away. But I think you're right. You've done enough. I don't see why you should feel you owe any loyalty here.'

'I don't owe loyalty anywhere!' He had a sudden wish for a row with this damned woman who so calmly wrote off him and all his months of slaving as though they had never existed.

'But after all, as you say, why shouldn't you think of yourself for a change? All the others did. Why should you stay on in a place you don't like, just for the natives? As you say, they couldn't care less. They didn't ask us to come here. Sometimes you wonder if they're really worth working for; trying to save.'

'You have *kai* early?' said the edentulous whale. 'Cinema tonight.'

'You want to go?'

'Yes please, Leicester. You like to come with me?'

'Not tonight, thank you. You can go. What's my *kai* tonight?'

'Tonight is special. Corned beef.'

'All right. Leave it on the table. I'm going for a walk.'

Strange to pass Temata's house and find no feeling remained; to see undisturbed, the little brothers and sisters playing among the piglets. Where was Temata now? He did

213

not really care. That should be shocking but it meant nothing; no more than the sandy spit where, in an earlier incarnation he had proposed to her. Temata and that life were gone and with it the Leicester who had loved her. He sat down under the casuarina trees, feeling old.

The sun, dying across the lagoon, dragged shadowy fingers over the sand. In the copper light massive Gauguin women squatted, boneless, immobile, embowered in children.

Did the islanders really not care at all? Was it true what that horrible woman had said ... they were not worth working for? Were all his efforts thrown away? Too late now to care.

The sun dropped out of sight and at once it was dark. The Gauguin women gathered their children and waddled across the beach. '*Kia orana*,' they murmured as they passed. '*Kia orana*, Leicester.' When you needed to hate a place it always showed its best side.

Singing began; too far away for the shrillness to penetrate; not far enough to disguise the heartbreak. Behind him, a silken whisper of casuarinas; on the short green grass, bare Laocöon frangipani trees, flowering Queen of the Night, *tiare Maori* ... all Aratoa's beauties combining to make painful his farewell.

It was true, after all, what people said. It was Polynesia one fell in love with.

He sat up, wiping his eyes as a yellow light moved down the beach. Girls and boys, going reef-fishing, perhaps to dance and make love. Gentle, melodious voices came through the darkness.

'Good night, Leicester. Good night, Leicester.' Brown legs gleamed in the swinging circle of light. 'Good night, Leicester...' The murmur passed and was gone.

Who spoke to you like that in the Wellington streets? Who lulled you to sleep with singing, greeted you in the morning with flowers and smiles? Frustrating, baffling, bewildering, thoughtless, carefree, unreliable children, with children's faults, vulnerability. Not worth working for, according to cynics like Judy Pollock. Not worth saving.

He stood up. He must write out his resignation before bed. He was not going to stay, for all Aratoa's beauty, its soft murmuring voices. Work, talk, teach; think you have convinced, then turn your back for an instant and see what happens. Squeeze the sponge, the water runs out.

Yet they hadn't asked us to come here; they hadn't asked to be saved. Was it their fault that we expected them to be like us? To want what we want? Were they not wiser perhaps than we thought ... accepting what suited them, rejecting the rest; retaining their own way of life in spite of us?

A clatter; a cry. Raucous laughter from a lamplit cottage. An empty tin sailed from a cookhouse to lie, offering sanctuary to *anopheles*. Essence of pig, village latrines counterpointed the flower-scents, burning coconut husks in the unmistakable olfactory fugue of the islands. They'd never learn. Never.

'I'll ask for a passage in the next *Marinda*,' he decided, and at the same instant, 'Why not build Joseph a schoolhouse of coral aggregate, in a modern design! There's plenty of coral on Manu—pandanus for thatch ... so cheap and cool, if properly used. Then he could afford a big building and all the equipment he needs; and as many latrines as he wants.' His feet crunched, unnoticed, into water-filled shells. 'I must have a look at the budget tomorrow ... if I called a meeting with Vincent and Wilson and told them straight ... if I could get *one* decent Maori nurse from the hospital ... if I spent three months on Manu, with Government supporting me ...'

Darkness had blotted the lagoon. Enormous stars shone out, too close, almost too beautiful. Smoke drifted, the smell of oil lamps. The reef moaned and sighed, coconut leaves clattered gently in the night wind. Soon there would be singing, guitars, ukeleles, familiar rattles and thumps from the village where Items were once more in hand.